JANE BETTELEY

Luisa Mulligan Can't Keep A Secret

When secrets unravel, lives unravel.

Contents

Acknowledgement

The last twelve months have been a whirlwind for me. I've received an overwhelming amount of support from so many people, and I'm incredibly grateful to everyone who has reached out to me. Whether it was to tell me that they've read my book, to encourage me to write more, or just to congratulate me, I appreciate all of it.

Self-publishing can be a lonely road, but it's also empowering. The community of independent authors is very special, and I want to give a huge thank you to all of my cheerleaders who have given me advice and guidance over the past year. I will forever be in awe of my fellow indie authors, especially Ross J Kinnaird, Cassie Steward, Arini Vlotman, and Matthew R Burton. Thank you for all of your help, guidance, and support, and for being brilliant people.

I started writing this book after my first book, These Thoughts Are Yours, was published. I love writing short stories, but I wanted to get my teeth into a whole novel. Short stories can often skate over the surface, and feedback from These Thoughts Are Yours showed me that readers wanted to know what happened next. When I sat down to write this book, I had no idea where it was going or what was going to happen. I've started many books that never got past the first few chapters because I had no clue what was happening next. You hear of authors planning their stories, their characters, and each chapter. I don't do any of those things, but what I realized was that it's okay. It's perfectly okay to just sit and write and see where it takes you - for me, that's all part of the fun.

I've had the privilege of talking to some people who have provided me with insightful perspectives on the themes in this story. Your honesty, raw emotion, and vulnerability have left me speechless at times, but I will always be grateful for your assistance. Thank you for sharing your stories with me and helping me to understand.

I have some people to thank as well. To my team of BETA and ARC readers, thank you for giving up your time to read a story that began in my head, for providing me with valuable feedback, and for pointing out my horrendous errors. I hope the final product doesn't disappoint.

To David, you never cease to amaze me with your unwavering support. I love you. x

To O, M & T, you will never know how proud I am of you all. Keep being brilliant. x

And finally, to my mum, who will kick off if I don't mention her.

Chapter 1

'Bloody hell,' Luisa muttered as she hobbled the short distance from her car to the front step of her house. She closed her eyes. The frustrations of the working day were weighing on her like a wet blanket. She let out a long, measured sigh and closed her eyes. The balls of her feet throbbed, and her toes grumbled at the lack of room in her black patent heels, which were an inch and a half too tall to be the 'guaranteed comfort' the display stand had promised her when she purchased them.

The green paint on the front door was also starting to look tired, she pondered, head tilted, as she lingered for a moment on the doorstep. On a good day, Luisa would tell you that the paint was sage green; however, on a bad day - she would describe it as the colour of flu-season snot. Luisa described her world very differently on days when she wasn't quite feeling it, and even more so when she was pissed off with life, or the people in her life, or just life in general - which seemed to happen quite a lot lately.

It had been ten hours since Luisa closed the front door behind her as she left for work that morning. Now she was back, standing in front of the door, key in hand, building up the courage to enter the house she had called home for the last sixteen years.

The only sound she could hear, as she stood still with the late afternoon sun's warmth on the back of her neck, was the faint hum of distant traffic, the sporadic ticking of her car engine as it cooled down, and the odd chirp of a bird. Other than that, nothing; no radio, TV, shouting, blaring sirens, or barking dogs. She rubbed her eyebrows with her forefinger and thumb. How she would love this peace to last more than the brief couple of minutes she stood at the front door. Once that key went in the lock, who knows what would greet her on the other side? Given the mood her fifteen-year-old daughter, Lucy, was in as she left the house for school this morning, it would go one of two ways. There would either be a tirade of shouting and tears or a sulky, moody figure following her around the house like a dark shadow, sighing and huffing and giving one-word answers to questions she clearly didn't want to answer.

All Luisa really wanted to do was go in, take off the godforsaken shoes that were slowly cutting off the circulation to her toes, make a brew, slump on the sofa and lie in silence. Actually, what she *really* wanted was someone to make her a brew, ask her how her day was, and massage her feet while asking what she would like for dinner. *Fat chance of that happening*, Luisa brooded, rubbing the back of her neck and rolling her eyes.

She dismissed the thoughts to the back of her mind, pulled her shoulders back and raised the key to the lock. *No point standing here fantasising about a life that doesn't exist*, she thought. The key didn't even have a chance to engage before the front door was flung open from inside.

'Why are you just standing there staring at the door? You are so embarrassing!' a voice, edged with disdain and frustration, barked. 'What are you even doing?'

And there she was, her first and only child, reminding her that she was, in fact, a complete embarrassment to her. I mean, God forbid anyone saw her standing at her own front door, the door of the house that she paid the mortgage on, as she returned from the job that gave her the money to pay the mortgage on the house that had the door that she was standing at. There was no need to respond to this declaration as Lucy had already stomped up the stairs and slammed her bedroom door shut behind her.

Luisa finally kicked off her uncomfortable shoes into the cupboard under the stairs. She padded down the hallway, taking a moment to enjoy the feel of the beige carpet on her feet before she stepped on the grey lino of the kitchen floor. It was a joint decision, the flooring, and despite wanting to remove all traces of her former life, she didn't replace it like other things they had bought together for the house. This was partly because of the expense and partly because it was convenient to keep it that way. She lifted the kettle to check there was water in it and flicked the switch. She grabbed her favourite 'World's Best Mum' mug from the cupboard and flung in a tea bag. 'Oh, the irony', she laughed as she recalled the doorstep statement. She was actually glad that Lucy had taken herself up the stairs; at least she would get half an hour to herself before she had to attempt to converse with her about dinner choices, one of the many topics of conversation that was guaranteed to end in a row.

She took her freshly made tea, strong with a splash of milk, and ambled into the living room. She sat on her usual spot on the sofa, tucking her feet under her, and hugged the mug with both hands. She could hear the muffled thud of something masquerading as music from the bedroom above her. Still, other than that, it was peaceful. Luisa took this as a bonus as she enjoyed fifteen minutes of indulgence. She reminded herself that you've got to take these moments when you can. *It's not being selfish; it's self-care.* She tried to block out the ironing pile in the basket behind the living room door that was trying to signal her that it was still there. She closed her eyes to avoid the task at hand. *It's just fifteen minutes, you can take fifteen minutes, Luisa.* But no, it was no good; she knew that Lucy would need some of the items in the laundry basket for the weekend. So tea, half drunk, Luisa picked up the basket and set herself up for an hour with the ironing board.

After half an hour of heat and steam and tiny items of clothing that Luisa couldn't make head nor tail of, Lucy reappeared, drawn out of her lair by hunger and boredom.

'What are you doing?' Lucy asked as she sat with her elbows on the work surface, her face squished up by her hands, her long dark brown hair hanging on either side of her head.

Luisa looked up with the iron still in her hand, 'what does it look like I'm doing?' she asked, raising her eyebrows and smiling.

'No need to be sarcastic, I was only asking,' Lucy huffed predictably, her brown eyes squinted.

Luisa continued with the ironing and persevered with the conversation. 'How was school?'

'Boring' Lucy responded.

'What homework have you got?' Luisa continued, desperate to find a topic of conversation that warranted more than a one-word answer.

An exaggerated huff signalled her question wouldn't open up a productive exchange.

'You're always on at me about stuff; can't you just give me a break? I never get this much stress at Dad's,' she huffed as she crossed her arms.

Luisa placed down the iron. 'Sorry Luce, I'm just taking an interest, that's all', she told her softly, desperate not to let the conversation end in a row. Lucy had already moved on and was opening the kitchen cabinets and promptly shutting them again.

'There's never anything to eat in this house' she exclaimed.

Luisa, knowing this to be untrue, picked the iron back up. She knew what was coming, that age-old question that every parent dreads...

'What's for tea?' Lucy asked.

Luisa admitted defeat, set the iron down, unplugged it from the wall and folded the last item of clothing before putting it in the basket. *Here we go. Take a deep breath, Luisa.*

'I don't know, love, what do you fancy?'

'Anything' Lucy shrugged.

'Spag bol?'

'No'. Lucy screwed up her face.

'Chicken nuggets?'

'Mum, I'm not eight'. Lucy genuinely seemed offended by this last offering.

'Sausage?' Luisa was losing the will to live.

'I've gone off sausages'

'Since when?' Luisa asked

'They have stuff in them, stuff you shouldn't eat, like stuff off the floor. Feet and stuff,' Lucy stated. 'I'm not actually sure I want to eat meat anymore anyway; Maxine says it's horrific for the environment'. At this point, she crossed her arms and tilted her head to the side.

'OK, well, you tell me then,' Luisa sighed, refusing to give any fuel to the 'no meat' conversation.

' I don't know - anything,' Lucy shrugged.

'But nothing I suggest,' Luisa said under her breath, avoiding eye contact with her daughter.

Her eyes met her mother's with a look oscillating between indifference and annoyance. 'It's not my fault you haven't got anything I want - there's never anything to eat in this house', she repeated with more venom than was necessary.

'OK, well, I'm going to make egg and chips, so if you want that, I'll do you some.'

Lucy curled her lip. 'Forget it, I'm not hungry anyway,' with that, she flounced back out of the kitchen, stomped up the stairs and, for the second time in an hour, slammed shut her bedroom door.

Chapter 2

Luisa's move to Copcut Green, a picturesque village in the heart of Worcestershire, marked the beginning of a significant new chapter in her life. With its tree-lined avenues, the village captured Luisa's heart from the moment she and Jon, Lucy's dad, arrived. She pictured herself in a white linen dress, lounging on a plaid blanket under the shade of the towering oak tree at the centre of the village, her baby gurgling contentedly beside her. And now, with a thirty-four-week bump, her dreams were slowly becoming a reality.

Luisa and Jon had been together for just over a year when two blue lines appeared on a test, taking them both by surprise. Jon was not entirely on board at first, expressing concerns about the responsibility of parenthood and home ownership.

'It's not that I don't want kids, just not yet; we're not even living together properly; we haven't even discussed this', he insisted when Luisa told him her happy news.

'It's a bit late for that now', Luisa responded, chewing her bottom lip and clasping the test between her fingers.

'What I mean is, we don't have to go along with it', he said, frowning. 'You know as well as I do that we still have options'.

Luisa was devastated. 'So what are you saying? That we get

rid of it? Are you being serious?'

'We must think about it sensibly; we're still young. Do we need a baby right now? Can we even afford a baby?'.

'We're twenty-seven, Jon; we're not exactly young. Meg had Izzy when she was twenty-five, and she manages just fine!'

'You honestly think so?' scoffed Jon, 'didn't stop her calling you every five minutes to help out, though, did it? Are you sure you haven't been friends for so long because all she does is use you?'

Luisa threw him a look. 'Megan manages brilliantly, actually, *and* she's on her own', she snapped in defence of her best friend of nearly twenty-five years.

Jon rolled his eyes. 'I'm only saying, why do you always have to overreact? You can never just have a normal conversation, can you?' he sneered. 'I suppose you'll start crying next.'

Luisa swallowed the emotion that was building inside her chest, desperate not to give him the satisfaction of being right and furious at herself for, yet again, being unable to have a conversation without being reduced to tears.

The subject of options wasn't addressed again. After the initial early doctors appointments, Jon started to spend more and more time at work, and Luisa would be asleep on the sofa by the time he got home most evenings. Despite this, Luisa was grateful that he was at least stepping up and providing for them, even if it meant they spend much time together. She understood that he had important work commitments to fulfill and she couldn't expect him to prioritise everything at once. Moreover, she appreciated the fact that they had a roof over their heads and a steady income. Truly, Luisa was grateful for everything.

An unexpected modest windfall from a distant relative on Luisa's mum's side gave them the push they needed. The money certainly softened the blow for Jon. Combined with a small amount of savings from Luisa, they had scraped enough for a small deposit.

They put in a hesitant offer on a house on the edge of the village. Although not one of the pretty cottages overlooking the village green that Luisa set her heart on, she was overjoyed when it was accepted. Luisa felt a sense of contentment and giddy excitement as she awaited the birth of their new arrival, and Jon became increasingly distracted by the financial constraints of his newfound domesticity.

Number 82, their new home, was a standard three-bed semi situated at the end of a rather long and sometimes seemingly endless street. Luisa often thought it could have benefited from being about thirty houses shorter. Driving down wasn't much of an issue, but walking from one end to the other on foot took forever. The entire road, despite its name "Foley Street," was more of a cul-de-sac or a dead end, depending on Luisa's perspective and how she felt about it on any given day.

Moving into their new home was a relatively smooth process, mainly because Luisa and Jon didn't possess a lot of belongings of significant size or value. Their modest possessions mainly consisted of baby paraphernalia, generously handed down from Megan, rather than tasteful adult furnishings.

Luisa made it as homely as possible with an ever-expanding bump, and Jon went off to work, as he did, a lot. They needed every penny to pay the mortgage and survive while Luisa was on maternity leave. She never did get to sit on the blanket in the shade of the Oak Tree. She never got to own a white dress, either.

It was hard work in those early years; Luisa was, for all intents and purposes, a single mum with Jon working all hours. Jon's parents moved away to Spain before he and Luisa got together, so there were no grandparents to help on either side. Luisa never met her dad, Mario, but from what her mum, Trish, told her, and as his name suggests, he was of Italian descent (hence the spelling of her name, a name that Luisa spent a lifetime having to correct when people got it wrong). From what she understood, in the early days, her parents' relationship was a love story that could have made the big screen. The pair were very much in love; it wasn't just a short fling or a whirlwind romance. Trish had set her heart on a white wedding, being welcomed into a huge Italian family and spending holidays on the Amalfi coast. Mario had wooed her with tales of endless summers and crystal clear seas, a far cry from the River Severn that ploughed through Worcestershire. He told her she would sit beside him as they meandered up the roads that snaked along the coast, sunglasses on and headscarf tied with a bow. 'I'll be just like Audrey Hepburn,' Trish told her parents, her eyes wistful and her chest heaving with excitement.

Her grandparents described him as handsome with dark hair, olive skin, and a thick Italian accent. 'He might have been a looker, but he was bloody useless at everything else', her Grandad told her. There was one crucial turning point that steered away from the fairy tale narrative. A week or so after

Trish told him they would be a family of three, he flew back to Italy for a relative's funeral and never returned.

Luisa's mum, Trish, never overcame the overwhelming sense of abandonment and betrayal. She was forced to move back home to her parents, Luisa's grandparents, who weren't entirely thrilled with the whole situation. Trish spent the next eight months planning what she would do after the baby was born, plans which didn't lend themselves to life with a baby. Predictably, Trish very soon lost interest in being a mum after Luisa was born and spent more and more time away from the family home, craving a life that didn't involve nappies or formula. Luckily, Luisa's grandparents were happy to take charge and raise Luisa.

Trish would reappear every so often, the odd birthday or Christmas, but never long enough for Luisa to build any sort of relationship with her. Trish became preoccupied with trying to reclaim her lost youth, attending parties with people who had no responsibilities, and losing whole weekends to a heady mix of alcohol and substances that she didn't understand but took anyway. Her youthful complexion that initially won Mario's attention became sallow and grey, her zest for life replaced with an intense need for escapism that can only be found in powder form. It could be months between visits to see Luisa, by which time Luisa hardly even recognised her. Until she stopped coming, and Luisa stopped asking about her.

Trish's battle with addictions finally caught up with her and led to her untimely death at the age of fifty-one. Luisa was informed of Trish's passing through a distant cousin, who had taken it upon herself to sort the logistics - Luisa was grateful; for all intents and purposes, she was estranged from her mother and wouldn't even know where to begin. Jon had told her to find out what was in the will; being an only child, it would all surely come to her. There was no will. There was nothing left to show for Trish's life, only Luisa and a trail of powder.

Luisa attended the funeral. She missed most of the service, throwing up behind a tombstone, partly due to morning sickness but primarily due to the overwhelming anxiety of burying her own mother. Luisa's grandparents died a few years earlier, both within a few months of each other. They were spared the pain of officially losing their only child. However, many years before, they had accepted that they would never have a conventional relationship.

Without her parents and grandparents and a partner who spent more time at work than at home, Luisa was left holding her baby and facing a future of uncertainty.

Chapter 3

Luisa collapsed into her office chair, tossing her handbag haphazardly into the open drawer beside her. With a frustrated motion, she slammed the drawer shut with her foot and slumped forward, resting her head in her hands.

'Blimey, someone needs a brew?' a friendly voice enquired. Luisa looked up to see Janet holding a Yorkshire tea bag in one hand and her 'I'd rather be drinking gin' mug in the other. Luisa smiled, 'absolutely'.

Luisa followed Janet into the tiny kitchen area at the back of the office. Luckily, there was a whole school assembly that morning, so Luisa and Janet had half an hour to themselves. The phones still needed answering while everyone else belted out 'Shine Jesus Shine' from the school hall.

'Come on then,' asked Janet as she filled the mugs from the water heater on the wall, desperately trying to avoid the excited spits of boiling liquid that came with the first use of the morning.

'Oh, I don't know,' replied Luisa despondently, 'ever feel like you're just getting by?'

'Explain', Janet instructed as she added milk to the two mugs.

'Well, Lucy hates me, the ironing pile is multiplying, my kitchen floor needs mopping, and I haven't had sex for....' Luisa started to count on her fingers but gave up 'forever'. Janet started to laugh.

'Right, firstly, Lucy doesn't hate you, she hates everyone, she's a teenager, that's normal. Secondly, ironing is an activity invented by bored housewives with no job; it isn't a necessity. The kitchen floor only needs cleaning if you plan to eat off it or have sex on it, and given your last statement, I don't think there's any chance of the latter happening anytime soon'. Janet tapped the spoon on the edge of the mugs and picked them both up, nodding toward their desks.

Luisa's laughter echoed in the office as she followed Janet back inside. Janet had a knack for lifting her spirits, and Luisa cherished their friendship. Janet's brutal honesty was balanced by a genuine kindness that made her a trusted confidant. From an outsider's perspective, their banter might have seemed cutting, but Luisa knew that Janet held her in high regard, just as she did for Janet. Their unique bond was forged on Luisa's first day at the job, a day forever marked by a hand sanitiser mishap in the toilet that left Luisa embarrassed and self-conscious about the ambiguous stain down her black trousers.

As the years passed, their friendship continued to grow. 'Ever get the feeling you're just existing, though, Janet? Like you have no purpose in life other than to make sure everyone else is happy, and I don't even feel like I'm doing that very well.' Luisa took a sip of her tea and set it down on the 'World's Best Teacher' coaster on her desk. There was always an abundance of this particular type of coaster at the end of term. 'Best School Office Admin' was clearly too niche to be a popular gift option.

Janet wheeled her chair over the grey carpet tiles and positioned herself at the opposite side of Luisa's desk.

'Not really,' she said, 'I don't actually give a flying fuck if other people are happy or not if I'm honest, that's not really my responsibility'. Luisa knew that Janet didn't actually mean this; it was all part of the facade she put on to make people think she was devoid of emotion. She did it quite a lot and earned her a reputation for being a ball-breaker. Luisa knew there was more to her than that.

'Not even Simon? Surely you care if he is happy or not?'

'Well, we're still married, so I assume if he wasn't happy, he would have either started sleeping with someone else or left me. He hasn't done either of those things, so he must be OK.'

'That you know of', said Luisa, raising an eyebrow.

Janet laughed, 'Well, just because you didn't see the obvious signs that your fella was playing away, I think everyone else did'.

Luisa rolled her eyes. Janet was right. Her friends hinted at the possibility of Jon playing away. There was never any proof, but if she was honest, all the signs were there: the late nights at the office, the 'just popping out' and returning six hours later, the unexplained transactions on the bank statements, the effort he put into his appearance when he went to fill up the car. But Luisa never wanted to believe that her partner of five years would cheat on her so soon after giving birth to their only child. Either way, their relationship didn't last past the nappy stage. When Lucy was only eight months old, Luisa solidified her self-proclaimed title of 'single mum', a title she didn't want but rose to valiantly.

'OK, well, what about your kids? Don't you care if they are happy?' Luisa asked.

'At twenty-four and twenty-seven, they can make their own happiness', replied Janet, very matter-of-factly. 'Again, not my responsibility anymore'.

'But they're your kids!'

'Correct. But it's not up to me to make sure they are happy. That's just weird at their age. The only thing that makes them happy at the moment is cash, and I don't have any. So yes, I hope they are happy, of course I do, but it's not up to me to make that happen anymore.'

Luisa couldn't help but reflect on this as she sat at her desk. The prospect of Lucy turning twenty-four seemed like a distant future, especially when Lucy was just fifteen years old. At this moment in time, Luisa's greatest desire was quite simple: for Lucy to be happy, or at the very least, to see her smile occasionally. They once shared a close bond, filled with laughter over the silliest things, finding amusement in the quirkiest moments, giggling at roller skating dogs and brides fainting at the altar on 'You've Been Framed'.

But those days felt like a lifetime ago. Now, their home oscillated between eerie quietness and eruptions of teenage temper and tantrums, all accompanied by a whirlwind and fizz of hormones. Lucy fully embraced the mood swings and challenges of being a teenager, creating a void in their relationship that Luisa struggled to navigate. Lucy often complained of boredom, yet whenever Luisa suggested doing something together, she was met with resistance. Whether it was exhaustion, lack of interest, or the excuse of having homework, Lucy always seemed to find a reason to avoid spending time with her mum. It left Luisa feeling adrift, unsure how to reconnect with her daughter and struggling with this new phase of their relationship.

There was a sudden rumble of noise and a distant chatter of excited children on the move. Janet got up and made her way over to the other side of the office,
    'You know what you need, don't you?' she said
    Luisa didn't reply; she already knew what Janet was going to say again.
    'A good shag'

* * *

Janet's words played on Luisa's mind as she drove home from work. Janet's solution to most problems had always been to find a partner. While Luisa knew it wasn't quite that simple, she couldn't deny that she missed the intimacy, the companionship, and the simple joy of having another person to talk to about everything and nothing. The idea of having another heartbeat in the house, apart from hers and Lucy's, held a certain allure.

But the reality of dating and intimacy as a single mother was far more complex. Luisa hadn't had any romantic or intimate encounters since Jon left over fourteen years ago. It wasn't because she was prudish or inhibited; she enjoyed her fair share of excitement as a teenager. However, her life has evolved significantly since then. She no longer had the body or the confidence she possessed at nineteen. She also had the responsibilities of a teenage daughter, a mortgage, a job she enjoyed (even if it was demanding), and the looming worries about her bank balance and lack of pension.

The thought of dating seemed daunting, and the idea of introducing another person into her and Lucy's lives was a challenge she hadn't yet found the courage to tackle. Instead, she found solace in the occasional fantasy of winning the lottery or meeting a wealthy suitor who could whisk her away from her financial worries. Or, perhaps, she thought with a touch of dark humour, she might not live long enough to reach pensionable age, sparing her the need to worry about retirement.

The memory of Jon's quick rebound and the string of significant others he paraded through their lives over the years still stung for Luisa. She lost count and, truth be told, interest in keeping up with his ever-changing partners. Lucy was initially curious about them, talking about them for the first week or so, but as they stopped making an effort with her, she grew uninterested and distant.

Luisa tried to communicate her concerns to Jon, asking him to take things slower when introducing new women into Lucy's life. Lucy only spent half the week with him, leaving plenty of time for him to nurture his new relationships without causing undue disruption for their daughter. But Jon, true to his nature, always put his own desires first, even at the expense of his own child's feelings. He never prioritised Lucy's emotional well-being, nor had he shown much regard for Luisa's feelings, then or now.

Luisa and Janet had discussed the possibility of online dating. After watching a few true crime documentaries on TV, Luisa dismissed this and exclaimed, 'It's a minefield out there. The internet is full of nutters.' Janet laughed and jokingly asked, "Are *you* a nutter?'

'Well, no, obviously, not in the online serial killer type of way anyway.'

'So if you went on Tinder, would you automatically want to chase vulnerable men in an attempt to capture them and hold them hostage?'

'Errr, no'

'So how many other men do you think are sitting at home thinking the same thing about crazed women on the prowl for their next victim? It's not a thing, Luisa! It's no different to meeting someone in the pub, actually no, it's safer than meeting someone in the pub as this way you get to vet them a bit first.'

Luisa had to admit, she was coming around to the idea, maybe if only to just chat with someone, albeit virtually, when she was home alone. So that night, after she'd cleaned the kitchen and Lucy was barricaded in her room, she sat with her phone in hand, debating on what dating site to go for. She was hesitant to spend any money and was just testing the waters. She searched for 'best dating apps' but quickly changed her search to 'best free dating apps'. Her screen was suddenly awash with options. She clicked on Grindr, and it became apparent that this would be a perfect option if she were a gay man looking for a hookup.

DateMyAge, *hmmm, an option,* but she wasn't overly sure what age she wanted to date. Was she looking for the same age, an older man, a younger man! No, she didn't want to be too specific at this stage. Tinder, *ah, here we go,* a name she recognised. One of the teachers, Pauline, used that one and spent a rather lovely summer with a man named Geoff. It turned out that Geoff liked to be Steff at the weekends, and although very open-minded, it wasn't really what Pauline was after. Janet and Luisa found the whole situation hilarious and teased Pauline for some time. Luisa hovered over the 'install' button as she recalled the story. But Pauline *did* say she had a summer she'd never forget and had no regrets at all, apart from lending him her expensive foundation and him never returning it.

'Surely that was a big red flag, Pauline?' Janet asked. 'The fact he wanted to borrow your foundation?'

'He told me he had an allergic reaction to my perfume and wanted something to cover it as they had staff photos at work,' Pauline struggled to hide her embarrassment. 'We all know the pressure of school photo time, I felt sorry for him'.

'But what about when he asked to borrow your shoes, Pauline?' Luisa added. 'Did you not wonder then at all?'

'Not really, he was always, you know, trying new things'. Pauline blushed a little before adding, 'He was very adventurous in many ways. As I've said before, I'm very open-minded about things, but I just couldn't get past him wanting to wear the shoes in bed. And he asked me to call him Steff. And he asked me to wear the harness. It left an awful mark on my thighs where it rubbed. I have a nickel allergy; it would never have worked.' Pauline straightened her A-line skirt and adjusted her tweed blazer. 'Anyway, I just hope he found happiness in the end'.

'So, has it put you off internet dating?' asked Luisa, genuinely interested in her response.

'Not at all!' exclaimed Pauline. I have had lots of dates since. I'm going away next weekend with a lovely man named Colin. We're going to the Cotswolds, staying in a charming sandstone cottage,' she gushed.

'Oooh sounds lovely', said Janet. 'Romantic night in a cosy country pub followed by an early night, eh?' she winked.

'Oh no' replied Pauline quite sternly. 'Colin doesn't drink; he has a heart condition and a prosthetic leg, so he needs to keep a clear head'.

Luisa dared not look at Janet at this point for fear of releasing the explosive giggle gathering momentum inside. Thankfully, the registration bell trilled and saved them both from falling apart with laughter as Pauline sashayed down the corridor back to her classroom.

'Blimey', stated Luisa. 'She certainly knows how to pick them - a heart condition AND a prosthetic leg,' her eyes widened.

'At least she's getting herself out there, Luisa, you know, rather than sitting at home doing absolutely nothing.' Janet declared while tapping away on her keyboard.

As Luisa watched the installation of her new dating app complete, she couldn't help but feel a sense of accomplishment. She contemplated sharing the news with Janet, imagining her friend's proud reaction. However, Luisa quickly realised that there was more work to be done – adding photos and a profile description for starters. Luisa decided it was best not to rush the process; she'd take small steps.

She set her phone down on the sofa and turned up the volume on the television. The app could wait until tomorrow, but the next episode of "Peaky Blinders" couldn't. Luisa settled in with a cup of tea, fully immersing herself in 1920s Birmingham. As she watched, she couldn't help but daydream about her future dating prospects. Still, she had to admit, anyone she dated next would have quite a high bar to meet, especially when she was swooning over the charismatic Tommy Shelby on the screen.

Chapter 4

By 16.00, the school office regained a sense of calm, other than the various after-school activities. Pauline donned her navy polka-dot wellies for a Forest Schools session, an activity she absolutely detested but participated in because no other staff member wanted to do it. As Pauline was the only one who hadn't already bagged a more favourable activity, she was named Forest Schools Champion, which basically meant she had sole responsibility for supervising groups of children who found great pleasure in covering themselves in mud.

This week, Year 3 was traipsing across the wet grass to find various shaped leaves in the woods behind the school. Last week, a child in Year 2 proudly came back with a 'balloon' that looked suspiciously like a used condom. Pauline confiscated it immediately, much to the dismay of little Lola Jackson, who wanted to take it home to show her mum.

'Honestly ladies, she came running over like she'd found a golden bloody ticket', Pauline retold, shaking her head. 'Swinging it around like a bloody helicopter propeller. I really do not get paid enough for this sort of trauma'.

'Shall I make you a brew, Pauline?' offered Luisa sympathet-ically to divert the conversation away from Janet, who found the whole incident hysterical.

'I don't know what you find so funny, Janet', snapped Pauline. 'I could have caught something nasty, and so could the children'.

'I can't imagine who would think having a shag in the woods behind the school was a good thing to do anyway', Luisa said, handing over a sweet tea. 'I mean, it's not exactly the height of romance, is it?' she questioned, one eyebrow raised.

'Oh, I don't know,' laughed Janet. 'I've done it in worse places', she added, much to the disgust of Pauline, who pursed her lips and shook her head.

'And knowing the Jackson family', Janet continued, 'I suggest that if we ran a DNA test on that 'balloon', we'd find it belonged to one of them anyway'.

The three of them stifled a giggle. It was true; it wasn't unusual to have four or five siblings at the school at one time, let alone cousins. 'I don't know how they do it', Janet puzzled. 'I only had two, and I was bloody knackered, let alone four or five'.

'Mmmm' pondered Luisa. 'I guess that maybe we should commend them for at least attempting to use contraception then.'

'Well, whoever it was, next time they should bloody take it home with them', Pauline snorted.

Year 5 football was in full swing, but they had been banned from entering the school building due to the amount of school field that they brought back in with them. Janet was gutted when the new rule was implemented, primarily because Adam, the young man who came in to do the coaching, was just her type despite being a good twenty years her junior.

'Well, that's fucked that up for me then', she had declared when she was told of the new procedure. 'Because I'm sure, given time, he and I would have ended up getting it on, he clearly has a thing for me'.

'Janet! You can't say that; he's at least half your age, and you're married!' Luisa laughed.

'I'm telling you, Lu, another six months and he'd have fallen head over heels with me'. She shuffled the papers on her desk and put them down, looking across at Luisa knowingly. 'Maybe it's for the best because we both know I'd have destroyed him'. The ringing of the office phones reigned them back from their hysterical giggling.

'No, sorry, Mrs Lewis, nothing has been handed in here, although we do insist that if the children do need to bring in their phones, they are to leave them with us at the office when they come in', Luisa reiterated, rolling her eyes at Janet.

'We haven't had a coat handed in here today, Mr Royle, but if she has her name in it, we will be sure to get it back to her.' Janet mirrored the eye-rolling back at Luisa.

'Imagine how quiet it would be here if the bloody parents and kids actually followed the procedures? Honestly, it really yanks my chain,' Janet stated.

'Literally', agreed Luisa.

'I really can't be arsed with it' stated Janet, shaking her head.

Janet had been particularly sharp today, blaming a stinking headache from the cheap wine she'd had after dinner last night.

'It does the job, but I will be honest with you, Luisa, it tastes like absolute cat's piss.'

Luisa shook her head, 'I don't know how you manage to drink a bottle of wine full stop on a school night, Janet; I'd be like the walking dead in the morning if I did that'.

'I'm immune to it – I'd go into some sort of cold turkey if I stopped now', Janet joked.

Luisa studied her face across the office. Something had changed over the past few months; she was starting to look older. Luisa wondered if Janet was actually unwell; her hair was not as styled as it used to be, the lines on her face seemed to trench across her skin, and her eyes often resembled those of a bloodhound first thing in the morning. She looked worn out most of the time. Luisa, being the sort of friend who had everyone's best interest at heart, broached the subject in a supportive friend way. Still, Janet's response was always the same 'Wait until you're my age; it all goes to shit. The only thing left is alcohol,' she stated.

'I'm sure there are other alternatives,' Luisa suggested.

'Nope, nothing that wipes you out so you don't notice how you're feeling or, better still, knocks you out', she replied thoughtfully.

The ping of her desktop alerted her to an email. 'That's odd', she said out loud, not to anyone in particular. Janet shut the filing cabinet with her behind, and it slammed shut. 'What now?'

'I've just had an email from Head Jackie (as opposed to Cook Jackie, who worked in the canteen) asking me to go in and see her tomorrow at 9 a.m'.

'Oh? Wonder what that's about? Maybe they've cottoned on to the fact that you're rubbish at your job, and they're finishing you,' she joked.

Luisa took in a deep breath. 'Don't say that! Oh my God, do you think I'm in trouble?'

'Bloody hell, Luisa, no! As if! You'd know if you'd done something bad enough to be sacked for.'

Luisa sat tapping her pen on the desk. 'I did forget to pass on a message last week, the one about Tom in Year 1 and his P.E. kit'.

'Not sackable,' replied Janet, sitting back at her desk, frowning at her computer screen. 'In any case, if you are getting the sack, I am too; I've had the same email.'

They both made eye contact over the top of their screens. 'What? At 9 a.m?' inquired Luisa.

'Yep. Maybe they've hidden secret microphones in here, and they've been listening to us for months,' Janet laughed.

'That's it then, we're definitely getting the sack.' squeaked Luisa, and she put her head in her hands.

Chapter 5

Crosslands had its heyday as a bustling carpet town, an offshoot of nearby Kidderminster designed to accommodate the carpet industry workforce. Over time, the factories shifted overseas, leaving numerous families without their primary breadwinner. The town's structures crumbled, once thriving streets emptied of shops and shoppers, and the dearth of opportunities failed to draw new families to the area. Apart from a handful of takeaways, a few pubs and the occasional off-licence, there was little to speak of in Crosslands. It became a transient stop with no compelling reason to linger.

The first five minutes of Luisa's commute home took her through the centre of Crosslands, before taking the B-road, which ran straight through to Copcut Green. Leaving behind the oppressive buildings and dimly lit streets, she emerged into sunlight, where grey buildings gave way to vibrant greenery. It had been a typical summer, marked by ample rain and sunshine. As a result, the hedgerows along the road were lush and full, and dandelions nodded their approval as cars sped past.

'She's a waaterrfallllll, ' Luisa belted out, unable to listen to the Stone Roses classic without joining in, a throwback to her teenage years. The late summer sun was still intense, forcing her to reach for her sunglasses stashed beside the car door. The sun's warmth caressed her face as it pierced through the windshield, fueling her excitement for the impending summer. One of the perks of an administrator working in a school was that her six-week summer break meant just that: six weeks of freedom. No marking, lesson planning, display board upkeep, or early get-ups orchestrated by the shrill alarm. Luisa had big plans this year - a thorough house clean, wardrobe organisation, and a deep dive into the neglected cupboard under the stairs. She even considered regular walks to finally hit her daily step goal. And then, of course, there was still online dating; she could always arrange a couple of dates if she wanted to pass the time. With Lucy spending time at her dad's house, Luisa intended to prioritise self-care, investing in herself and taking things easy. Yes, this summer held the promise of being truly exceptional.

Truth be told, Luisa knew she'd likely start feeling restless around week three. During Lucy's visits to her dad, she often found herself lying on the couch for hours, sometimes forgetting to eat, shower, or occasionally, even go to bed. She could go days without speaking to anyone or hearing her voice. Four weeks marked her limit, beyond which things tended to spiral into a muddy mix of not getting dressed, falling asleep in the afternoons, forgetting to put the bins out and eating leftovers for breakfast. Fortunately, Luisa's best friend, Megan, understood her struggle with solitude and would occasionally swoop in, urging her to get dressed, brush her hair, and leave the house.

Luisa grabbed many items from the pocket on the side of her door: an empty water bottle, a handful of chocolate bar wrappers and something that may possibly have once been a boiled sweet, everything but her bloody sunglasses. 'Where the fuck are you?' she said out loud, 'I know you're in there somewhere'. She glanced down and spotted the dark glasses hidden behind a pile of used tissues. 'Ah, there you are', she said, relieved, but also disgusted with the state of her car, and pulled the glasses from their hiding place. As she glanced back to the road and gasped, 'Shit!' Out of nowhere, right on the bend, a figure dressed in dark clothing appeared, inches from the front of Luisa's car.

Luisa spun the wheel to avoid a collision with the shady figure and slammed down on the brakes. The car came to a sudden halt, jerking Luisa's head forward. 'What the actual fuck!' she shouted. Luisa felt an instant surge of anxiety and a painful pulsing behind her eyes that told her that this could have ended very differently if there had been an oncoming car. She sat still for a moment, her heart pumping furiously. The young man glanced back briefly, raised an apologetic hand, then broke into a jog and continued his journey. 'Oh right, yea you trot off, you little shit, never mind me!'

She positioned the car to the correct side of the road and turned off the engine, needing a moment to calm herself from the tight feeling in her chest and the nauseating dizziness pulsing through her. Her limbs suddenly felt very weak. What the hell was he doing walking along that road? And on a bend? Crosslands was a good ten miles away, and this wasn't the kind of road where pedestrians walked; there wasn't even a pavement. She tucked her hands under her legs to stop them from shaking. Her throat felt sticky and constricted, and a film of sweat was forming in the small of her back.

After taking a few minutes to compose herself, Luisa took a deep breath and put her car first gear. After pulling back onto the road, she turned the stereo off to allow total concentration on the road ahead. Her heart was still thumping harder than it should have, and beads of sweat were gathering on her fore-head. She inhaled a deep breath and let it out slowly, replaying the near miss in her head, anxiety building as she thought about how close she had come to knocking the stranger over. She couldn't shake the eerie feeling she experienced as she approached that young man. Their brief, locked gaze sparked a recognition that sent a shiver down her spine. Why was his face so familiar? She didn't know who this person was, yet there was an uncanny resemblance that she couldn't put her finger on.

Chapter 6

When Luisa first left college, she worked as an indoor sales rep for a large storage company. She hated every single minute of it. Two things kept her there: the monthly wage, which with the commission was pretty good for a nineteen-year-old, and her co-corker Megan. Apart from that, it was, according to Luisa, the worst job in the world. She didn't stay there long, maybe eighteen months in total, give or take a couple of weeks, but her friendship with Megan continued from that point on. They shared all of their life events together: new relationships, breakups, weddings, babies, divorces, drunken nights in, drunken nights out, illness, bereavement and everything else that twenty years of life throws at you.

Megan stretched out on Luisa's living room floor, arms above her head and toes pointed. Megan would never make a catwalk model at just over five feet tall. Nevertheless, she possessed all of the attributes of someone whose face would grace the cover of a glamour magazine. Perfectly proportioned, they call it, legs the right length, slender torso, perfectly sized chest and petite, doll-like features. Her naturally blonde curly hair bounced just above her shoulders. She really was picture-perfect.

'Oooh, that's nice', she wheezed as she stretched and exhaled. 'I went to the gym again last night, and I'm stiff as a board today'.

'I don't know how you do it,' Luisa replied. 'I'm absolutely knackered when I get in from work - raising sweat is the last thing I think of doing'.

'I only do it because I've nothing else going on in my life', Megan stated. 'If I didn't go to the gym, I'd end up like...' she stopped sharply.

'Like me?' Luisa offered.

'Sorry, I didn't mean it to sound like that, but yes. But then I'm not so at ease with my own company as you are, Lu; I'd end up going mad staring at the same walls all evening'.

'I may have already gone mad,' Luisa replied sadly. 'I just can't seem to get anything right at the moment.'

Megan winced as she sat up, giving Luisa her full attention as she settled on the sofa beside Luisa.

'Come on then, what's going on? Spill.'

'Urgh, I don't know. Everything. And Lucy. She's so stroppy lately. I know she's a teenager, but even so, it's relentless. Is it wrong to say that I don't feel like I even like her at the moment?' Luisa could feel herself welling up. 'God, I'm such a shit mum'.

Megan saw the floodgates about to open and scrambled up off the floor. She sat down just as Luisa let herself let go and let the tears cascade from her eyes. Megan stroked the back of her head.

'You are NOT a shit mum Luisa, you know you aren't, it's just a shit situation. It's hard doing this alone.'

'She hates me though.'

'She doesn't hate you; she's just trying to find her place in the world, pushing boundaries - and also, just being a twat because she's a human being. Christ, we can all be a twat now and again, you should know!'

Luisa attempted a laugh between the tears, which sounded more like a snort.

'You dare get snot on my new top, and I'll be fuming', joked Megan, 'come on now, sort your face out.' She peeled Luisa off her shoulder and wiped away the hair that stuck to her damp cheek.

'Sorry,' whimpered Luisa. 'I didn't want to cry on you; I don't know what's the matter with me lately.'

'You know what you need, don't you?' asked Megan, purposely ignoring the apology.

'Don't you dare say a shag', Luisa stated, half smiling.

'Sorry to disappoint Lou, I was only going to suggest a cup of tea'.

Luisa laughed. That's exactly what she needed.

Megan set the two mugs of tea on the kitchen table. The cooker hood light left a warm glow across the kitchen, and Luisa felt herself relax as she cradled the warm mug between her hands.

'Enough about me', Luisa stated, 'tell me something exciting; how's Izzy getting on at college?'

Izzy was just over two years older than Lucy. One week after she was born, Luisa had been met by frazzled-looking Megan answering the door with one boob hanging out of her vest top, a sanitary towel stuck to her leg and a pool of baby sick on her shoulder. She'd burst into tears the minute she saw Luisa.

'She won't stop crying. My fanny hurts, and my boobs won't stop leaking,' she cried out loud.

'Oh shit', Luisa panicked. 'I don't know what to do - what do we do?? Shall I call someone? Why is she crying? Why won't she stop? Where is she??' Luisa did not have much experience with babies. Without speaking, Megan opened the door wider, and Luisa raced in. She followed the wailing and found Izzy in her Moses basket, red in the face, arms and legs thrashing around like she was trying to fight her way out of a boxing ring. Luisa instinctively picked her up and jogged her up and down on her shoulder. Izzy immediately calmed down, and Luisa fell in love with her right then and there.

'She hates me,' Megan wailed. 'She just hates me. You take her - she likes you, look, she's happy. TAKE HER PLEASE,' Megan begged.

Luisa laughed. 'She doesn't hate you, Meg; you can't have pissed her off that much in a few days, surely?'

'I have no idea about babies, but my first suggestion would be hunger - can you feed her?' She handed Izzy over to Megan on the sofa, 'You feed, I'll make tea'.

They muddled through the first couple of years together, and not long after, Luisa announced she was pregnant with Lucy. Megan cried; Luisa couldn't tell if she was happy, sad or still crying as she had done since Izzy was born. The truth was, it was all of those things.

Their friendship had continued to grow over the years. They were there for each other as they brought up their girls as single parents, navigating toddler tantrums, first days at school, first periods and teenage tantrums.

'Izzy's OK', Megan replied, stirring sugar into her tea. 'She's turned a bit of a corner since she started college; I think a new set of friends helped. She's just getting on with it.'

'What are her plans?' Luisa asked, 'I can't believe she's

nearly finished school! Where has the time gone?'

'Who knows?' Megan looked up at Luisa. 'One minute, she's taking a gap year. Next, she's getting a job, then she's going off to uni.' Megan shrugged her shoulders. 'Changes her mind like the bloody weather, that girl', she joked.

'Wonder who she gets that from?' Luisa grinned.

'Sod off, I was never that bad!' Megan protested.

'If it wasn't your choice of career, it was your sexuality. One minute you were after the boys; next minute you were after the girls, ' Luisa relayed.

Megan laughed, 'I can't help it if I am indecisive. And given my track record with men, maybe I would have been better off sticking with girls'.

Luisa looked at her friend. There was an air of sadness about her last statement. Megan had not been with Izzy's dad long before she got pregnant, and although he said all the right things at the time, he didn't stick around for more than the nappy stage. Megan had been in a few relationships since, but none of them lasted for long. Even though she had many potential options waiting for her, none of them could ignite anything in Megan that would make her want to pursue them. Luisa noticed Megan's gloominess and reached across to take her hand. She gave it a gentle squeeze to show her support. Luisa was always fiercely loyal to her friends, but she struggled with other people's emotions as she never knew what to say.

Megan broke the silence. 'So, are you going to crack open the biscuits?'

Luisa was grateful for the interjection and got up a little too quickly. 'Yes, yes, of course, sorry.' She reached up to the biscuit tin. 'Oh shit, hold on, no, sorry, for fucks sake, this was full yesterday! Lucy's been at them! They were bloody chocolate, too,' Luisa declared as she set the biscuit tin down a little too hard. 'Bet she doesn't do this at her bloody dad's house.'

'Bet her bloody dad doesn't buy chocolate biscuits in the first place, Lu, you know how tight he is.'

They both laughed. They both knew all too well how tight *he* was.

'You'll miss her eating all the biscuits one day', Megan said sadly, feeling the ever-impending departure of Izzy to Uni.

'Yea, I know,' replied Luisa, echoing Megan's tone. Megan felt the weight in Luisa's response. She returned to the table and hugged her almost a little too hard.

'We've got this, Lu, ' she whispered in her ear.

Luisa didn't reply, but she held on as hard as possible.

'Ow, blummin 'eck Lu, not so hard, I've been to the gym, remember!' Megan winced in pain and pulled away.

'Oh god, yes, sorry', laughed Luisa, 'remind me why this is good for you again?' she teased.

After another few rounds of tea and tears, Luisa felt like every last ounce of energy had drained away in her tears. She flopped onto the sofa, exhausted and fuzzy with the aftermath of letting her emotions go. She loved it when Megan came over but was annoyed with herself for crying again. She was tired of the constant circle of wanting to be happy but not allowing herself to change things for fear of upsetting Lucy. She lived in fear of losing her relationship with her only child; she feared Lucy deciding she didn't want to live with her anymore. She didn't want to rock the boat. She felt anchored with the responsibility of being a constant but also wanting to set sail for adventure. At what point in her life did she lose that spark that ignited behind her glassy blue eyes whenever there was an opportunity for fun.

She couldn't remember the last time she actually went out and enjoyed herself without checking her phone to see if Lucy had messaged or left early to make sure she wasn't too tired for when Lucy returned the next day. She never let herself go anymore and felt trapped in a cycle of wanting more but not willing to put her needs first, any of them. What she didn't realise was that she needed the most was the one thing she would never allow herself to be. And that thing was simply to be happy.

Chapter 7

Lucy sat perched on her bed in her lavender-painted room, her lilac duvet cover contrasting with the feelings of frustration that enveloped her. Year 10 had become a tiresome, monotonous routine. In just a year, she'd finally be free from the clutches of school, exams, and endless revision. The thought of having an entire summer to herself was a tantalising prospect.

Opportunities for jobs were scarce, especially without access to reliable transportation, and apprenticeships were far from plentiful. Lucy, though, had her sights set on something more significant—university. She yearned to break free from the confines of Crosslands and explore a world filled with fresh experiences, diverse people, and new perspectives.

Her aspirations led her to dream of attending university in a distant city, far removed from the familiar streets of Crosslands. It wasn't that she disliked her hometown; she simply craved more. She hungered for a life surrounded by like-minded individuals who shared her passions and interests. Above all, she yearned to paint, a creative outlet that captivated her soul.

In her daydreams, Lucy envisioned herself waking up in a chic loft apartment in New York City, the tantalising aroma of freshly brewed coffee wafting through the air as she indulged in a leisurely breakfast of sausage and pancakes. From there, she'd make her way across the city to her art gallery, where her paintings would grace the walls, fetching prices in the hundreds of thousands of dollars. The reality at her school, however, was far from ideal. GCSE Art wasn't offered, leaving her to make do with textiles as the closest alternative. But Lucy remained undeterred, determined to pursue her artistic dreams and break free from the confines of her small town.

Lucy's heart was set on pursuing Fine Art at university, envisioning herself as a student in a vibrant city like Liverpool or Manchester. The one silver lining to living in Crosslands was its central location in Worcestershire, making it a gateway to the rest of the country. Regardless of which direction she chose, a pulsating city lay ahead, waiting to be explored. Excitement beckoned, and Lucy was determined to answer the call. She was resolute in avoiding a fate like her mother's, trapped on the outskirts of a picturesque village bordering a less-than-desirable town. She refused to be tethered to a dead-end job in a stifling office with no social life. Lucy yearned for adventure, a chance to traverse the globe, savour foreign cuisines, and embrace local traditions. She craved life's experiences in all their vibrant diversity. Above all, she yearned for the exhilaration of it all.

'I can't believe we'll be going into Year 11', chirped Sally.

'I can't believe we're going to have to sit our exams this year', winced Kate.

'I'm excited', guessed Lucy, 'we'll get to go to all the parties'.

Kate and Sally exchanged glances.

'What? What's up with you? You two need to let loose a little; you're becoming really boring,' Lucy added.

'We're not going to get invited to any parties, Lucy', Kate added.

'*I* am!' Lucy snapped back, 'Evie Stretton has already asked me to go shopping in Brum with her and Layla.'

'Evie Stretton? Evie' My skirt is so short you can see my arse' Stretton?' Kate frowned, 'why on earth would you want to do that? She's probably only asked you to carry the stolen goods so she doesn't get arrested again,' she said cruelly.

'Has she actually?' added Sally.

Lucy nodded. 'I haven't said I'd go yet, but I think I will; I mean, it's not like there's anything else to do around here'.

'She was vaping up the rec the other night,' Kate added.

'And?' asked Lucy.

'Just saying,' huffed Kate.

'And what? You think just because she was vaping that I'm going to start?'

'No, just saying, she was smoking. Bet she's having sex too,' she added.

Lucy shook her head. 'and what if she is?'

'we don't actually know that she is', chipped in Sally.

Kate sighed. 'Well, if you want to be friends with them, then I doubt we'll do anything together this year. I hate the lot of them, and why they have to wear so much make-up to school, I don't know. My mum says they're trouble'.

'Or maybe they're just having fun,' Lucy said. 'Like we should be doing.'

'Well, if that's your idea of fun, then crack on', sulked Kate.

'Do you think I'll get an invite to these parties' asked Sally hopefully.

Lucy shrugged, 'no idea, Sal, but I'm telling you now, they won't have to ask *me* twice'.

Lucy couldn't help but notice a striking lack of ambition among her friends, and their indifference towards leaving town began to frustrate her. Their lack of enthusiasm for her plans was increasingly evident.

'No way I'm going to uni', Kate told her. 'I'm not getting saddled with a load of debt before I've had a chance to enjoy myself'.

'You don't have to pay it all back, you know', retorted Lucy. 'It just comes out of your wages. You don't even have to pay anything if you don't earn enough.'

'So what's the point if you're going to come out of it with a job that pays so little you don't earn enough to pay it back? I thought you were supposed to get paid loads of money if you've been to uni?'

'My cousin went to uni and spent five years signing on because he was overqualified for every job he went for', added Sally. 'My mum says I can go if I want, but she won't support me financially.'

'You could get a job?' offered Lucy. 'That's what most students do.'

'So study and work? Or, just work. You'd earn more money in four years working than you would at uni,' Kate stated

Lucy rolled her eyes.

'I don't even know if I'm going to go to college, let alone Uni', Kate said boldly. 'My dad says I can do an apprenticeship in the office'. Kate's dad ran a modest transport business in town. Her whole family worked there in some capacity, and it was assumed that Kate would end up there, too.

'The wages will be crap, but I'll get a qualification at the end of it, and then I'll go somewhere else', she stated, having clearly already thought about this.

'And you reckon your dad will be OK with that?' Sally added, laughing. 'Everyone knows that if you're a Smithson, you work at Smithson's haulage yard' (she sang the last three words, mimicking the radio advert that seemed to play every 10 minutes on the local radio station. Kate reached across, grabbed a pillow, and hit Sally with it playfully.

'Right then, when *I* go off to Uni, you can all come and visit me if you can drag yourself away from Crosslands, that is', Lucy declared.

'As if you'll still want to be friends with us when you're in the big city with your uni friends', said Sally sadly.

'And all this talk may be totally irrelevant anyway because you're assuming we're going to pass our GCSEs, let alone A Levels', interrupted Kate. 'And if I have Mr Waton for English again next year, then you can guarantee I will fail.' Lucy and Sally laughed. Kate had disliked Mr Walton since he asked her to read a chapter of The Great Gatsby. The line, 'the orchestra leader varies his rhythm obligingly for her, and there is a chatter as the erroneous news goes around' became 'erogenous news', and the whole class fell apart laughing.

'Well, we've basically got one school year left, and after that, who knows what's going to happen', Lucy said.

They all looked at each other. They knew their friendship would change forever over the next few years.

Chapter 8

Jon, Luisa's ex, returned home from work that evening with a heavy cloud of frustration hanging over him yet again. He carelessly hung his worn rucksack on the back of the kitchen chair, impatiently flicked on the kettle, and slumped into a seat at the small kitchen table.

'Maxine!' he bellowed. He didn't expect a prompt response; Maxine had always been somewhat of an enigma. Her life followed no discernible routine except for the sporadic openings of her shop, which seemed to happen whenever she pleased. She relished the freedom of owning her own business, and predictability rarely followed any routine.

In stark contrast to Maxine's passion for her business, Jon harboured a profound disdain for his office job. He loathed every job he'd ever taken on and never managed to stay in one for more than a couple of years. His mantra became, "I just haven't found my thing yet," which he regularly shared with anyone who inquired about his career path. He'd tried his hand at various roles—a stint as a teaching assistant, a brief interlude as a cinema usher, and a foray into the world of recruitment. All, he swiftly concluded, were 'a waste of time'. His frustration was palpable as he confided in Maxine,

'I don't understand why people don't recognise my potential. I'm clearly wired differently; I could do these jobs standing on my head.'

Jon's charisma and quick wit invariably secured him a spot in nearly every interview he was invited to. Each time, he embarked on a new career with boundless enthusiasm and grand aspirations, only to confront the disheartening monotony that inevitably led him back to square one.

Jon endured a whole year at the insurance company. The job, while mind-numbingly dull, did have one significant advantage: its proximity to his home. He could easily walk to the office, saving him from a daily commute and allowing him to squeeze in an extra twenty minutes of sleep each morning. This arrangement also spared him the hassle of worrying about driving, an absolute convenience, especially after one of his frequent late-night drinking sessions. Given his unreliable camper van, walking to work ensured he made it on time most mornings.

The office occupied a building that had likely once been a residential dwelling. Downstairs, there was an unmanned reception area, while a dated kitchen at the back of the building housed a kettle and a microwave. The main office was upstairs, adorned with a moss-green carpet and garish orange curtains valiantly clinging to a broken curtain rail. Jon's office was a shared space, and he found himself in the company of three elderly men who seemed content to spend their days planted firmly in their seats. Their primary task involved making phone calls to individuals who were often less than thrilled to engage in conversations about insurance they neither wanted nor needed. It wasn't the most stimulating job, but Jon had the benefit of constant access to a computer, which provided a welcome diversion when he grew weary of the monotonous telephone calls.

The longest Jon had ever remained in a job was when he and Luisa first moved into their house in Copcut Green. He was determined to be the best father he could possibly be to Lucy, which meant he had to work diligently to provide for his family. And that's precisely what Jon did. He put in long hours and often worked on weekends to ensure he earned enough to cover Luisa's wages while she was on leave. The sense of responsibility finally motivated him.

Jon had an innate talent for making friends and found himself enjoying the company of his coworkers. He liked one particular person a hell of a lot. In fact, he wanted her so much that he spent every spare minute he could with her. She was exciting. She made going to work exciting. On the other hand, home presented its own challenges, especially with a baby. Luisa had high expectations and a desire for perfection. Jon started feeling stifled by the relentless routine and lack of sleep. While he adored Lucy, he found it increasingly difficult to handle the pressures of being at home. Luisa became needy and emotional, and Jon felt ill-equipped to cope with that level of emotional intensity. It was unfortunate because he did genuinely love Luisa at the beginning. She was a firecracker when they first met, a burst of energy that drew him in. However, the stress of having Lucy took its toll on them both. Luisa gained weight, and her mood became increasingly unpredictable, which wasn't something Jon had much time for.

Jon poured himself a coffee and went to his home office, which he set up in the corner of their bedroom. He fired up his PC and set his coffee on the 'coolest dad ever' coaster. He sat back in his leather-looking office chair and smiled to himself. His bitcoins were gaining momentum, and his investments were moving in the right direction. He started dabbling in stocks and shares a while ago, not knowing what he was doing initially. He soon got to grips with the bucks in trends and the unexpected successes. On paper, he was, at this moment in time, quite a rich man. Of course, it was all virtual. He had no cash to pay the mortgage or replace his car. 'One day', he told Maxine, 'one day we will reap the benefits of all this, and all those doubters will be laughing on the other side of their faces. Maxine smiled. 'You are so clever, sweetheart.'

Jon was feeling quite pleased with himself. Unlike his previous girlfriends, Maxine had a relaxed attitude towards everything. Jon had a history of being a serial dater, ending his relationships within a month or two, and that suited him just fine. He would get bored easily and preferred the initial excitement of a new relationship, the thrill of the chase, and the excitement of the first times. After that, he would become frustrated with the need for commitment or labels. He would often tell his partners, 'I just want to have fun, I don't want to settle down again.' When Maxine entered his life, she was distant and difficult to get a hold of. Jon found this alluring, and before they knew it, they had discovered a happy medium.

Maxine ran a small shop in Crosslands selling nick-nacks,

crystals, handmade clothing and incense. She made enough to cover her rent, but that was about it. She didn't need material things; she just wanted to have fun. Jon was all for that. They would take off in her camper van and spend the night at various places, enjoying copious amounts of alcohol and often smoking something herbal that Maxine kept for special customers behind the counter.

Maxine was a free spirit. She didn't want to settle down any more than he did. Still, ironically, a short time later, they found themselves living together. Maxine moved in with Jon, combining their income so that they could enjoy themselves with their newfound disposable cash.

Despite being utterly unreliable as a partner, Jon had always taken care of Lucy as best he could. He paid his child maintenance (although begrudgingly and often not on time) and always had Lucy a few nights a week. He enjoyed having her there, being 'dad' for a couple of hours. Jon did love Lucy; he loved how quiet and awkward she could be. He loved that she just went along with his plans and seemed to take to every girlfriend he introduced her to. She was easygoing. He liked that.

He saw Lucy grow from a quiet, sensitive young girl to an inquisitive, engaging young lady. She spent much of her time in her room with her sketchbook at Jon's house, but since meeting Maxine, she started wanting to spend more time with them. Jon loved watching Maxine and Lucy together; Maxine would teach her all about the healing properties of her crystals and how aromatherapy can help with various ailments. Lucy would drink it all in, taking a sincere interest in whatever Maxine told her. They talked into the early hours about Maxine's time in Thailand and her trek across the Sahara. She helped Maxine finish off her handmade clothes (her GCSE textiles coming to some use at last).

Maxine arrived just in time for Jon as he started to tire of the dating game. He had always been attracted to petite women, and Maxine, with her yoga-toned body and slight frame, ticked that box. She never married, had children, or wanted to be tied down. But she, too, was getting to the age where she just wanted a quiet life and some company. No pressure, no expectations, just a bit of affection and someone to talk to. Lucy was an added bonus, another voice, another opinion, and much to Maxine's delight, someone who took a vested interest in all of the things important to Maxine, her alternative lifestyle and a carefree view of the world. There were no boundaries with Maxine, no rules and no structure, the exact opposite of the world that Lucy lived in.

Jon heard the front door shut. 'Maxine!' he called again. He recognised the familiar sound of light footsteps on the stairs. Maxine opened the bedroom door wearing a long, floaty blue chiffon dress with a scarf on her ash blonde hair.

'Good day at work, hunny?' she enquired as she climbed onto his lap and nestled herself into his neck.

'Better now it's over', he stated.

'Bet I can make it even better', Maxine whispered as her hand found its way along his thigh and onto his crotch.

'It's Wednesday, Max; Lucy will be here in a min.'

Maxine immediately stopped what she was doing. She knew

where she stood in the pecking order when Lucy was around and was at peace with that.

'Oh yes, I've brought more material from the shop for her to show her how to sew a sleeve.' She jumped off to find out her wares.

Jon laughed to himself. Maxine really was a stick of dynamite. He just wasn't sure if he would ever have control of the fuse.

Chapter 9

As it was Lucy's night to spend with her dad, Luisa didn't need to re-balance herself before opening the front door. Luisa would only be exposed to whatever mood Lucy was in for an hour at the most. There was just enough time for Lucy to get her things together before Luisa would drop her off at Jon's.

'Lucy? Have you got your stuff ready?' Luisa asked as she shut the door behind her and dropped her keys on the hallway table. She was met with silence.

'LUCY!' Luisa repeated. Why did it always take a second call until she raised a response?

'Why are you shouting at me?' Lucy retorted from the kitchen. 'I'm literally right here'.Lucy threw her arms down for dramatic effect.

Luisa was determined not to react; she hated parting on bad terms.

'Just checking you could hear me - you'll never guess what just happened to me on my way home?'

Lucy rolled her eyes.

'Go on then, at least attempt to guess', Luisa pleaded.

'You just said I'd never guess, so why bother trying?' Lucy stated.

'OK, so I was on the bed at Hall Farm, and I wasn't speeding or anything, but then I had to slam my brakes on and swerve across the road. I'm lucky to be alive, actually,' embellished Luisa. 'Aren't you going to ask me why?'

'Why?' repeated Lucy.

'Because then I can tell you?'

'No, mum. Why did you slam your brakes on and swerve?' Lucy was losing patience, as she often did when conversing with Luisa.

'Oh right, yes. Some lad was walking along the road; how I missed him, I have no idea. Who even walks along there? It's miles to Crosslands! I literally had to swerve right across the road. Good job nothing was coming the other way, can you imagine? Daft sod. If I'd have run him over, I'd have felt awful. Dressed in dark clothes too! I didn't really stand a chance,' Luisa rambled, grateful to retell the story to ease some of her anxiety.

Lucy stopped searching through her bag. 'Where did you say it was?' she asked, chewing her bottom lip.

'Hall farm, right on the bend!'

'What did he look like?' asked Lucy, pretending to be disinterested in the answer.

'I don't know! It all happened so fast. Youngish, I'd say. Early twenties? Dark hair. I didn't really stop to look at his face; I was too busy trying not to run him into the hedge. Why? Any idea who it was? I didn't recognise him from the village,' Luisa stated.

Lucy glared at Luisa. 'I'm just asking. Obviously, I don't know who it was. Why would I?' she snapped defensively. Luisa was a little taken back. She also noted the look on Lucy's face, which she recognised and made her insides knot slightly. The look she inherited from her father. Luisa knew in an instant that Lucy was lying.

The car journey to Jon's was silent, apart from Luisa's failed attempts at a conversation. As she drove, she glanced over at her teenage daughter. When did she get so tall? It seemed like yesterday that she was toddling around in her wellies, pointing at everything and babbling away to herself. She was so quiet now, only speaking to retort to something Luisa requested or to moan about something. Luisa tried hard to put it down to the teenage phase, but it still hurt. All she wanted to do was laugh with Lucy, spend some time together, and do something fun. They seemed to clash about everything, even when Luisa specifically tried to do something she knew Lucy would like, such as getting her favourite tea or suggesting they go to the cinema, it was either she had gone off whatever it was she bought or that she had too much homework to do. Looking over at Lucy, her eyes fixed through the passenger window, Luisa felt that this was a passenger sitting next to her, not her daughter.

'Here it was, love,' Luisa offered as they came around the corner, where she nearly swiped the legs of the young man walking along the road.

'Here what was?' replied Lucy, not even directing her voice in the right direction.

'Where I nearly ran over that lad'.

Lucy shrugged her shoulders.

'Don't you think it's odd that someone would be walking along this road, though? I mean, it's a fair old trek into town from here, isn't it?' Luisa continued.

'I don't know, mum, maybe his lift let him down, or maybe, just maybe, he fancied a walk. Comes to something when you can't even walk down the road without someone thinking you're up to something. You're all the same; you think all teenagers are up to no good.'

'I never said he was a teenager, Lucy', said Luisa, matter-of-factly.

'Yes, you did.'

'No, what I said was, he looked early twenties.'

'Same thing, in any case, he was old enough to walk along a public road without supervision. Or judgment,' Lucy stated, folding her arms.

The next ten minutes passed in silence.

Lucy opened her door the second Luisa pulled up outside Jon's.

'See you tomorrow night then', she offered as she went to slam the door shut.

'Hold on, wait a minute!' Luisa shouted

'What?' Lucy turned around, clearly aggravated at the three-second delay in her plans.

'Love you.' Luisa smiled.

'You too,' Lucy muttered, letting herself through the ter-raced house front door. The door slammed shut, and Luisa sat in the car for a moment, grounding herself. It didn't matter how many times she told herself that this was a phase; she couldn't help but feel that she was losing her relationship with Lucy.

Chapter 10

Right, OK, so here we go. Luisa had been scrolling through her camera roll for a good forty minutes when she eventually found a photo she was happy with. *There, upload, crop. OK, that looks OK.* She stared at the photo of herself, dressed in a cobalt blue wraparound dress at the wedding of one of the teachers last summer. That was a lovely weekend in the end. She wasn't going to go because although Lucy was at Jon's that weekend and everyone from work was invited, she felt a little anxious about social situations.

'Luisa', Megan said sternly, 'What is the problem? You'll know loads of people there'.

'But I will have to go in on my own, and it's just awkward; I could just stay at home with my PJs on and watch a film.'

'What? Like you do every weekend?' Megan stated, one eyebrow raised. 'Stop being ridiculous, get your glad rags on, get some slap on your face, and go! Have a glass of wine while you're getting ready, put some tunes on!'

Luisa sighed. 'I'll have to drive Meg; I can't afford a taxi there and back.'

'Bollocks to that, what time do you have to be there? I'll take you.'

Megan was always on hand to prize Luisa out of her bubble.

Given the choice, Luisa would choose to stop at home at every opportunity. And Luisa didn't want to miss out on all the gossip, so she made a real effort to leave the house.

As she climbed into the front seat of the car, Megan exclaimed, 'Jesus Christ, you look fucking gorgeous, Lu!'.

Luisa giggled and blushed before she realised a gym-gear-clad passenger was sitting in the back of the car.

'Oh shit, sorry, hi' Luisa stumbled.

'Lu, this is Susie, we've just done a circuit session'. Megan explained.

'Yeah, excuse the sweaty top lip', Susie responded from the back, locking eyes with Megan in the rearview mirror and laughing.

'Susie, Lu, you know all about her already', she said as she pulled off. Luisa watched Megan's face turn a shade of pink, which she couldn't help but think had nothing to do with the circuit session.

'Right, now get out and have a bloody good time', Megan instructed as she pulled up at the venue.

'Oooh, this looks bloody posh', Susie observed from the back of the car.

Luisa smiled. 'Thank you, Meg, honestly, I really appreciate it'. She leaned over and kissed her cheek.

'Go!' Megan instructed, 'Get yourself a drink and have a bloody great time - and if you want a lift home, just let me know'.

It was one of the times that Luisa was really glad that she had listened to Megan and had made an effort to leave her house. The wedding was at a stunning venue, a beautiful rustic barn in the rolling Worcestershire countryside. There were ivory and blush peony-topped barrels at every turn, and twinkly fairy lights festooned over the courtyard. Miss Crossly, sorry, Mrs Catagna married the son of an extremely wealthy businessman, and although her husband had a modest office job, they still benefited from the extended family wealth. The warm summer weather meant most of the evening reception was set outside. The wine was flowing, and photos were taken, many of them without Luisa knowing, so there was no awkward posing, just natural happy faces. This photo she used was not posed, not strained, just a smile taken from her good side.

Janet made full use of the free bar and got so drunk she dropped her handbag into the large fishpond in the middle of the courtyard, and the venue staff spent a good hour trying to fish it out. She then had the whole reception party looking for her phone after she declared it had gone missing from the table where she was sitting. Janet accused one of the waiters of stealing it to 'bump up his petty little wages'. She had become quite nasty when the manager asked her to calm down. Luisa took her outside for some fresh air, and that's when Janet found her phone tucked into her bra. She bought a round of drinks for everyone to celebrate finding it. The poor young waiter, who had avoided Janet ever since the accusation, found himself sitting with them as Janet insisted he have a glass of wine as an apology. Luisa locked eyes with him. 'It's fine, just tip it away, she won't notice'.

* * *

Right, what's next? Bio – tell us a bit about yourself. *Oh crikey.*

I thought the photo was going to be the hard part. OK, so, middle-aged mother of one seeks. No. Delete. It's not a dating ad from the back of the paper in the 80s. Concentrate Luisa. OK, divorced mum looking for fun. No. Delete. It sounds like I'm after a one-night stand; maybe I am - no. No, I'm definitely not. OK, so fun mum of one looking for someone to share the odd evening meal and maybe more. Eesh. Delete, delete, delete. No, I can't do this. Luisa slammed the laptop lid down. Why was she doing this? She should really be worrying about the meeting tomorrow morning, not setting herself up for online dating.

The meeting *had* been bothering Luisa. Normally Head Jackie would just come into the office if she ever wanted to speak to them. It was strange that she had called them both into her room. There really wasn't anything that had happened that warranted a reprimand, not that they would get one. Head Jackie didn't work like that; she was firm but fair and dealt with situations professionally. She was the most supportive boss Luisa ever had. Even when Janet forgot what day they returned to work after Christmas and didn't show up, Head Jackie was extremely understanding. And then again, when Janet turned up a little worse for wear at the Year Six leavers' party. It was always Janet in trouble, never Luisa, which made it even more intriguing why they were both required in the meeting.

Luisa's phone jumped to life and snatched her from her thoughts; it was Megan.

'Are you out partying because it's Wednesday and you are child-free?'

'Yes, I am currently standing on a bar coyote ugly stylee

grinding myself against a rather buff looking chap with a penchant for cocktails', Luisa humoured. 'Actually Meg, you can help me. I need to write a bio for this stupid dating app.'

'Oh yes, oh yes yes yes yes yes yes yes yes, I am so here for this. OK, are you ready? I'm going straight in. Fun-loving forty-two-year-old..are you forty-two?

'Yes'

'OK, I'm a fun-loving forty-two-year-old who loves nothing more than a good night out - even better if it includes good food and expensive wine. Weekends away are a must, as is a love of cheesy pop.'

'Hold on a minute, Meg, expensive wine? I don't know the difference between a Claret or a Zinfandel, let alone anything else.'

'Yes, but it shows you have high standards.'

'In men maybe, but not wine!'

'Trust me, it gives an air of sophistication.'

'Which is then ruined by the cheesy pop reference.'

'Oh no, this is genius because otherwise you end up with a really boring suit; no one wants that.'

Luisa sighed. This wasn't such a good idea after all.

'That's that sorted then. Keep me posted. Anyway, the actual reason I am phoning is to ask when were you going to tell your best friend that her second favourite teenager in the world was dating?'

Luisa paused momentarily, confused by Megan's long-winded way of asking a question.

'What are you wittering on about?'

'Lucy! When were you going to tell me that Lucy had a boyfriend?'

Luisa felt a lead weight deposit itself in the pit of her

stomach.

'I'm not sure she has. What makes you say that?'

'Izzy saw her up the rec earlier - with a boy. Are you still there, Lou?'

Lucy never talked about boyfriends; she doubted if Lucy even fancied anyone, and she certainly never discussed it with her.

'I don't know Meg, she's never said anything to me. And define *with a boy.*'

'OK, well, they weren't snogging or anything, but they were sitting together, up on the rec, you know, by the old playground. She was sitting on the swing, and he was standing talking to her.'

'Right, so not actually doing anything to suggest that he was her boyfriend?'.

'Well, no, but how often does Lucy go out full stop, let alone on her own with a boy?'

It wasn't that unusual for Lucy to be out when she was at Jon's; all her school friends came from the Crosslands estate, so she saw more of them when she was with him. Sometimes, Kate and Sally would get a bus to the village, but it wasn't a regular thing.

'It was probably just someone from school, ' Luisa said sharply, hurt that she felt so out of the loop.

'Yeah, probably', replied Megan, sensing the tone in Luisa's reply.

'Anyway, let me know who you get on with the app!'

'Yeah, yeah, will do. Speak soon.'

Luisa ended the call and threw her phone down on the sofa. How did parenting become so complicated? She never felt so distant from Lucy, and it scared her. When would it stop?

When would she get her daughter back? When would they sit in the kitchen together, drinking tea and dunking biscuits again?

Luisa felt relieved when Lucy went to Jon's, giving her an evening of not having to tread on eggshells in fear of saying the wrong thing. It was like living with a black cloud sometimes, which was starting to bring Luisa down. And then the mum guilt consumed her for feeling that way, and she would feel like the world's worst parent. At times, she felt it was a competition, and she couldn't compete with Jon. More was going on at his house; he was the fun parent, rules were lapse, Lucy had more freedom, and Maxine had way more in common with Lucy; they shared interests, and she was exciting. All Luisa could share was the oxygen in the house.

A mug of tea, as always, passed the half an hour it took for Luisa to wallow in self-pity and come out of the other side. She picked her phone back up and texted Lucy.

'Just checking you're OK x.'

Two blue ticks appeared, but no reply. At least she's alive, Luisa thought.

She then went back to her unfinished profile. Right, it's now or never.

Fun-loving 42-year-old. Love nights in and out and am pretty partial to a glass of wine. If it ends with a boogie to cheesy pop – even better! Would like to meet someone who shares my interests – reading, live music, and good food. Looking for the occasional night out/in, but nothing too serious.

Submit. Done.

Luisa then turned her phone on silent, placed it face down on the sofa, and turned up the TV.

Chapter 11

When Luisa realised that the reason she had no message notifications from the dating app was that she hadn't actually swiped right for anyone, her disappointment lifted. Once she got her head around the fact that it was just a swipe and not a marriage proposal, her finger was getting quite the workout. She soon had five whole messages in her inbox, waiting for her to read.

'Hey you? Bit jaded from the dating game so fancy some no-strings-attached fun?'

Luisa felt her cheeks flush a little. This really wasn't what she was after, and she wasn't sure what the etiquette was in this situation. Nevertheless, she found herself checking out his profile. She may have been persuaded if he was ultra-good-looking, but he was more Tom Thumb than Tom Hardy. She then spent a good twenty minutes berating herself about basing this on looks alone. *Does this make me shallow? Would I judge a man if he was selecting a potential partner based solely on looks? Am I insane?* He'd taken the time to message her, so the least she could do would be thanks, but no thanks reply. *'Hi. Thank you for your reply. I'm not really looking for no-strings-*

attached fun, so good luck.'
She moved quickly on to the next message.

'Hey babe. Would luv to get to no you more. I'm looking for someone to go out with and have a beer with to. I have kids but they stay with there mum alot so plenty of time for some fun. You up for it? Let me no'.

Luisa sucked the air through her teeth. One thing she detested was poor grammar. She found herself marking his work in her head. Luisa wasn't a teacher, but she was sure he wouldn't score very high if this was a literacy test.

'Thank you for your message; unfortunately, I don't like beer, but I wish you all the best.'

Messages three and four were not actually messages at all but pictures. Quite graphic images of things Luisa wouldn't expect to see until after a fifth date, let alone pre-date. Message five, however, was promising.

Hello Luisa. Nice profile picture. I am Martyn, 43, a single dad of one. I, too, enjoy fine dining and wine. Not sure about the cheesy pop, though? What counts as cheesy? If we can find some common ground music-wise, maybe we could discuss it over dinner? And a glass of wine? Anyway, hope you've had a good day. Hopefully, speak soon. Take care.

OK, this is promising, she thought, eyebrows raised. His spelling and grammar were spot on, not too pushy, and no explicit photo was attached. A solid score on the looks front.

Yes, well done, Martyn.

Luisa felt a little fizz of something she hadn't felt in a while. Someone had seen a picture of her; they liked it and were now chatting her up via the medium of text. That's the equivalent of seeing someone in a bar and offering them a drink. Now, she was toying with the idea of replying. It was much easier when she wasn't interested, but now she had no idea what to say to him. *Also, why did I tell him I liked cheesy pop?!*

She smiled to herself as she climbed into bed, connected her phone charger and turned her ringer on. She always did this when Lucy was at Jon's in case of an emergency. Not that she thought Jon couldn't cope in an emergency, but it made her feel better. It made her think that although her only child was not in her home with her mum, Luisa was still being a responsible parent.

Thoughts of the meeting had been pushed to the back of her mind for an hour or so, but just as her head hit the pillow, they decided that now would be a good time to resurface. What could the meeting possibly be about? She racked her brain to think what she may have missed; had she not passed a message on? Had someone overheard her and Janet talking inappropriately in the office? Had she not been dressed professionally enough?

Her go-to was always a negative; it stemmed from her being a people pleaser. She hated the thought that she had upset someone, often overcompensating with over-the-top gestures or putting herself out just to make things better. Nine times out of ten, she hadn't even upset them in the first place; she'd just created a situation in her head. She sighed. Making her wait was just cruel. She could have just come in and spoken to her if it was that important, not make her wait until the next day.

The last time she checked her phone was 3.45 am. There was still no reply from Lucy, but she had received thirty-four messages from Tinder, thirty of them from the same person. Brian from Derby sought a long-term commitment for him and his cats. No Brian. No, thank you. Your blurb about your interests in live music and books was promising. You didn't disclose that you had ten cats or that the live music you mentioned was actually you playing your electric keyboard repertoire every night before bed. The book comment was promising, though, but unfortunately, the nail in the coffin was the photo of him sitting at his keyboard with a cat in one hand and his other hand proudly wrapped around his massive erection. Luisa closed her eyes and shook her head, trying to eradicate what she had seen that she could not unsee. Despite not wanting to seem rude, she couldn't muster up a reply to this one.

Luisa put her mobile phone back on the bedside table and turned to lie on her back. Her mind was still active and it reminded her of the incident on her way home, where she nearly sent a young man to his untimely death. She felt the familiar prickle of panic set in once more. What if he had gone into shock and fainted at the side of the road? Had he been there all night? At one point, she considered getting up and driving to the spot just to check he wasn't lying in the bushes. Had she clipped him? Could she be sure? What if he took her number plate and reported her for a hit-and-run?

She rolled over onto her side and tried, in vain, to slow her breathing down. Her heart was now pounding, and catching her breath felt like a struggle. She sat upright in an attempt to let more air into her lungs. Why did she always do this? This overthinking always made her feel like this. No, she was sure she hadn't hurt him, and if he had gone into shock, that wasn't her responsibility, not entirely; he really should have been wearing something more reflective if he was going to be walking along the road like that. She lay back down and closed her eyes to force herself to sleep, which she must have done at some point, if only for an hour or two before the alarm jolted her back awake.

Chapter 12

As Luisa drove to work, the near miss of the evening before played on her mind yet again. As she approached that same corner, she was mindful to be extra cautious as she relived the moment. Why did that boy look so familiar to her? She had no idea who it was, but something about it stuck in her mind. His face was so familiar, and it shook her. It could have very easily been a different story if she had been going that little bit faster, and he was that little bit further into the road. Who was he? What was he doing there? Why did she feel that she knew him? There were so many questions, but at least it kept the meeting anxiety at bay for a while longer.

She pulled up at work, noting that Janet's car was not in the car park. 'She better not be off,' Luisa thought. She really didn't want to sit in this meeting by herself. Luisa didn't make herself a drink that morning as she would typically; her stomach was churning, and her anxiety was making her breath too heavy. Her eyes were locked on the display on her watch as she saw 8.57 change to 8.58. When it gets to 8.59, I'll go and knock on Head Jackie's door,' she thought. Still no Janet. 08.59, Luisa stood up, wiped her sweaty palms down her navy trousers and walked along the corridor. When she arrived, the door was slightly ajar, so her gentle knock opened it slightly. Head Jackie was sitting at her rather too-large desk, which was covered in a sea of paperwork and books. She was looking for something frantically, and papers fell from her desk, floating to the floor, grateful to be excused from the chaos. A somewhat awkward Luisa stood in the now open doorway.

'Oh, gosh, yes, morning Luisa, is it that time already? Of course, it is, yes; thank you for being so prompt. No Janet?'

Luisa felt her chest tighten as various potential answers to that question flew through her mind. Luisa was very loyal, but she was also very honest.

'Not yet' was all that she managed.

Head Jackie looked at her watch. 'OK, well, I did really need both of you here, but I don't have much time, so I'll start, and I'll fill Janet in later.' Jackie set her forearms on the desk in front of her.

'Before I begin, can I just say how much we appreciate all you do for us, Luisa. I know the office can bear the brunt of a lot of paperwork and last-minute requests, but we all appreciate it, and you and Janet.'

This is it; I'm being made redundant.

'And as you know, the creation of the Crosslands Trust has been gaining momentum.'

Just say it. Just tell me now. Rip off the plaster, for god's sake

We now have five schools signed up and another two in the pipeline, which obviously means we have many office staff all doing similar roles across the county. This means...'

'I am so sorry, traffic through town was a nightmare this morning,' interrupted Janet as she breezed through the door and sat next to Luisa.

'What have I missed?'

Head Jackie looked over the top of her glasses at the windswept Janet, whose hair was falling out of her ponytail and whose blouse, although very clean, was untucked and creased. Luisa couldn't be sure, but she could smell something suspiciously similar to alcohol.

'I was just explaining to Luisa how the trust is growing.'

'Yes, it is, isn't it! It's all very exciting. I always said how this would be good for the town,' babbled Janet.

'Precisely', agreed Jackie, Head Jackie. 'Which is why we need to be strategic about our plans moving forward. The thing is, the admin of each of the schools is all done slightly differently at each setting....'

'You're telling me! They use register codes at St John's down in Lower Crosslands that I've never even heard of!' added Janet, her voice getting progressively louder.

Luisa could feel herself cringing inside. *Shut up, Janet, just let Jackie get to the point.*

'Yes, and moving forward, we want to bring these all in line so everyone is doing the same thing. Standardise it all, keep it all the same. It will mean that our data can be analysed more effectively. I won't bore you with all the details, but to get to the point of our meeting this morning...'

Finally

'The Trust is looking to appoint a Senior Office Manager, someone to oversee all of the settings, who will coordinate the admin and the staff. It's a big job, but I am letting you both know before the advert comes out. So as a gesture of goodwill, shall we say, if you wanted to pop in an application, I could, well, you know, see that it is looked upon favourably, so to speak.' Head Jackie started to laugh.

Janet looked at Luisa and shrugged her shoulders. Luisa wasn't sure what was so funny, so she and Janet sat in silence for what felt like a very long time.

'Any thoughts?' Head Jackie asked when she finally stopped laughing.

'No offence, Jackie, but I'm not really looking to advance my career. As soon as my mortgage is paid off, then I'll be looking to step down, not up.'

Jackie smiled and then raised her eyebrows.

'And that is entirely your prerogative, Janet. I am just letting you know, given that this will affect both of you either way.'

'Thank you', said Luisa. 'I appreciate you taking the time out for us this morning. It is definitely something I would like to know more about.'

Janet shot her a look, which Luisa consciously ignored.

'Well, the advert will be out soon, but if your application was, you know, acceptable, then there is no need to look externally, Luisa. Anyway, thank you both; I am due on a Teams meeting in the next few minutes, so if you don't mind,' she started pawing over the melee of paperwork across her desk.

'Oh yes, of course, sorry,' apologised Luisa, confused by the instructions she was given. Janet was already back through the door and heading to the office.

Back at her desk, Luisa felt unnecessarily awkward. She hadn't expected Janet to be so openly dismissive in front of Jackie.

'So what do you think about that then?' she asked.

'Nothing. Not interested,' said Janet. 'And you'd be mad to even consider it.'

'How come?'

'Imagine how much work is involved in that?

'But imagine how much more the salary would be! Lucy wants to go to Uni, so I'm going to need every penny I can get.'

'Well, I think you're daft. And also, I'm not entirely sure Jackie is even allowed to do that.' she said abruptly.

'Do what?' Luisa replied, still frowning.

'She's clearly not following policy. I'm sure there's something official that says you have to give everyone equal consideration. She can't just give you the job because you're the only one who applied, before it's even advertised'.

Luisa was hurt. 'So you don't think I'd be in with a chance if others applied?' she asked.

'No, I'm not saying that Lu, of course not; I just think it seems a bit underhand, that's all', she sniffed while trying to open her desk drawer.

Luisa was still hurt. She hadn't any plans to become manager of the year, but she did think that when Lucy was older, she would do something more with her career. This seemed like an opportunity too good to miss. She was hurt that Janet was being so dismissive.

'Wouldn't hurt to throw my hat in the ring, though', she stated stubbornly.

'Are you actually being serious?' Janet questioned, abruptly letting Luisa know she was annoyed at her considering it.

'Why wouldn't I be? Even if I'm not in with a chance, I don't want people to think I'm not interested in moving along the career ladder.'

'Unlike me, you mean.' said Janet, still trying to prise open her drawer.

'No, I don't mean that. I just mean that by applying, it looks like I'm interested in staying.'

'And I'm not?' retorted Janet again, kicking the drawer.

'Come on, Janet. I'm not saying anything about you; I'm just going to consider it, that's all. And even if neither of us gets the job, someone else will be our boss, so we better acknowledge that change is on the horizon.

Janet scowled. 'We've run out of sugar'

'what? '

'Sugar! We haven't got any.'

'You don't even take sugar', stated Luisa, confused.

'I know that. I'm just saying.' And with that, Janet picked up her bag and walked right out of the office.

Luisa sighed. Janet was never usually this tetchy. She was used to her early morning moods but never directed at her. She made her way to the kitchen to make herself a drink now that the anxiety had subsided. She stopped in her tracks. There on the side was a full bag of sugar.

Chapter 13

Luisa hit the 'send' button and closed the laptop lid. She spent all evening on the job application. Megan cast her eye over it and was pleased with the result.

'It looks good to me, Lu; it's a strange application, though, don't you think?' Megan asked.

'In what way?'

'Well, usually you have to give more than a written statement; where's the section for qualifications and training and stuff?'

'I guess as it's internal, they already have all that?' Luisa suggested, and there was no reason to question it further.

Salary had yet to be discussed, but there was bound to be a raise, meaning she could put by a little more each month. Jackie mentioned that she would be based at the high school for part of the week if successful. She wasn't sure how Lucy would feel about that, but it wasn't enough to prevent her from applying.

Janet had not actually been back to work since the sugar remark. Apparently, She called in to say she would be off for a while. And despite being good friends, Luisa was secretly relieved. Janet was being quite obnoxious recently, picking at everything Luisa said. Some tasks were incomplete, messages had not been passed on, and it was starting to grate on Luisa. Working with someone you classed as a friend could sometimes get tricky, especially when one of them isn't pulling their weight. A bonus of a new job would be that Luisa would only need to spend a couple of days in the office working with Janet - the space would do them good.

The downside of Janet not being in, was that Luisa had no one to discuss her forthcoming date with. She had finally plucked up the courage to arrange a date with Martyn, whose grammar was impeccable and who didn't seem too keen or desperate.

'So I was thinking, if it were OK with you, we could meet for coffee or a drink? He asked. Luisa sat contemplating this for what felt like an hour, her fingers poised over the keys and her heart beating faster and faster. Lucy was with Jon this weekend, so worrying about her was unnecessary. Her fingers started to type 'Yes, OK, how about this weekend, I'm free on Saturday?' and hit send before she realised what she was doing.

Her breath got louder and louder as she waited in anticipation for a reply. She didn't have to wait long.

'Really? That's great! Should we say coffee, then? There's a place on the other side of Crosslands that's just opened that sells amazing cakes. Should we try there?'

Luisa smiled to herself; she knew exactly what he was talking about. The cake slices were at least six inches tall, and she'd been trying to get Lucy to go with her for ages. Lucy declined, stating that sugar was a drug, a silent killer, an indication sign that Lucy had clearly been in conversation with Maxine. Luisa thought it had more to do with the fact that it was so close to Crosslands that she wouldn't want to be seen out with her mum by her school friends. Anyway, it was a good choice, and she was relieved it wasn't an offer of a drink; that seemed a little too much too soon for Luisa.

'I know it, yes that would be great. One-thirty? Two? I can meet you there?'

'One-thirty would be perfect. Looking forward to it already.'

Phew. Luisa felt a flutter of excitement or nerves, she wasn't sure which, in her stomach. A date. She was going on a date! Well, a coffee with a man, but that was as close to a date as she had come in a very long time. She knew that Jon and Lucy had made plans this weekend. Maxine was giving a yoga masterclass at a festival in Bristol, and they were given free wristbands for the weekend. There would be no chance of being spotted and having that awkward conversation. Luisa was conflicted. She didn't want to hide things from Lucy. Still, she also didn't want to cause any unnecessary anxiety – this may not come to anything, and he may not be her type. It was a coffee, not a wedding. There was no pressure.

An hour later, Luisa had second thoughts about everything. As if sent through the ether via the medium of psychotic thoughts, Megan called her.

'Have you sent it then?' she asked, hopefully.

'I have, yes, but do I actually want it, Meg, really? Am I ready for it? Do I want the extra responsibility? Could I even do the job? I'm rubbish at interviews. What if I mess it up, and everyone sees how stupid I am?

Megan interrupted her with laughter.

'OK, firstly, you haven't got an interview yet, let alone the job. And secondly, you aren't stupid because if you were, Jackie wouldn't have encouraged you to apply.'

'And if that isn't stressful enough, I've done something stupid and agreed to go on a date on Saturday.'

'Wait, what? Er, backup Lu, say that again.'

'A date, on Saturday.'

Megan was speechless.

'You have actually arranged a date on Saturday with a man without any discussion with me, and you're actually going to go?'

'Well, I don't know now, I feel silly. What would we talk about? I don't even know anything about him!'

'That's what the date is for, stupid. Oh my god, this is so exciting. What are you going to wear?' enquired Megan, giddy with excitement.

'I don't even know if I will go yet!' stated Luisa.

'Yes, you blummin well are'.

'I'm busy.'

'Doing?'

'Stuff.'

'Such as?'

'Arghh, stop! 'Luisa was exasperated.

'Lu, I love you, you are my best friend in the whole world., But please stop being a dick and just go on the bloody date,' Megan pleaded.

Luisa laughed. 'OK, OK, I'll go. But if I end up getting murdered, then I'll tell everyone it was your fault.'

'Deal. But you do know it will be OK, don't you? And if it isn't, then at least you're out of the house for a few hours, and someone is buying you coffee and cake. And you never know, you might even let your guard down and have a nice time?'

Luisa was not at all comfortable with this impending feeling of nervousness. A potential new job and boyfriend in the same week; this was not something Luisa was accustomed to. She was aware of Lucy upstairs doing her homework or whatever it was she did up there that meant she couldn't converse with her own mother. Luisa shouted up and asked her if she wanted a brew. Apparently, she was only drinking herbal tea after Maxine introduced her to green tea the other evening. And not just any green tea, the top-of-the-range green tea you could only get from the herbalist shop. 'Are you sure it's tea?' Luisa asked. Lucy rolled her eyes. 'What else would it be?'

'I don't know, you know what Maxine is like with her hippy-dippy ways and her crystals and incense -could be something hallucinogenic in there', Luisa joked.

'For God's sake, mum, for your information, Maxine is actually really cool. She's travelled all over Asia and experienced so much life. Just because you're happy in the same town and job you've always been in doesn't mean everyone else has to be,' Lucy spat.

Luisa was stunned. Where has this come from? She was just kidding and faced with a tirade of teenage emotion.

OK, I'd suggest you watch your tone Lucy, I was just joking,' Luisa said slowly.

Lucy scowled at Luisa, holding her in a gaze she didn't recognise. Her eyes were fierce, and her face indignant. Luisa wasn't sure who this person was in front of her, a million miles away from her fresh-faced Lucyloo who used to wrap her arms around her neck and tell her that she was her favouritist person in the whole widest world.

'So you don't want a brew then?' Luisa asked, trying to break the tension of the moment.

'No'.

Luisa raised an eyebrow.

'No, thank you'. Lucy added, rolling her eyes.

Luisa left her bedroom, a red rash rising up her chest, bringing an emotion that Luisa had no control over. She went to the bathroom, locked the food and sat on the toilet, the tears spilling from her eyes. She let them flow before she wiped her eyes, washed her face, flushed the chain and faced the rest of the evening alone on the sofa; a teenage daughter whom Luisa didn't recognise upstairs alone, on her bed, wishing she was somewhere else.

Chapter 14

'So, how did it go? Do I need to buy a hat?' Megan joked as Luisa poured the boiling water into two mugs. 'Hold on, don't tell me yet, let me get comfortable'. Luisa,laughing, stirred the tea, set the spoon on the side and carried the mugs to the kitchen table.

'OK – you may begin'. Megan sat, mug cradled between her hands, her eyes wide with anticipation and excitement.

Luisa laughed and looked at Meg fondly. She was always so invested in her life and interested in what she was doing. Luisa was looking forward to chatting to Megan about her coffee with Martyn. Megan drove over to Luisa's house first thing the following day for a debrief.

'OK, so I'm trying to figure out where to start.'

'At the beginning. I want all the details. Did he meet you outside? Did he stand up when you walked in?'

'Really? You want every single detail? We could be some time.' Luisa laughed, secretly enjoying the attention and the opportunity to talk about something other than her stroppy teenage daughter. She spent the next half an hour explaining the minor details.

Megan approved of Martyn's jeans, jacket, and trainers combo;

it was smart but not over the top and still trendy enough to be cool without trying too hard. She was also glad that she persuaded Luisa to wear the blue satin top they bought when they went shopping together earlier in the year.

'What about baggage?' Luisa frowned as she said this, taking a sip from her mug.

'Ex-partner, split up six years ago, same as me and Jon, one son, Zach, fifteen, same age as Lucy.'

'And do they get on?'

'Yes, he stays with him most weekends and a few nights in the week.'

'Not his son silly, his ex-wife'.

Luisa giggled. 'They seem to, he didn't talk much about her. She still lives in Crosswich and Zach goes to Heath High rather than Crosslands. Martyn moved to a rental on the other side of town and has been there ever since.'

Megan frowned. 'Is that far enough away to not bump into her?' she enquired.

'It didn't sound like there was any animosity between them, so I don't think it's an issue, ' Luisa replied. Crosswich was the neighbouring town, and Luisa knew it well; Jon worked there when they first bought their house in Copcut Green.

'So what happened between them?'

'He didn't say much about it, he wasn't bitter, I think they just grew apart. He said that after Zach was born, there was a distance between them. Didn't sound like either of them wanted to rebuild their relationship.'

'So he has Zach a lot, then? '

'Yes, I think they're quite close.'

'So how is that going to work?'

'What do you mean?

'When things get a bit, you know, physical.' She mouthed this last word as if trying to conceal what she was saying.

'It was one date!' Luisa laughed. 'I'm not thinking about stuff like that.'

'But will there be another one?'

Luisa giggled like a schoolgirl.

'Potentially, yes. I liked him. He was funny, and it felt effortless. I was so nervous, but he made me relax, and I really enjoyed his company.'

'Oooooooooo' Megan wasn't used to hearing Luisa talk like this. 'This is progress indeed,' she declared as she put her mug down.

'And any news on the job?'

'Closing date is tomorrow, so I guess I'll hear something after that,' Luisa replied.

'New job, new man, it'll be a new baby next', Megan said, raising her eyebrows.

'Oh shut up,' smiled Luisa. She had no intention of having any more children, but the thought of another date with Martyn and the excitement and nerves of applying for a new job left Luisa with a fizz inside that she hadn't felt in a long time.

Luisa stood at the sink, swilling out the mugs. The nervous excitement took over from the usual anxiety inside her. She heard the telltale thud of Lucy emerging down the stairs.

'Has Megan gone?' she enquired.

'Yes, just', Luisa replied. 'She said to say bye'. Lucy didn't respond to this and opened the fridge door. She closed it again with a huff.

'Why is there never anything to eat here?' she asked.

'Are you being serious? The fridge is full!' replied Luisa

'Yea, but it's all crap', Lucy stated. 'It's no wonder you're overweight. You should try going vegan instead of eating all this shit'.

Luisa was stunned. OK, so she wasn't the size she was five years ago, but she wasn't overweight by any stretch.

'Who says I'm overweight?' she snapped back, genuinely hurt by Lucy's comments.

'OK, maybe not overweight, but you're not toned like Maxine. She does yoga five times a week, and there's not a bit of fat on her – she looks great. She's vegan; she swears by it.'

Luisa could feel the rage building inside of her. She was sick to death of hearing about Maxine and her alternative ways. And Luisa wasn't sure that she wanted Lucy to be so obsessive about her diet at fifteen years old. Luisa tried to make sure she ate a balanced diet and exercised.

'Lucy, the fridge is full of fresh food. The cupboards are also full. There is definitely something here that you can eat that is healthy.'

'Like what?' Lucy replied indignantly.

Luisa placed her hands on the table in front of her. 'Lucy, can you watch your mouth, please? I'm getting a bit tired of your attitude.'

'And I'm getting a bit tired of you – you never listen to me, you have no interest in anything I do!'

Luisa's eyes grew wider.

'Are you actually being serious? You never talk to me, you spend every night in your room! Do you do this at your dad's?'

'No, because they actually talk to me and support my choices. Why can't you just be more chilled out like them? It's like living in a prison here. In fact, prison would be more entertaining than this boring house.'

Luisa took a deep breath for two reasons: to stop herself from crying and to stop her from saying something she regretted. 'I do support your choices, Lucy. Why are you saying this? Where has this come from?' she continued.

'You never do anything, mum. You sit on the sofa constantly; when was the last time you even went out? Just because you never want to leave the house doesn't mean I don't want to. I hate living here; there's nothing to do, all my friends go out in town, and I'm just stuck here, doing nothing, sitting in my room every night.'

Luisa took yet another deep breath.

"For your information, I don't go out much because I'd rather spend my money on you, and when you're here, that's my time with you. Or it would be if you came out of your room occasionally. And you DO get to see your friends when you go to your dad's. You can't see them every night of the week!' Luisa exclaimed, still blindsided by the outpouring.

'Oh, you're fully aware that I go out with my friends at Dad's. Don't think I don't know that you sent Izzy to spy on me up the rec the other night; I suppose Meg came running to tell you about that too?' shouted Lucy. Luisa shook her head.

'I don't know what you want me to say, Lucy. You have everything you need; you have a nice home and parents who love you. What is it you want me to do?' Luisa was getting exasperated. She hadn't prepared herself for this conversation; she had no idea where it came from or where it was going.

'Oh, forget it, you don't understand,' Lucy turned to exit the kitchen.

'Try me', proposed Luisa, lowering her voice in an attempt to diffuse the tension in the air.

Lucy stopped in her tracks and turned around very slowly. Then, she was measured and calm for the first time since the start of this exchange.

'There is one thing you can do for me,' she stated. 'You can let me go and live with my dad'.

Chapter 15

Luisa saw the email drop into her inbox at precisely 11.32 a.m. Meeting request. This was it; this would be the result of quite possibly the worst interview experience of her life. She had participated in many interviews over the years, but never one quite like this. The face-to-face interview was in Jackie's office, in front of a panel of one; Jackie took an extremely informal approach to the whole affair, so relaxed that they had to pause at one point as Jackie was struck down with a fit of the giggles. Luisa tried to take it as a positive sign and not take it too personally.

The worst part of the interview was the role play, Luisa's idea of a nightmare, where Jackie insisted on playing out a scenario of an angry parent. Luisa wasn't quite sure what the relevance to the job was but went along with it anyway; after all, it was an interview with her boss; how could she not. They abandoned the role play because Jackie kept going off-piste and losing her train of thought.

Luisa questioned herself at one point: did she really want this job - was it worth it, putting herself through the stress of this process? Her finest moment was her answer to 'What can you bring to the role?'. Luisa physically winced as she recalled her response, 'Myself'. She would prefer a 'thanks but no thanks' email; she really didn't think it was necessary to humiliate her face to face.

Luisa let out a long sigh; what was done was done. She sat alone in the office; Janet still hadn't returned. Luisa was told that she was off sick long-term, and Janet hadn't returned any of Luisa's calls or messages. Luisa could have done with someone to debrief with, but given Janet's reaction to her applying for the job, it was probably best that she was on her own. Luisa checked her watch. It was 11.35 a.m, meaning she had exactly twenty-five minutes until her fate was sealed.

She went to the kitchen to make a drink; the only way she could think would take her mind off the wait. Opening the cupboard door, she realised that she hadn't picked up the new box of teabags from the kitchen counter that morning. The morning routine was thrown into disarray since Lucy decided to stay at Jon's. Ironically, Luisa now had much more time in the morning. Still, she struggled to find a routine that worked for her that didn't highlight the void of the empty house, reminding her at every turn that she had failed as a mother. Luisa reapplied her makeup twice that morning to cover her blotchy skin and puffy eyes. She recalled the box of Yorkshire tea on the side. *Damn it.* She opened up all of the cupboards, but not a teabag in sight. There was a jar of coffee that looked like it had been there for a couple of academic years that had turned black and smelt like coal. It was that time of year, just before the summer when there was a universal lack of quality tea bags, and only broken, rich tea biscuits were left in the barrel.

Luisa suddenly remembered the emergency stash that Janet had kept in her drawer. Luisa was sure Janet wouldn't object if she took one; she could replace it before anyone noticed. The pair only drank Yorkshire tea so there would be no cross-contamination of brands, which, according to Janet, was 'criminal'. She kept them hidden away as she didn't want them wasted on visitors, 'they can have the Tetley; the Yorkshire is the tea of Kings,' she once told Luisa. Luisa found herself smiling at the memory; she really missed Janet, or rather, she missed the version of Janet from a year ago.

Luisa took the key to Janet's drawer (Janet always blu-tacked it to the bottom of the painted pebble on her desk), and she yanked on the handle. 'Bloody thing', she muttered under her breath. Something was jamming the slider, and the drawer wouldn't budge no matter how hard Luisa pulled. She gave it a desperate kick and then checked her watch. 11.40 a.m. T minus twenty. Literally. She gave the drawer one final yank, and it flew open, propelling Luisa into the filing cabinet behind. Head Jackie popped her head around the door. 'Everything OK in here, Luisa?' she inquired.

'Yes, sorry, just looking for something!' Luisa responded. She did not want to admit that she was trying to get into an absent colleague's drawers. There was only so much humiliation she could take in one day.

'Still OK for twelve?' she raised her eyebrows as she asked. Luisa desperately tried to read her facial expression to gauge her mood. Still, Jackie wasn't giving anything away at this point.

'Yes, no problem at all', Luisa answered, trying to sound as calm as she could after careering with the furniture.

She waited for Jackie to get to the end of the corridor before fully opening the drawer. It was full of bits of paper, old letters, pens, a calendar from two years ago and a packet of outdated throat lozenges that had turned to seeping syrupy balls. There was a bottle of mouthwash, an empty water bottle and three boxes of soup sachets – all minestrone. Luisa was surprised at the chaos; Janet was always very insistent about cleanliness; her desktop was always pristine, so the drawers juxtaposed her outward need for tidiness and symmetry. As Luisa reached down to the back of the drawer, desperately feeling for a telltale shape of a teabag box, her fingers came across something cold and hard. She grasped it, and she pulled it out of the drawer before she realised what she was doing.

'Jesus Christ,' Luisa whispered in disbelief at the item she held in her hands.

Jackie reappeared in the doorway at that exact moment, and Luisa kicked the drawer closed.

'Actually, Luisa, if you're free now?' Luisa got the impression this was an instruction, not a question. She held the item behind her, praying that Jackie hadn't seen it. That would be a complicated conversation.

'Yes, absolutely'.

'Come on then, no time like the present!'

Luisa was grounded to the spot. Jackie wasn't moving.

'OK then, shall we?' she continued, gesturing for Luisa to join her.

Luisa felt the prickles of sweat build on her back and suddenly felt extremely nauseous.

'Yes, I er, I just need to visit the bathroom first, if that's OK.'

Jackie frowned. 'Yes, of course, I'll meet you in my office then, shall I?' To Luisa's relief, she turned and walked away.

Luisa suddenly became very hot and queasy. *What the heck was Janet playing at?* Luisa went to reopen the drawer. 'Bloody thing', she whispered. It was no good; it was jammed shut; she must have lodged something when she kicked it shut. What the hell was she going to do with it now? Luisa's only option was to stash it in her own drawer. She covered it with paper and closed the drawer.

Janet often sneaked extra cakes from the staff buffet to her desk or even took one more glass of wine than the allowance at the end-of-term get-together. Still, there was absolutely no reason for her to have a near-empty bottle of vodka in her desk drawer.

'So thank you for your application, Luisa; you have proved to be a valuable team member over the last few years.

'Thank you', replied Luisa, wishing she would just get to the point.

'And we would hate to lose you from the office,' Jackie continued.

'Yes, of course, I understand', nodded Luisa, relieved and gutted simultaneously. She always knew it was a slingshot applying for the role. There were much more experienced people across the trust than her. A new job and a new love interest may be one step too far in one week. Of course, she wouldn't get the job. She suddenly felt an air of embarrassment sitting across the desk from Jackie.

'But obviously, the role would mean working from the high school most of the week.' Jackie was looking through some papers on her desk as she said this.

Luisa nodded again. *OK Jackie, I get the hint; you don't have to keep going on about it; let me just get back to my desk so I can wallow in the shame in peace.*

'So if that's all OK with you, then congratulations,' Jackie chirped.

Luisa's head shot up. What had she missed? Was she actually offering her the job? She wasn't entirely sure what just happened and found herself saying out loud, 'So, just to clarify?'

'Yes, the high school would be your base, and you'd be over here once, twice a week, hardly at all actually, just now and again. A change of scenery would be good, wouldn't it? What do you think?'

'So you're offering me the job?' Luisa asked, needing confirmation of what she thought she was hearing.

'Yes, absolutely, congratulations again. You interviewed extremely well, Luisa. We had a giggle, didn't we, eh? I'll write to you to confirm the change in contract and salary, but as of September, you'll be, errr, what was the title, Senior Trust Administrator — something like that, anyway. Well done!'

'Really? Thank you, thank you very much,' said Luisa, still in astonishment.

'But Luisa, can I ask one thing of you, please? Our interview, or rather your interview, we'll just keep the details between us, OK?' she lowered her voice and narrowed her eyes.

'Yes, yes, of course', she whispered back, not entirely sure what the need to keep quiet was, but she certainly wasn't going to start questioning Jackie now.

Luisa sat back at her desk, a little shell-shocked and desperate to tell someone her good news. She pulled her mobile from her bag and scrolled down her contacts. There was no point texting Lucy, her first choice; she'd be in class. She scrolled to Megan's number instead.

Hi Meg, guess what??? «send»

She sat for a minute, waiting for the two ticks to turn blue. Nothing. She also noticed that Meg had not been online since 9.33 a.m. that morning. She then scrolled to Martyn's name, and her finger hovered over his number. Should she text him? They were messaging each other but had yet to arrange another rendezvous. Luisa wasn't sure if he was losing interest. 'Ah sod it,' she said under her breath, 'seize the moment and all that'.

'Hi Martyn, you know that job I applied for? Well, I've only gone and got it! «send»

She sat again, waiting for the blue ticks. Nothing. She popped the phone back in her bag and closed her drawer. She'd have to celebrate with a glass of water. There was no way she was going back into Janet's drawer today. She had just been given the best news she had received in a long time, making her feel she was finally doing something right. Still, as Luisa sat back in her seat, she suddenly felt very alone.

Chapter 16

Luisa checked her appearance in the bathroom mirror. Martyn had insisted that he took her out to celebrate her promotion, and Luisa counter-insisted that he should come to the house and she would cook for him. And now she was wondering what the hell she was thinking of, suggesting such a thing.

Luisa kept it as simple as possible without it appearing like she'd made no effort. She didn't want Martyn to think she had pulled all the stops out. A ham and leek pie with carrots and peas and a warm chocolate brownie for dessert. All ready to go, just a quick warm in the oven. She checked her watch: 19.16; in around fourteen minutes, Martyn would be knocking at the door. She applied yet another layer of lipstick in her go-to shade, Hidden Vixen (a slightly subdued red that Luisa hoped gave an air of sophistication), and sprayed yet another spritz of perfume (a knockoff version of La Vie Est Belle that she got from one of those online fragrance sites that sold the idea of a designer fragrance for a fraction of the price) and took a deep breath. She then spent five minutes coughing after inhaling said cheap perfume, as it hit the back of her throat like a veil of poison.

The thought process behind her outfit had taken some time. She wanted to look effortlessly sexy but didn't want to scream desperate. She thought about a dress and tights combo but felt that was too much. She'd consulted with Megan, obviously, who suggested some skinny jeans and a nice top.

'It's such a cliche though, Meg, jeans and a nice top,' she groaned.

'It's classic though, Lu, and you can dress it up.'

Luisa sighed. 'But what if we move to the sofa? The jeans will dig in, and I'll be uncomfortable – maybe I should wear leggings?'

'Absolutely not, I forbid it!' screamed Meg. 'Have I taught you nothing!?'

Luisa laughed. 'Just kidding', she replied (she wasn't kidding but knew deep down that leggings did absolutely nothing for her, so she didn't protest).

'OK, let's compromise then. Do you have any cargos?' she inquired.

Luisa stalled.

'I'll take that as a no then, shall I?' she continued. 'Just go for the jeans option and floaty top; that way, you can unbutton the jeans if you eat too much'.

Megan knew Luisa all too well. They then ran through the menu, and both agreed that there was no need for a starter; more effort should be made with the main course and dessert. Dessert *must* be served with a spoon so that it could be used as a flirting tool.

Luisa took a final outfit check in the bedroom mirror. She went for a black top with a slash neck that was floaty and just skimmed her bum cheeks and a pair of black jeans that weren't actually 'skinny' but gave that illusion on Luisa as she was probably more of a 14 than the 12 she was trying to squeeze into. Maybe Lucy was right; maybe she had noticeably put on weight recently?

The dilemma of what she should wear on her feet caused her some anxiety. Ideally, she would have worn heels, but that seemed ridiculous when they weren't even leaving the house. The only socks she owned either had pug dogs on them or were neon - not really the vibe she was going for. There was no way on earth she was wearing slippers, so she opted for bare feet and added a slick of pale pink nail polish to her toes. She smudged one foot slightly on her jeans as she battled with getting them over her backside, but it was too late to do anything about that now.

Her newfound confidence that came with her new job was slowly evaporating away and drifting up to the extractor fan along with the scent of dinner with haste. She was doubting her ability to pull this off. There was no time to deliberate further as the rapping on the door announced Martyn's arrival.

Once the pleasantries were out the way, the gifted wine was opened and poured, and the flowers arranged in a vase (huge brownie points for the last one), they sat at the kitchen table and talked while they ate a rather spectacular (his words, not Luisa's), ham and leek pie. Luisa couldn't help but notice the sharp blue of Martyn's eyes as he spoke to her, boring into her as if he was delving into what was going on behind her mask. It gave her a warm, fluttery sensation inside, and if she was honest, she quite liked it. Luckily, Martyn was a huge fan of pie, which was lucky, really, as Luisa hadn't even considered his tastes. She knew he wasn't a vegan as they'd discussed steak strangely during their first meeting. She knew he was a 'medium rare' kind of guy, which she found strangely attractive.

Once the main course was done and Luisa and Martyn cleared the plates away, they both decided they were too full for dessert at that moment and moved to the sofa. The two rather large glasses of Pinot Grigio dampened her nerves, and she felt quietly confident that this was going better than expected.

'So', Martyn said quietly, 'some big changes coming up for you then, eh?'

'I guess so' Luisa responded. 'I mean, it's not like it's a new job as such. I will know quite a lot of people already, but it's more hours, more money, and more work, obviously', she giggled.

'Sounds like you really impressed them though?' he offered

Luisa laughed, not wanting to correct his 'them' to 'her'. 'Apparently so!'

'Well, you've certainly impressed me…' he looked down at his wine glass, waiting to see if Luisa responded or brushed him off.

'Well, thank you', Luisa said, eternally grateful the two glasses of wine were working their magic. She allowed her eyes to lock with his for just a moment longer than she felt comfortable.

'I think the universe must be looking down on you at the moment; you should buy a lottery ticket', Martyn laughed, his eyes still fixed on her, intently.

Luisa suddenly felt a weight in her stomach, the reality of

Lucy not living at home suddenly reminding her that if this was the universe looking down on her, then the universe was a bitch.

Martyn was telling Luisa all about his fishing hobby. She wasn't really interested in fishing, so she took the opportunity to study his face. He wasn't Luisa's normal type; she normally went for dark-haired men. Megan said she had daddy issues and was looking to replace the Italian male in her life. Luisa thought it actually had more to do with George Clooney's smouldering looks. Martyn was more Jason Donovan than George Clooney. His complexion was pale, but not ill pale, more like the hue of margarine, and his hair was as close to being blonde as you could get without actually being blonde. His blue eyes darted about the room as he became more and more animated about the 12lb barbel he once caught on the Severn. He was the exact opposite of Jon, and Luisa liked that. Time for change in every sense of the word.

The subject turned to children, and Martyn asked about Lucy.

'So how often does Lucy stay with her dad?' he asked.

'Quite a bit, we have a very flexible agreement', Luisa replied. She wasn't lying, but she wasn't telling the truth either. She genuinely wanted to start this relationship off with transparency, but she didn't want him to judge the fact that her daughter moved out to live with her dad. She felt that was a reflection on her parenting, and who wants to date a failing parent?

'That's good that you have that relationship', added Martyn. 'Zach and I spend a lot of time together, or rather we used to. I think he might have discovered the joys of the opposite sex,' he chortled.

'Oh god', laughed Lucy. I am dreading Lucy getting to that point, although I suspect she already has,' she stated, not wanting to sound like she had no idea what was going on in her own daughter's life. That is not an attractive trait to a seemingly fantastic dad who has his shit together.

'Well, he's a little coy about the whole thing, but just lately, he's been cancelling our boy's nights. Can't imagine what could be more important than a night out with your old man, eh? Unless it's a girl. Or a boy, actually,' he added.

'Oh?' Luisa raised her eyebrows.

'I'm not sure, actually. It's not really anything we've discussed, but if he's happy, then I'm happy', Martyn stated confidently.

A smile spread across Luisa's face. This man got better the more she got to know him. How refreshing to meet a man who was so open-minded. He really was ticking all of her boxes.

'I have no idea about Lucy, but my friend's daughter said she had seen her out with a boy the other week. Quite handsome too, apparently,' she added as if that was important.

'Well, I guess it's only going to get worse the older they get, eh? Zach will be sixteen soon, although he thinks he's already an adult. We clash sometimes, but he's a good lad overall.'

'I hear you', Luisa sighed. 'It's hard, isn't it, this parenting malarkey'.

'It is, but I always thought I couldn't have children, so when Zach came along, I was just blown away', stated Martyn. Luisa looked at his face; he was so genuinely proud of his son, and it was lovely to see. The guilt pierced her stomach again as she thought about Lucy over at Jon's, her own daughter not even wanting to live under the same roof as her. She really should have told him, but now really wasn't the time.

'Ready for dessert now?' she asked as she got up, desperate to change the subject and lighten the mood. Martyn smiled at her, a smile that took her by surprise. A smile that said that this was going to be more than a casual arrangement, and she smiled back. 'I take it that's a yes then?'

Chapter 17

It had been nearly two weeks since Lucy moved in with Jon. Luisa had hardly spoken to her during that time, despite calling her every evening and texting multiple times throughout the day. She really needed to talk to Lucy about the job, especially the part where she would be around the High School in the new term. When the phone went to voicemail again, Luisa decided enough was enough, and it was time to speak to Jon. Conversations with Jon, even now, still made Luisa feel anxious and on edge.

'Hi Jon?'

'Yep. Hi Lu' She hated it when he called her that. That was for friends, not him.

'I really need to speak to Lucy. Is she there? She's not answering her phone.'

'No, she's out at the moment. Shall I ask her to give you a call?'

Luisa could hear Maxine laughing in the background, making her feel paranoid. Was Lucy there? Was she avoiding speaking to her? Was Maxine laughing at her? A million thoughts suddenly rushed into her head. Where was Lucy? Who was she with?

'Any idea when she will be back?' Luisa asked bluntly.

'No, not till late, probably,' he replied.

'How late is late?' Luisa asked, annoyed at his flippancy. She heard Jon sigh on the other end of the phone. *Luisa reminded herself that asking what time our fifteen-year-old daughter is due home* is not unreasonable.

'I don't know, 10 pm? 11 pm? She's fifteen years old, Lu; she's out with her mates.'

'But you don't know where she is?' Luisa was getting frustrated. 'Is she normally out that late?'

'Sometimes, yes. She needs to spend time with her friends. It's the whole reason she moved over here in the first place. You need to give her a break, Lu, and calm it down a bit. You'll just push her further away if you don't.'

'Do you even know who she is out with?' Luisa persisted. She could feel the anger bubbling inside of her. How dare he give her parenting advice.

'The usual crowd,' he replied, before taking a drag from a cigarette. Luisa wondered if this boy that Megan had told her about was part of the 'usual crowd'.

'Right, well, can you get her to call me when she gets in, please?' she asked.

'What, at 11 pm? You'll be in bed by then, surely?' Jon laughed. Luisa hated that he still felt he had a right to comment on her routine. He was right, though, and she hated him for it.

She responded with a curt 'no'.

'OK then, I'll ask her to call you. See-ya'. The line went dead.

'Twat' Luisa said out loud and threw her phone onto the sofa. Who the hell did he think he was?

Luisa desperately wanted to text Martyn, to speak to someone who would listen to her concerns and not make her feel like she was overreacting. However, she also didn't want to come across as a bitter, controlling ex. Luisa checked her watch; it was 8.45 pm. It could be a couple of hours before Lucy called her back. She decided she would text Martyn - it could be a nice distraction and she would refrain from bringing up the Lucy situation. Things had been going really well between them; she hadn't felt so at ease with someone for what seemed like forever, and Martyn was so kind and unassuming. He made her feel something that she hadn't realised she could feel.

'Hey you,' she texted.

Her phone immediately sprung to life with the Top Gun theme tune blaring out into the otherwise silent room. She answered immediately, assuming it was Lucy. 'Hi Lucy, sweetheart,' she began, without thinking.

'Errr, sorry to disappoint, it's just me,' Martyn laughed.

Luisa felt embarrassed at being unprepared for the situation and, if she was honest, a little disappointed that it wasn't Lucy returning her call.

'Oh God, sorry Martyn, I was expecting a call from Lucy,' she stammered.

'Hey, it's OK; I'm in the car, so I can't type a message. How are you?' he asked, his voice calming Luisa down with every syllable. He had the most soothing tone about him - creamy, Luisa had described it.

'Ah, you know, this and that. What are you up to?' she enquired.

'Just dropped Zach back off at his mum's; we've been out to the cinema,' he told her.

'Ah, that sounds nice,' Luisa replied, not wanting to hear about him spending time with his son when she couldn't even get her daughter to answer her phone. She spent the next 10 minutes listening to him telling her all about how Spiderman spans many different universes. Luisa couldn't give a shit about Spiderman. Or the fact that he and Zach had watched every film together. She didn't care that they agreed that Toby Maguire was the best Spiderman. What she hated most of all, though, was the disproportionate air of resentment that she was starting to feel toward Martyn for having a good relationship with Zach. What sort of person resents that? It's no wonder she had been single for so long. Who'd want to be with someone like her?

'What do you think then?' Martyn asked.

'Errr, I don't know, maybe Val Kilmer?' Luisa offered, seriously hoping she was still on the right track of conversation after losing her train of thought and going down a rabbit hole of what a crap parent she was.

'What? No, what do you think about bowling? Me, you and Zach? I'd love for you to meet him. Not straight away, obviously, but in a month or two? Maybe Lucy could come too?'

Luisa felt a surge of irrational rage developing inside her. 'What do you mean, *maybe Lucy could come too?*' she burst. 'Why would you think we could meet, and she wouldn't be invited?'

Martyn hesitated before responding, 'Sorry, that didn't come out right. Of course, Lucy is invited. I was just thinking about Zach. I apologise if that sounded selfish.'

Luisa didn't respond. Of course, sweet-natured didn't mean anything by it.

'Luisa? Are you still there?' Usually, if Luisa had been in this sort of conversation, she would cut off the call, block the number, and never contact them again. It was her defense mechanism. She hated being so defiant and recognised that she needed to stop doing it. Megan used to joke and say, 'Oh, here she is pulling down the shutters again.' Luisa really did like Martyn; it was probably the first time since Jon that she felt like it could go somewhere. She desperately didn't want to sabotage the relationship before it started properly.

'Yes, sorry, I'm just tired; it's been a long day. Yes, definitely, maybe in a few months.' She replied.

'Ah, OK, don't worry. Listen, that's down the line; let's just concentrate on us for a while first, eh? Are we still OK for dinner tomorrow night?' he enquired.

'Yes, yes, absolutely. I'll see you tomorrow then. Seven?'

'I'll be there....and Luisa?'

'Yes?'

'Val Kilmer was Batman, not Spiderman.'

Chapter 18

Luisa was jolted awake by the Top Gun theme. She sat upright in bed, disorientated and panicked by the phone ringing so late. She grabbed her mobile from the bedside table and saw 'Lucy' flash up on the caller display. She answered immediately.

'Lucy? Is that you? Is everything OK?' she spluttered, still dragging herself from the deep sleep that she had been in.

'Mum, calm down; Dad told me I had to call you.'

Luisa checked her watch. 'Where have you been, Lucy, it's 12.30 am? Your dad said you'd be back by 11 pm,' Luisa asked.

'Well, I don't know why he said that to you because I never said when I'd be back,' Lucy responded matter-of-factly.

Luisa took a deep breath. She didn't want this conversation to end in a row.

'OK, well, where have you been? Anywhere nice?' she asked, trying to keep her voice as calm as possible.

'I went into town, then round to a mate's house.'

'Which mate?'

'You don't know them.'

'OK, well, have you been there all night? Don't her parents mind?' she asked, hoping that Lucy didn't catch on to her trying to find out if she had been alone with whoever this 'friend' was.

'I wasn't there all night; I went over later. I've been up town with Mia and Jade, and then I went to a friend's house as I said before. Luisa could sense Lucy rolling her eyes at the end of the telephone.

'And is this friend a boy?' enquired Luisa, a teasing tone in her voice which fell flat when Lucy didn't answer. 'Well? at least tell me that!' Luisa insisted.

'Yes, OK, it's a boy- but don't start lecturing me, mum, I'm fifteen.'

Luisa smiled to herself. Fifteen. Just a child. Lucy said, 'I'm fifteen' in a tone that suggested Luisa had no right to question what she was up to.

'OK, right then, glad we've sorted that then' Luisa continued, not really sure what to say.

She was aware that the point of her request for Lucy to call her back was to discuss her new job, but it wasn't a conversation she wanted to have over the phone in the middle of the night. 'So anyway, I needed to talk to you about something, how about you come over at the weekend? We could go shopping or have lunch in Worcester or something? Or the cinema? I've heard the new Spiderman movie is good,' asked Luisa, jumping on her conversation with Martyn to sound like she knew what she was talking about.

'I'm going with Maxine to a Yoga retreat on Saturday morning for the weekend, so I can't. In any case, I've heard the Spiderman film is crap,' Lucy replied.

'OK, well, what about tomorrow night? You could come for tea then if you didn't fancy the cinema?' Luisa knew that she would have to put off her dinner with Martyn, but that time with Lucy obviously ranked much higher.

'No, I can't; I have plans tomorrow,' she added. 'Sorry, mum'.

Luisa was a little taken back by the last couple of words. She felt Lucy's tone soften slightly and sounded genuinely sorry that she couldn't make it.

'Nothing that can be rearranged?' Luisa asked hopefully.

'No, sorry,' she continued. 'Maybe Monday?' Lucy continued.

'Yes, yes! That's perfect, OK then, I'll call you over the weekend then, shall I?' Luisa asked, hardly able to contain her excitement.

'Yes mum.' Lucy sighed.

'And you'll answer the phone? Only you haven't the last ten times I've called,' Luisa said, glad to have lightened the mood slightly.

'I just said I'd answer, didn't I?' Lucy snapped back. That didn't last long.

Luisa decided to quit while she was ahead. She really didn't need a row at this time of the night, and she'd managed to tie Lucy down to a visit, so she was taking that as a win.

'OK Luce, I'll speak to you soon, see you Monday. Take care, love you.' Luisa offered hopefully.

'See ya,' and the line went dead.

Luisa lay back down in bed and wondered how she had suddenly become this version of a mother who she vowed she would never be. Lucy's lack of availability now left Luisa with a problem -she was due at the school on Monday for an informal introduction to the team based there, and she ran the risk of Lucy seeing her there before she could explain about the job. She wondered when she became scared of what her daughter may say. Luisa lay in bed, each of her thoughts fighting to get heard first, leaving her with a head full of static energy and nowhere for it to go. Deep breaths, Luisa. Count to twenty.

1.....2......3.......but what if Lucy sees me and causes a scene because she thinks I am spying on her? I'd be mortified. How would I explain that? What would that say about me as a parent?

OK, start again. 1....2....I know - maybe I will tell Jon, and he can tell her. But then Lucy will have a tantrum that I haven't told her myself. But she may understand because she knows I've been trying to get hold of her. Yes, that's what I will do.

3.......4.......5, but do I want Jon thinking that I can't even have a conversation with my own daughter? No sod that, I don't want to give him the satisfaction.

6....7.....I could text her. That could work.

8....is it something I can text to her? Would she think I was rude by not having the decency to call her?

.....9.....10 I'm the adult here, for god's sake. Not her. I should have insisted she was coming round, end of.

11....12....13 Why does she hate me?

14.......15 I'm such an awful person; all my relationships break down. I must be a terrible person. I'm sure Megan is only friends with me because she feels sorry for me. Maybe I should just turn vegan and have done with it, then at least me and Lucy would have something in common.

16....17......what do vegans eat? Is it just no meat, no hold on, that's vegetarian? Plant-based only, isn't it? Is it? So chips. And lettuce. No bread? Or can you eat bread? Is bread vegan?

19.......oh fuck it. Luisa sat up, reached over for her phone, loaded Google, and asked whether bread was vegan or not. Turns out that it isn't quite as clear-cut as she thought. It was at that moment, as Luisa was reading about additional sugars and fats that may be animal-derived that she spotted the notification. How had she missed that? Lucy had sent her a message right after they had ended their call. There she was, contemplating the origins of the humble loaf of bread, and Lucy was reaching out to her. Typical. World's Worst Mother strikes again.

She opened the message.

'Can't make Monday, sorry. I forgot I promised Maxine I'd help her with something.'

Maxine. Fucking Maxine. Or Waxine, as she and Megan had named her based solely on the fact that she sold wax melts in her shop.

Well, you can't say that I didn't try, Luisa said to herself. And the consolation was that she still got to keep her date with Martyn - at least someone wanted to spend time with her.

Chapter 19

Luisa returned to her car and closed the door, relieved for two reasons. Firstly, the admin team at Crosslands High was lovely, if not a little odd. And secondly, she had managed to get back to her car before the end of school.

Pat, the longest-serving admin, had been there for twenty-five years and knew absolutely everything and everyone. But what she didn't know was who Luisa was and why she was there. Luisa didn't want to say too much as she wasn't sure if there would be some announcement. Pat had taken Luisa aside and told her she'd give her the heads up on who is who 'if you know what I mean' as she tapped the side of her nose. Luisa instantly decided she liked her, even if she was a little odd. Karen was part-time and had a fascinating love life (Pat's words).

Kim was the office apprentice who needed 'reigning in' now and then (again, Pat's words). Luisa's initial nerves had quickly evaporated as she realised that actually, she knew more than most and although Luisa didn't have a great deal of management experience, she was good with people and that went a long way. She would have liked to have introduced herself with her proper title, but it still needed to be confirmed, and Luisa was still uncertain of her start date, so her morning was mainly spent exchanging pleasantries and asking what people did.

Luisa checked her watch. 14.59. School finished at 15.10. She looked around; she was parked between two cars on the row furthest away from the building due to the visitors' spaces being full when she got there. She wasn't conspicuous. She debated waiting until the students started leaving, hoping she would see Lucy.

How ridiculous that she was skulking in her car in a car park to catch a glimpse of her own daughter. No, she'd go; she didn't want to risk Lucy seeing her and accusing her of invading her space before she could explain. She was just about to turn the key in the ignition when a sudden banging on the window made her jump out of her seat. 'Jesus Christ,' she gasped, seeing Pat stood gesticulating as she wound the window down.

'Sorry Luisa love, but you forgot your phone and someone's been trying to call you. Seems important. I would have answered it, but you know, didn't want to overstep the mark so early on.'

'Thanks, Pat, much appreciated,' replied Luisa, irked at Pat's use of 'love.' She desperately wanted her to leave so she could get out of the car park before the end-of-day bell went.

'The caller ID said Work, so I assume it's important? And not to worry you, but they've called the office here too,' Pat continued.

'Yes, again, thanks, Pat. I must get off.'

'Oh, you won't get off now,' Pat interjected. 'Kids will be out in a bit. You'll be here for a good ten minutes, like a swarm of bees they are, and no road sense whatsoever, especially the year eights. Saw one of them run straight out in front of a car the other day, didn't even look, not once. Then the little bugger had the audacity to stick up his fingers before he ran off. Daft sod. Didn't realise it was Mr Jackson. He's the head of Year Nine, by the way. Lovely man, likes his food he does.'

The Top Gun theme started, and Luisa waved Pat away from the window while pointing to the phone and mouthing, 'Sorry, need to get this.'

Pat had been correct; it was work, and she'd had eight missed calls.

Luisa answered the phone just as the uniformed mass filtered across the car park. Her eyes flitted back and forth in a desperate attempt to spot Lucy and ensure she wasn't seen at the same time.

'Hi Jackie, yes, just left; I'm in the car park,' Luisa responded to a rather somber-sounding Jackie. 'Is everything OK?'

Apparently, everything was not OK and Luisa had been summoned back to the office immediately. Her heart was pounding, and her palms were sweating, and she immediately started to play out the worst-case scenario possible. Someone has died; that must be it. Or a child has gone missing. Or maybe someone is leaving. Oh god, she hated this anxiety that started pulsing around her body like a rough barb, taking her breath now and again, and it tried to find an escape.

A young boy, probably a year seven, given the neatness of his uniform, suddenly fell onto the bonnet of the car after being jovially pushed by a group of seemingly older lads who quickly ran off. The young, floppy-haired boy held his hand up as an apology, and he raced off, swinging his bag around his head as he went. Luisa couldn't help but smile. She remembered Lucy when she first started high school. She was so excited on her first day. Luisa was a bag of nerves. She had been left on the playground as Lucy skipped in and didn't even look back. Luisa had spent the short walk to the car wishing that Lucy had at least attempted to cry, and then she spent the whole journey home feeling guilty for thinking such a thing.

The older kids were noticeable by their attempt at adapting their uniforms. Extremely short skirts and hair that was certainly not 'natural colour' as defined in the uniform policy. The make-up was immaculate; Luisa didn't even manage to perfect it on a big night out, let alone every day. She noticed a massive group of girls walking by, noticeable by the telltale plume of smoke coming from the huddle's center. They must only be year 9 or 10, Luisa thought to herself, rolling her eyes. One of the group threw her a look as she walked past, which Luisa couldn't interpret, but it had an air of disdain about it. Another of the girls at the back of the group glanced over and scowled before flicking her hair and rejoining the group. Luisa held her breath. Shit. That was Lucy, had she seen her? Christ. What the hell was she doing with those girls? Luisa hadn't recognised any of them. Was it her who was smoking or vaping or whatever it was? Why had Jon let her leave the house with her skirt that short? No, she wasn't having this. She was going to call Jon as soon as she got home. They needed to unite themselves as parents and get her back on track. She was going to demand she come home this weekend so she can keep her eye on her. Jon and Maxine's alternative view of parenting clearly wasn't working.

She had no time to think any more about this, conscious that Jackie was expecting her back ASAP, she pulled out of the car park and made her way over to the primary school, a nervous anxiety building again as she considered what on earth could be so important that it warranted eight missed calls and a call from the main office.

Luisa immediately knew something was amiss the second she swiped in through the main doors. The receptionist had picked up the telephone as soon as Luisa got through the door, and Luisa had made enough fake phone calls to know that this was an attempt at one of them. Jackie stood waiting for her, ushered Luisa into her office, and closed the door behind her.

'Take a seat, please,' Jackie indicated, requesting Luisa to sit on the seat at the other side of her desk. Luisa didn't feel able to speak at this point. She sensed that Jackie had something unpleasant to discuss, her inability to make eye contact making her stomach flip over and over as she sat waiting for something to break the silence in the room.

'Luisa, I have something extremely important to ask you.''

'OK...' answered Luisa, not knowing where this was going.

'Can you please tell me why you have a half-drunk bottle of vodka in your drawer?'

Luisa didn't flinch and looked right at Jackie. She could tell the truth, but that would land Janet in deep trouble. She could lie, say she found it, or say it was hers. Whatever Luisa said, this didn't look good. She toyed with the idea of telling the truth and the idea of covering for Janet, but maybe Janet *did* have a drinking problem; that would explain quite a lot, and this was a way of getting her some help. Luisa took a deep breath.

'I found it in Janet's drawer. I couldn't put it back because the drawer jammed shut, so I put it in mine,' Luisa gabbled, aware that she sounded like a schoolgirl who had just been caught stealing. Jackie raised an eyebrow.

'So you're telling me this does not belong to you?' Jackie asked.

'Yes, I mean no, I mean yes, it doesn't belong to me.'

'OK, thank you. and can you tell me what you know about this?' Jackie held up a second bottle of vodka, this one empty. Luisa shook her head slowly. Maybe this was worse than she thought. Had Janet got a drinking problem?

'This was found stuffed behind the sanitary bin,' Jackie said, her lips pursed.

Luisa's eyes widened. 'OK, well, I don't know anything about that either. *Oh god.*

'OK, thank you. That's all.' Jackie swung her chair around and started shuffling some papers. Luisa sat momentarily, unsure whether to get up and leave.

'That's all Luisa. You can go. But can I please ask that this is kept confidential? As you can imagine, we are dealing with something quite sensitive here.'

'Of course, yes, absolutely,' Luisa replied.

She made her way to the door. Before she left, she turned to Jackie

'Is Janet OK?'

Jackie looked up at her and raised her eyebrows again. 'As I said, it's a sensitive matter'.

Luisa sat back at her desk. How had she not seen this coming? The parties where Janet had been bundled into taxis a couple of hours into the evenings, the morning hangovers, the weekends where Janet couldn't remember what she had done. It all pointed to the same thing. Luisa felt like the world's worst friend. She took her phone from her bag and typed a message.

'Hi Jan, just checking you're OK. Missing you!' and then proceeded to delete it. She had landed her in it; messaging her at this point was like shutting the stable door.

By the time Luisa had pulled up on the driveway, she had replayed the forthcoming conversation with Jon over in her head a hundred times. She could feel the fizz of anxiety rising in her windpipe, and she desperately needed something to ease her dry mouth. Altercations were not her favourite pastime, especially with her ex, Jon, who tended to turn it around and make her feel stupid. Meg had always said that he was a gas-lighter, but she had also always said he was a wanker, either way, Luisa hated confrontation with him.

She stood at the front door, took a deep breath, and planned her next move. 'OK, I'm going to put the kettle on and call, and then when it's over, I can make a brew straight away to calm the nerves.' She gave herself a pep talk. 'You can do this, Luisa; he has no power over you. He does, however, have your daughter who is in danger of being sent to a detention centre if she carries on the way she is going.' She pushed open the door, mobile in hand.

She didn't get as far as the kitchen. She heard the stomping on the stairs before she had even got halfway down the hallway.

'WHAT THE ACTUAL FUCK ARE YOU DOING SPYING ON ME AT SCHOOL?' a furious Lucy screamed. 'DO YOU KNOW HOW EMBARRASSING YOU ARE? I'M SO SICK OF YOU.' Her face was contorted, and Luisa had been caught unawares. She was trying to take in a lot of information at once. Firstly, Luisa was delighted to see Lucy at home but also horrified by the palpable fury emitting from her. Secondly, she was trying very hard not to stare at her extremely short skirt or comment on the eyeliner that was not what you would call discreet.

'Lucy, will you calm yourself down! If you had bothered to make an effort to meet up with me this weekend, I would have explained why I was there, but just lately, I am always at the bottom of your priorities.'

Lucy stood staring, clearly furious with this response. Luisa was surprised at her own retaliation. The practice conversation in the car was clearly still at the forefront of her mind.

'I'm nearly sixteen. I have a life. I'm busy,' Lucy stated.

'I am your mother,' retorted Luisa, furious that she dared talk to her this way. Enough was enough. She wasn't having this anymore.

'This has gone on for long enough, Lucy. I don't know what's going on; your dad doesn't keep me informed, and I have no idea where or who you are with. You're clearly dating, and I have no idea what is going on in your life.'

'That doesn't give you the right to spy on me,' stated Lucy indignantly.

'How many times, I was not spying on you. If you'd bother to contact me now and again, you would know that I have a new job which means that I will sometimes be at your school. That's why I wanted to see you, to explain, before you saw me there and wondered what I was doing there.'

Lucy took a moment to digest this latest piece of information.

'Great. Because that's not embarrassing, is it?' She eventually added.

'It doesn't have to be,' stated Luisa.

'So you weren't spying on me then?' Lucy softened slightly.

'No, of course not. I would have left before you left school, but I couldn't get out of the bloody car park. It's a nightmare at that time of day,' she stated. 'But on the plus side Luce, you could get a lift now and again?' she hinted.

'To Dad's house, which is literally around the corner? Or is this your way of ensuring I'm not spending time with my friends?'

Luisa sighed. She was so fed up with not being able to have a decent conversation.

'No. Obviously. But maybe you could come and spend some time here with me? Now and again, come for your tea? You're here now; why don't you stop and have something to eat with me? I could order Pizza. I thought you were helping Maxine tonight? Maybe that could wait?' Luisa was aware of the desperation in her voice.

'No, sorry, I can't. I promised.' Lucy replied. Since when did Waxine get to the top of the pecking order? Don't rise to it, Luisa, she told herself. Act cool.

'OK, well, never mind, another night, maybe then.' So much for Luisa laying down the law.

'Can you give me a lift back over then please?' Lucy added. Luisa felt herself fizz up inside. *She's basically come over to have a tantrum at you, and now she's done that, she wants you to give her a lift back so she can spend time with her dad's girlfriend rather than sit and eat dinner with you. Don't do it, Luisa, say no.*

'Yes, OK. Are you ready to go now?' Luisa found herself saying.

'I just need to get some stuff from my room.'

'OK, I'll wait in the car.'

Fucking Maxine

* * *

'So, how long do you think it's been going on?' Martyn asked as he handed Luisa a brew. She had asked him over after she dropped Lucy off, desperate to talk to someone who didn't detest her. He wasn't supposed to be free this evening but he'd text to see how Luisa had got on at her first high school meeting and explained how he'd been ditched by Zach in favour of the cinema with friends.

'not sure, but when I think about it, there have been many occasions where she's hit it hard - I just thought she loved having a good time; she's always been the life and soul of the party.' They had been discussing Janet and the bottles.

'It's a bit odd though, don't you think, how she just took your word for it? I mean, she didn't exactly challenge you, did she - especially as the bottle was in your drawer! ' he enquired. 'I'd hate for Jackie to be the judge if ever I was on trial!'

'Well, maybe I'm just exceptionally trustworthy,' Luisa laughed.

'I wasn't saying that,' Martyn laughed, 'what if she had asked Janet that, and she had said it wasn't hers? Where would that leave her then? Would you have automatically got the blame?'

He had a point. Jackie had only just asked her a question. It was as if she just wanted to say it wasn't hers. Now that she thought about it, it was all rather strange.

'You just don't know what goes on behind closed doors, do you?' he remarked.

Luisa sat back. You don't. She knew she had not been completely honest with Martyn about Lucy. As if he sensed what she was thinking, Martyn spoke.

'So what about you?'

'Well, I like a drink, but I definitely don't have a problem with it,' Luisa stated.

'No, silly, I meant any skeletons in the closet I should be aware of?'

Luisa laughed. 'No, absolutely not, what about you?'

'Nope. I have an ex-wife and a son; I've already told you that. I once got a telling-off from a police officer for peeing in the street, but I was only eleven at the time. Oh, and I may have been involved in a little altercation outside a nightclub once, but it wasn't anything to write home about.'

'Well, I have an ex and a daughter that you know about. Nothing really more than that. It's all very boring here.'

'Boring is good, Lu; boring is exactly what I need right now.' he leaned in to kiss her. She pulled away.

'Right, there's something I need to tell you. Lucy has moved in with Jon. She hates me. She's hanging around with girls at school who look like they want to commit a crime. One of them smokes. And there's a boy, and she's being very secretive, and she won't talk to me or see me, and she saw me at the school the other day, and now she thinks I am spying on her, and it's all such a mess.'

Martyn watched her unravel before him, trying desperately to take it all in. 'OK, breathe'. Luisa felt tears building, and she desperately didn't want to cry. 'I'm sorry, you don't need this. I don't know what I'm doing wrong. We used to be so close. She hates me. I bet you think I am a shit mum now too'. It was no use; the tears started. Martyn scooped her into his arms and held her, and for the first time in a long time, she let herself go and cried until there was nothing left to give. And Martyn held her, just hard enough to let her know she was cared for but not too hard that he took control. She was in the perfect balance of being cared for and wanted; although she didn't realise it, she was also fast becoming loved.

Chapter 20

'What about this one?' Megan held up a navy and white striped long-sleeved top.

'I'm meeting his son, not going yachting,' Luisa replied.

The dress code for meeting your new boyfriend's son for the first time is not something she had ever had to navigate.

'I'm not sure he's going to take too much notice of what you are wearing, Lu; he's a 15-year-old boy,' Megan remarked.

'Au contraire Megan - if young Zach thinks I'm an uncool Gen Z, then he'll be telling his dad to dump me - plus I want to make a good impression.'

'It's his dad you want to impress, and by all accounts, you have already done that; the man is crazy about you!'.

Luisa giggled, blushed, and wondered how a grown man had made a grown woman act like a schoolgirl going on her first date. Things couldn't be going better with Martyn, and they were at the point where they wanted to introduce the children. Lucy and Zach were the people most important to them, and it was equally important that they both got on with their respective partners' offspring. Luisa had always said that if it wasn't working for Lucy, then it would never work. However, she was also mindful that Lucy seemed to hate anything remotely connected with Luisa at that moment, so there was a very high possibility that she would hate both Martyn and Zach. She was prepared to take that chance, though, as Martyn had ticked most of the two hundred and eleven metaphorical boxes she kept for potential love interests (not that there had been that many over the years). There were a few boxes he would never tick; he couldn't play the piano, for instance, but Luisa was prepared to let that one slide. He did, however, make a mean curry, which hadn't even been on the list so swings and roundabouts. Luisa had agreed to a coffee shop meeting with Martyn and Zach first, and they would tackle Lucy after, as Luisa predicted she would take some pinning down.

'OK, but I still want to look nice, so let's keep looking,' Luisa replied.

'Oh, I meant to tell you, Izzy's got a place at Uni! She's going off to Liverpool! As long as she passes her A Levels, obviously. How mad is that? My daughter is off to Uni!'

'Oh my god, this is massive news, Meg!' gushed Luisa. 'How are you feeling about it?'

'Well, I know she's always wanted to go, so I am really pleased for her, obviously, but at the same time, she's my baby girl,' and with this, Meg stood in the middle of Dorothy Perkins, and the tears started rolling down her cheek.

'Oh fuck' Luisa declared. 'Don't cry, oh shit, Meg. Hold on, let me get you a tissue.'

They stood in the middle of the shop momentarily before Luisa declared. 'OK, sod the shopping, let's go and get a glass of wine. We can celebrate and commiserate at the same time'.

'Sorry', sniffled Meg. 'I'm not sure what came over me. It's just such a huge thing. Izzy's always been there. I'm not sure what I will do with myself - especially now that you've got yourself hitched practically. Sod's law, I'm suddenly at a loose end, and you're tying the knot.'

'Whoa, calm down, tiger,' laughed Luisa. I am absolutely not tying the knot, and Martyn spends enough time with Zach for me to have a few evenings free every week - now stop blubbing and drink your wine. She's going to university, not emigrating to Australia!'.

A couple of Pinot Grigios later, the pair were back scanning Primark's rails. Meg held up a lurid orange blazer - Luisa pulled a face. 'for me, not you,' Meg started laughing, 'I don't know whether I should be offended.'

Luisa checked her watch. 'Right, we need to hurry this along, Meg,' she stated. 'Are you trying these on?' She held up the basket she had been carrying around like she was some sort of personal shopper.

'Yes, come on,' she said, 'come in with me; I need your advice.'

'How has this happened? I thought we were shopping for me! Luisa laughed. Luisa hated clothes shopping with a passion. Her mother had always told her she had an odd-shaped body, and given the way high street clothes fitted her (or rather didn't fit her), it made her think that she may have been correct.

'But I'm traumatised about my daughter leaving me,' declared Megan. 'Retail therapy is the only thing that will get me through!'

Luisa rolled her eyes and laughed.

'While you're standing there doing nothing, go and get me this in size 12, the 10 doesn't fucking fit me, and I'm furious about it' Megan thrust her arm out from behind the curtain, and Luisa trotted off back onto the shop floor. She scanned the hangers; there were nine-hundred size tens and one thousand size fourteens, but nothing in a size twelve. 'Bloody hell,' she whispered as half of the tops slid off their hangers onto the floor. 'For fucks sake.'

She looked around to see if she could get away with leaving them there; that seemed to be the norm here, but her conscience wouldn't let her. She bent down to pick them up.

She scanned across the floor as she got up, narrowly missing her head on the chrome rail. Hang on a minute; surely it wasn't. She moved her head to the side to get a better look across the aisle at the boy walking towards her. It was him! The boy she had nearly ploughed into on her way home from work. She recognised his dark mop of hair and his features, which reminded her of Lucy when she was smaller. She had initially thought he was older, in his early twenties maybe, but on closer inspection, he was much more teenage, 16, maybe 17? Perhaps he was coming over to give her what for and to tell her to pay more attention when driving. (Overthinking was her specialty). 'How strange,' she thought as he disappeared up the escalators to the menswear section.

She went back to the changing room just as Megan came out. 'Fuck it,' she declared. 'None of these bloody clothes fit me – I can't be arsed. Let's go back to yours for a cup of tea. Who needs new clothes anyway? We'll look through your wardrobe and find something 'meet the son' suitable.'

Luisa thought about telling Megan about seeing the boy but

was aware that a story about nearly killing a teenage boy and then seeing him again in Primark wasn't the most remarkable tale ever told. Plus, she couldn't help but feel uneasy about seeing him again. Why did he seem so familiar to her? She often got this, working in a primary school. She would often see students later in life that she recognised. They would sometimes come up to her and say, 'Hello miss, remember me?' and more often than not, she would. Now and again, there was a drastic hair or weight change that meant she needed a clue, but this was different. There was something much more familiar to her than an ex-student, and it was more than the fact that she nearly ended his life prematurely. It played in her mind all evening, which was helpful as it took her mind off the fact that she still didn't have a clue what she was going to wear.

Chapter 21

Lucy sat in her room with her head in her hands and cried. The tears collected in her eyes and dropped, weighted with the sadness and confusion that was reserved for those in their teenage years. The relentless buzz of her mobile phone jarred her insides like a blunt knife poking at her. She could hear Jon and Maxine downstairs shouting about something that sounded like money. She heard her name a couple of times but couldn't quite work out what was being said. Maxine had been away all weekend. Lucy was supposed to have gone with her, but there was a mix-up with the accommodation, so she stayed home.

Home. Lucy wasn't sure what that word meant at this moment. She lay back on her bed, wishing she could have some silence.

'Just fucking ask her, you spineless shit,' she heard Maxine say.

'I'm not asking her for money, Max,' replied Jon.

'Why not? She's happy for us to feed her daughter while she sits at home without a care in the world!'

'Our daughter, not her daughter. She's mine too.'

'I'm fully aware of that, Jon. I never signed up for this. Not full-time. You used to be fun.'

'I don't want you doing that stuff in the house when she's here, Max. I've told you before,' Jon stated.

Lucy heard the slamming of doors and put her hands over her ears. This type of discussion didn't happen very often, but now and again, Maxine would lose her shit and start wailing like something had possessed her. The usual routine was that they would make up audibly, and a few hours later, she would calm down, really calm down, so calm that she often couldn't string a sentence together or get up off the sofa.

Lucy picked up her mobile and scrolled through the group chat. Her friends were at a party tonight, but she hadn't gone. She was getting tired of all the drama, the 'he said, she said' continuous saga that ran day after day after day. The group chat was quiet; it was only 9 pm. She pulled up her contacts and scrolled down. She stopped at the name Woody and hovered over the message icon. She knew he was out with his dad that evening, but she might squeeze in an hour with him if he got back early enough. He was a welcome break from the friendship group - going to the school on the other side of Crosslands meant he also came with an air of mysteriousness and a distinct lack of drama, which Lucy liked.

Of course there had been the rumours, the stories that he had been expelled and had to change schools, the rumours that he had slept with over ten girls, but that was par for the course whenever someone tried to infiltrate the group. And Lucy couldn't help but think that the others were jealous. Woody was handsome, with dark hair, and tall, like Lucy. They looked good together, and he made Lucy feel like she was the most incredible person in the world, something she hadn't felt in a long time.

She typed a short message, 'Call me when you're back,' and pressed send. She lay back on her bed and put her air pods in to drown out the loud moaning of the reconciliation that was currently taking place downstairs.

Lucy, as she often did, started to think about her mum. She had been so excited to move out of home and in with Jon and Maxine. There was always so much more going on here, so much life. She had freedom, something she could never have at home. Living so far from town meant she could only meet up with friends when she could get a lift or stay over at Jon's. Now, she could go out when she wanted and with whom she wanted to. Jon wasn't bothered. She was a free spirit, as Maxine would say. Free to find her way. And she had for a while; she had been to parties, she had been drunk, and she had even tried vaping. And she had met Woody.

It was a party at Justine Mitchell's house. She had moved to Crosslands from the other high school and had contact with another set of friends. Woody had arrived at the party quite late, and Lucy had spotted him instantly, drawn to his dark mop of hair. He was one of the popular boys, but it soon became apparent that he had no interest in the fake tan, hair extension, or lashes crew. He and Lucy had met at the drinks table, where they pretended to pour Vodka into a red plastic cup.

'I won't tell anyone if you don't,' he had said with a cheeky wink.

They had then left the thumping sounds of Taylor Swift singing about a Love Story to find somewhere to talk. The rumours that she had let him do more than talk had spread quite quickly around school and earned Lucy an air of respect from a particular group of girls who welcomed her into their fold. She had never been part of the 'popular' crew before and was suddenly thrust into what felt like a significantly grown-up world. Maxine's vegan regime had meant that she had lost a few pounds, her 'puppy fat' as Luisa had named it, and she felt like a woman rather than a schoolgirl.

A few months later, with more opportunities to meet, they formed quite a friendship. More than a friendship. Lucy had her first kiss and encounter with a boy she wouldn't want to tell her mum about. It was getting serious. He had been to Copcut Green several times, but the lack of buses made it hard to maintain. Moving to Jon's had catapulted their relationship.

She hadn't told Jon or Maxine about Woody. She wasn't sure they would be bothered, but she knew Maxine would ask her personal questions that she didn't want to answer. Maxine was an inquisitive person and believed that your body was a vessel of joy that should be shared freely - she often asked Lucy if she had discovered the joys of intercourse, much to Lucy's embarrassment. It wasn't unusual for her to walk around the house naked. Her friends never came around to her mum's, and there was no way she would invite them to her dads either unless she knew Maxine was away. Walking around with your boob hanging out while chewing on a vegan sausage was not something she wanted her friends to witness. She didn't want to see it herself, which is why she spent so much time in her room.

She instructed Alexa to play The Courteeners and felt herself relaxing to the soothing voice of Liam Fray, blocking out the noise with a song of the streets where he grew tall. She missed home. She missed the familiarity of her mum getting in from work and them struggling to decide what to eat for tea. She missed the quiet, the uneventfulness, her room, her bed, her journey home on the school bus where the drama of the day seemed to evaporate the further away from the town she got.

She looked at her phone; there was no reply from Woody yet, but there were a couple of photos in the group chat of Carly snogging some blond-haired lad she recognised from year 11. No doubt that would be all around school by the morning. She wouldn't have all this if she moved home, but did she even want to? It was all such a mess, and she was so confused. And now her mum would be working at her school, and she'd have to deal with everything that situation brought, knowing who her friends were and what she was doing. She missed her old friendship with Kate and Sally and being able to talk about her love of art without people mocking her and telling her that wasn't a 'vibe.' She missed talking about her plans to go to Uni; she was fed up with people telling her not to be such a 'sweat' at school. She was sick of having to pretend to enjoy being a dick to people who didn't deserve it. She also missed eating meat—a lot.

She closed her eyes, trying to block out the confusion of who she was supposed to be and where she was supposed to be going. Liam sang, 'I don't know if you would welcome me back with open arms through the door,' and Lucy drifted off to sleep.

Chapter 22

The situation with Janet did not sit right with Luisa. They had been colleagues for years and had drifted into that muddied category of friends who work together and socialise when there is a work event. She knew much about her life, her boys, and her husband. She also knew a lot about her sex life. They talked about many things in the office all day when there were no children around, but even then, they would use code for specific phrases. They had laughed together a lot and cried together. They always had each other's back, or rather they did, until Luisa threw her under the bus and basically told their boss that Janet was an alcoholic.

Luisa thought back over the last few months. It was true; Janet had not been herself lately. Her mood swings had been horrendous, with no one ever quite sure which version of Janet was going to present as when she came in. Thinking back, Janet had been quite confused at work, often forgetting the most straightforward things or getting tasks wrong that she had done correctly for years. She failed to input the registers, pass on messages to staff, and, on one occasion, told a parent that their child's name didn't appear to be registered at the school. Most of the time, Luisa would cover up the mistakes or put them right before anyone noticed. Could that have been a result of her drinking at work? Luisa could never recall smelling alcohol on her. There had been times when Head Jackie had an aroma of something boozy on her, but there were always so many trust events and lunches that she had to attend, which was easily explained. Not Janet, though; she had never given her reason to believe she actually had a drink problem.

Luisa pulled up outside Janet's three-bed semi, anxious that she may get the door slammed in her face. At this point, she had nothing to lose. She couldn't ignore the fact that Janet could be in trouble, and she wanted to help.

She walked up the neatly trimmed pathway to the red front door, knocked the brass knocker twice, and stepped back off the step. She could hear activity behind the door, and her heart beat harder.

The door opened slightly, and Luisa took a sharp breath.

'Janet?' she asked, hardly recognising the timid, casually dressed lady who answered.

'Hi,' Janet said, and after a little too long a pause, she followed up with, 'You'd better come in.' She opened the door wider and shuffled off down the hallway.

Luisa stepped inside and closed the door behind her. The house was a tip. There were coats scattered all up the stairs and piles of magazines on the floor.

'Excuse the mess, I'm having a sort out,' Janet called from the kitchen, 'do you want a brew?'

'Yes, please,' replied Luisa, unsure how this interaction would pan out. She had been to Janet's house many times but never remembered it being untidy like this. She entered the kitchen, which was equally messy, mirroring Janet's out-of-character appearance. Her jogging bottoms were ill-fitting, and there was a stain that looked like jam on her t-shirt. She also appeared to have put some weight on. It starkly contrasted with the Janet that paraded into the office in her brightly coloured blazers and matching eye shadow.

'How are things, Janet?' Luisa asked timidly.

'Oh, you know, pretty shit, Lu, to be honest,' she replied as she stirred the tea.

'I'm missing you at work,' Luisa offered. 'It's been very quiet without you.'

Janet set the kettle down on the worktop and sighed.

'I miss being at work, Luisa. Honestly, but I can't seem to get myself together recently, Janet replied, her honesty suddenly making her seem very vulnerable.

Luisa looked at her; she seemed sad, not intoxicated, and not even a hint of a hangover. As she scanned the kitchen, there was no evidence of empty bottles or glasses, just a few plates and mugs.

'So I suppose the rumour mill is going at work, is it?' Janet asked.

'Not really, people are just concerned about you; they miss having you around the place.'

'What's Jackie told everyone?' she asked.

Luisa dropped her gaze to the floor. She felt highly conflicted right about now between being honest with her friend and risking upsetting her or lying and potentially making the situation worse than it needed to be. She went for the first option, recalling her Granddad's phrase, 'Honesty is the only policy.'

Janet took a sip of tea and frowned quizzically at Luisa. 'Shall we sit down?' she asked. They moved some clothes off the kitchen chairs and sat at the breakfast bar. 'Well, the doctor tells me I will start to feel better in a couple of weeks, but honestly? I'm not convinced. I thought something was seriously wrong with me, Lu', Janet's sombre expression worried Luisa. And Luisa was also perplexed. Surely, it was a longer road to recovery than a couple of weeks? She'd had experience of her mother's alcoholism; she was no expert, but she did know that it wasn't a quick fix.

'Really? Well, that sounds positive. But do you think you're ready to come back to work? Has there been anything formal from work regarding, well, you know?' Luisa said, reluctant to refer directly to the bottle discovery.

'In terms of what?' Janet responded.

'The vodka in the drawer,' Luisa added sheepishly

'What vodka?' Janet asked, clearly confused. 'What drawer?'

'The bottle in your work drawer and the other one that Jackie found in the loos, ' Luisa informed.

'Luisa, I have no idea what you are talking about. Please, I know I may seem like I am losing my marbles, but it's nothing a bit of HRT, and some antidepressants won't sort out.'

Luisa sat staring at Janet. 'Wait, what? Hold on, start again.'

'I've been really struggling with everything, Lu. I've turned into a complete bitch; I fly off the handle at the smallest thing, the rage comes over me like a fucking tidal wave, and I shriek and wail like a crazy woman. And then I can't stop crying. All of the time. And when I'm not crying, I'm trying to find my glasses or the car keys, that's if I can even remember where I've parked the fucking car. I've doubled in size, nothing fits me, I feel shit, I look shit.'

'So you're not an alcoholic then,' Luisa got straight to the point.

'Chance would be a fine thing. I can't even drink wine without it giving me horrendous heartburn and an upset stomach, let alone Vodka - but I tell you what I am, though, I'm fucking menopausal! She replied. 'And what are you on about, Vodka in my drawer? What the hell has been going on?'

Luisa put her mug down and turned to face Janet.

'The bottle of vodka that you had in your drawer, Janet, and the one that was stashed in the ladies' loos,' Luisa confirmed.

Janet set her cup down with too much force, causing tea to splash on the worktop.

'Luisa, I am telling you now, I have no idea what you are talking about. Jackie knows full well why I am off work; I have a sick note for another two weeks. I know I haven't been completely on the ball lately but that has nothing to do with Vodka - as if I would keep a bottle in my work drawer!? At a primary school! I'm not insane - I'm bloody menopausal!'

Luisa rubbed her face with the palms of her hands. She hadn't got this wrong; she had seen the bottle of Vodka with her own eyes. She had sat in Jackie's office and had a conversation with her. It was Luisa who had told Jackie that it was Janet's.

'Right, well then, somethings not right Jan, ' Luisa stated. 'I found a bottle of Vodka in your drawer while looking for the emergency tea bags. I hid it. I was going to take it away before anyone else found it, but the next thing I knew, Jackie called me into her office and asked me what I knew about it. I'm so sorry, Jan; I told her I found it in your drawer. I didn't know what to do; I'd just got this job and didn't want to fuck it up. When Jackie said another one had been found in the toilets, I put two and two together and assumed that's why you were off work. Pauline said that she thought you'd been suspended.'

'Jesus Christ,' Janet exclaimed. 'So let me get this straight, you found a bottle in my drawer, which, can I just add for the record, I have absolutely no knowledge of. You find it, then Jackie asks you about it, and you tell her it was mine?'

'Well, no, it didn't happen exactly like that. I was holding it, and Jackie asked me where I got it.

'And again, you told her it was mine,' Janet questioned.

Luisa dropped her eyes to the floor, and her cheeks turned pink. 'Well, yes, I'm so sorry, Jan, I was in a really difficult position.'

'But it doesn't make any sense, Lu - Jackie knows why I've not been at work; it's written on my bloody sick note, for fucks sake, so why would she try to pretend that I'm off because I'm a secret drinker?'

Luisa's cheeks turned pink. 'Well, yes, I mean, you've been a bit snappy recently - not really yourself. I wasn't sure'.

Janet started to laugh. 'look, Lu, I know I must look a fucking state at the moment, but it's not because I'm an alcoholic. I'm struggling; It takes me all my effort to get out of bed in the morning. I get surges of energy when I go on a mission and start cleaning the house, and an hour later, I'm knackered, can't remember why I started clearing up in the first place, and then have to sit down, which then turns into a nap - hence the bloody piles of mess everywhere.'

'I did wonder,' Luisa nodded.

'And Simon has started a new job, which means he isn't here so much; truth be told, I reckon he's avoiding me. I'd avoid me, but I'm fucking stuck with myself.'

'What about the boys?' Luisa asked.

'Christ knows, I never see them - Tom has a new girlfriend - very horsey apparently, as in she has horses, not that she looks like one. She lives on the other side of Evesham in some converted barn. He's basically moved in. I bet he doesn't leave his dirty underpants lying around there like he used to here. She calls him Thomas. Little sod wouldn't even let his own mother call him that.'

Luisa laughed out loud. 'And what about Dan - what's he up to? she asked.

'Well, Daniel has a boyfriend, would you believe? I always said he was one for the boys. Simon wouldn't have it at first, but he's got his head around it - I told him to stop being a fucking bigot - he's gay, he's not a Nazi! Anyway, he spends most of his time with Peter -at the theatre, I expect.

'Not all gay guys like the theatre, Janet,' Luisa laughed.

'What do you mean? Peter's an actor! He works there,' she replied, throwing her head back and laughing.

They both sat there for a good few minutes, whooping with laughter.

'Oh Lu, I have missed you,' Janet gasped between giggles. 'enough about my shitshow of a life; tell me what's been going on with you.'

Luisa spent the next hour telling Janet all about Lucy, her job, and the gossip from the office. Janet had some curt parenting advice in terms of Lucy, which included the phrases 'you bloody tell her' and 'don't let her think she rules the roost,' and her favorite, 'Jon's still a useless piece of shit then.'

'I'm so glad you got the job, Lu, you deserve it; I'm so sorry I was a cow about it,' Janet said. 'I always thought I could have moved up the ladder by now, but the timing was wrong; there was no way I would have put myself through that when I struggled even to remember my own name some days.'

Luisa smiled at her. 'I'm so sorry you have been through such a time, Janet. I wish you'd have told me what was going on.'

'I would have done it if I'd known! I genuinely thought I was losing the plot; I even self-diagnosed myself with dementia at one point.'

'So how did you realise what was going on?' Luisa enquired as she took another biscuit from the packet.

'Well, Simon told me if I didn't go to the doctors, he'd leave me, which was tempting, but I thought if I did have dementia, I'd need him on my side. The GP was fab; you hear horror stories, don't you? He was very thorough. He suggested the Menopause, and I nearly knocked him out. I'm fifty Lu, I'm not old enough for that!

'I beg to differ, Jan - apparently, the average age in the UK is 51.' Luisa knew this because she had suspected she might be on the brink herself, but it turns out she wasn't; she was lacking in vitamin D.

'Anyway, they gave me some antidepressants to start with.'

'Are you depressed?' Luisa asked

'No, not for that; it helps with a few symptoms of Menopause, apparently. And then some patches which I stick on my arse cheek twice a week, and other than the excess weight which I can't fucking shift, I'm feeling much better.'

'But that still doesn't explain what's happening at work, Janet. I need to tell Jackie she's got it all wrong. Those bottles had nothing to do with you, and everyone thinks you're a steaming drunk!' explained Luisa. If nothing else, she hated injustice.

'It does seem strange,' agreed Janet. 'Why would Jackie let

you believe that?'

'No idea, Jan, but I'm going to call her first thing tomorrow and ask her what the hell is going on.'

Chapter 23

Martyn swished the hangers along the rail. This was a first for him - meeting someone special in his life and then introducing them to his son. Zach meant everything to Martyn. When he and Claire split up, he worried how it would affect him, a boy fast approaching those tricky teenage years without a dad in the house. So he made sure he was there for every moment he possibly could, even if that meant sacrificing his own independence and happiness.

Martyn tried dating in the past but never met anyone who was prepared to share him with his son. 'Zach time was precious', he would tell them, and although at first, they thought what a wonderful dad he was and how it was one of the reasons they liked him so much, the novelty soon wore off and the complaints of 'you never spend any time with me', and 'I'm sick of coming second on your list of priorities' started to emerge.

Martyn had no regrets; he'd done his best for his son and could hold his head high. As Zach approached his last year at high school., Martyn saw him less and less. Dad time was being replaced with friend time, and Martyn suspected he was in danger of being relegated further down the line by 'girl time'. Martyn didn't mind, though; he loved seeing Zach happy, which meant there may be a tiny opening in his life to share with someone else.

When Claire told Martyn she was pregnant, he was over the moon. They had stopped trying six months before to take the pressure off. It was getting Claire down, apparently. Martyn said that consistency was key, but Claire told him to back off, and that was that. He suggested that they should enjoy sex with the added stress of the outcome, but Claire wasn't in the mood for anything remotely related to intimacy. Then one month, out of the blue, Claire appeared at the bedroom door. 'Surprise!' she said, throwing the blue stick on the bed. Martyn was completely taken by surprise; intimacy between them was sporadic, and it took a moment for him to realise the significance of the blue lines on the stick. A few weeks later, a scan confirmed that they would be parents. Martyn threw himself into getting the house ready, painting the nursery and researching the safest travel systems. Claire had spent more time at home than she ever had. This baby is what they needed; it would bring them closer together. They had drifted over the last twelve months - yes, they needed this.

And they made it work at first. Claire became quite unwell with morning sickness, and Martyn took care of everything. He made sure she ate healthily, even though she threw most of it up; he cleaned, went to work, and decorated. Apart from actually giving birth, there was nothing more he could do. He and Claire were getting on, their relationship shifting from man and wife to co-habitants, making the best for their newborn. Martyn doted on Zach; he changed nappies, did night feeds, and walked for miles with the pushchair he'd spent months researching. It took Claire a few months to bond with Zach, but this little dark-haired bundle had captured both hearts. Martyn stared at him with his blue eyes, Zach's dark features staring back at him, studying his face. When Claire stared at Zach, she cried. It was expected, apparently, so Martyn had read. The baby blues, they called it. The baby blues seemed to last for quite some time, to the point where Martyn had sat Claire down to ask what was going on. He was concerned about her, about them. She started to bond with Zach, throwing herself into caring for him, taking him to mother and baby groups, and getting him weighed weekly at the clinic.

Martyn loved to watch them together, but Claire would shut down whenever he tried to join in or suggest they do things together. 'Just leave me to it', she would snap, 'I'm more than capable'. Martyn insisted that he would never suggest she wasn't, but Claire could be very difficult.

It turns out that Claire was so capable of doing things independently that she decided she didn't want to be with Martyn anymore. 'We've drifted too far', she declared. Martyn had pleaded with her not to let this end, if not for them, for the sake of Zach, but Claire was in the 'it's better to have two happy parents not together than two unhappy ones together' camp. And it was true, Martyn would only be staying for Zach; there was no love left in their marriage, only for the little dark-haired bundle of joy they each loved independently. It was time for a divorce while things were still amicable. They had shared custody of Zach, and Martyn moved out. And that was the end of that.

Luisa was the first person Martyn would introduce to Zach, and coffee and cake seemed the perfect first meeting. Casual, not too much pressure, not a sit-down meal where they were all stuck until the food was served. It was coffee and cake, and Zach could leave whenever he wanted. No pressure. Then why was he feeling so nervous? He knew that it would be over with Luisa if Zach wasn't on board with this. Martyn was also very aware that Luisa was the first person he could see a future with in a very long time. He checked his watch; in a few hours, he'd know whether his son would give him the green light. He looked upwards and whispered, 'Please, god, let this work out' to a god he didn't believe in but hoped would look down on him favourably, given that he didn't ever ask for anything.

The cashier swiped his navy polo shirt through the scanner. 'Must be your lucky day; this has been marked down by 50%,' she told him, her expression not changing, making Martyn wonder if she meant it to sound as sarcastic as it did. 'Thanks', replied Martyn, a little sidetracked by the thought that his prayer may have been answered incorrectly. He wanted his son to like his new partner, not 50% off the top he would wear to the event. 'Typical' he thought, the one time I prayed for something and get the wrong bloody result. He took the carrier bag off the counter and left the shop, but not before raising his eyes upwards again, at the risk of sounding greedy, to say 'thank you, but I still really want Zach to like Luisa', just in case of any confusion.

CHAPTER 23

Chapter 24

Luisa checked her watch. 1.30 pm. In thirty minutes, she would be in the coffee shop with Martyn and Zach. *Shit.* Of course, she had opted for skinny jeans with a plain white T-shirt and her trainers. She was going for Sophista-casual(a term she and Megan had created to describe Sophisticated yet Casual). They met at the same place they had their first date, which Luisa was pleased about. She liked familiarity and knowing where the toilets were without asking someone. She was a little nervous about the proximity to Jon's house. Although she knew Lucy was off to some Vegan food festival with Maxine today, the thought of her finding out that she was meeting her Zach before Luisa had even introduced her to Martyn made her feel a bit sick.

She parked and went to the coffee shop; she saw Martyn sitting with his back to the window. From what she could make out, it looked like he was alone. Luisa put her hand on Martyn's shoulder, and he stood up, kissing her on the cheek. She noticed he'd already got a Chai latte waiting for her. She loved that he was so attentive. She sat down next to him and exhaled. 'I have no idea why I'm so nervous,' she explained. Martyn put his hand on hers, 'don't be; honestly, Zach's a great lad;

he's going to love you,' he said reassuringly. Inside, he prayed again. 'He'll be along in a minute; you know what teenagers are like for timekeeping', he laughed, pushing the intrusive thoughts that Zach may not turn up to the back of his mind.

By the time Luisa had drunk half her latte, she was much more relaxed, and so was Martyn, after receiving a text from Zach to say he would be five minutes. Luisa excused herself, 'just nipping to the loo before he gets here,' she said. She didn't need the toilet; she just wanted to check herself in the mirror; she really wanted this to work. Each time Luisa saw Martyn, she felt herself wanting to be with him more and more. She loved the way he made her feel. She was already further in than she had ever expected, and to think that this afternoon's coffee could make or break their relationship made her feel anxious. She ran her hands under the tap and gave herself a pep talk. 'Come on, Luisa, you can do this. You're a strong, independent woman,' she told herself, quickly followed by 'your own daughter may not want to spend time with you, but that doesn't mean Zach won't' to bring herself back down to earth. And with that, she left the restroom and made her way back to the table.

As she made her way back over to Martyn, she cast her eye around the shop, her eyes suddenly stopping dead as she scanned the queue at the counter. It was him, there again, the boy she nearly ran over. Jesus, this was getting creepy now. There he was, standing at the counter ordering a drink. Had she actually run him over, and this was his spirit haunting her? She'd seen enough horror movies to know this sort of stuff happens. It was definitely him. She could tell from his dark mop of hair, and he was wearing the same jacket. It's incredible how much detail you can take in from a split-second incident, although she had replayed the near miss a few times since.

She made her way over to Martyn and sat down. 'Are you OK?' he asked. 'You look a bit flustered. There's no need to be nervous; honestly, he's here, just getting a drink.' He smiled at her and squeezed her hand. Luisa looked up at the queue; there wasn't anyone there but the dark-haired boy being served by the young blonde-haired barista. She looked around the room; no, there wasn't anyone else there who would be the same age as Zach. Confused, Luisa looked back at Martyn, who was now standing up. 'Zach, this is Luisa.' Luisa felt the blood pumping in her ears as she looked around. No, no, no, surely not. She automatically stood up and held a sweaty hand out. 'Hi, pleased to meet you,' she said quietly. The dark-haired boy whom she nearly killed replied, 'Hi, nice to meet you too'.

It was instantly apparent that Zach had no idea that Luisa had nearly killed him. Even when Zach had asked where she lived, he never mentioned that he had even been there, although Luisa couldn't help but notice him change the subject very quickly. Other than that, the conversation was relaxed and easy. She wished Lucy could have been here, although she was sure that the conversation may not have been so flowing if she had. They'd talked about Zach's plans for university; he wanted to get into graphic design, and he talked about possibly moving school to Crosslands for his A levels as they did not offer the right mix of subjects at his school. The conversation was all very organic. Luisa was mindful not to talk about herself too much; she wanted to know all about Zach, and she wanted him to know she was interested in him; she knew that teenagers loved it when people had a genuine interest, and she needed to gain as many brownie points as she could.

'So, have you considered where you may want to go to Uni?' Luisa asked.

'Not really; I'd like to move away but be close enough to be able to afford to get home whenever I want to', he explained.

'I wish my daughter thought the same', said Luisa, 'she tells me she wants to get as far away from Crosslands as possible'. She rolled her eyes as she took a sip of her latte.

'Luisa's daughter wants to study art', Martyn added.

Zach looked at Martyn and then back at Luisa, his gaze staying on her for a moment longer than was comfortable. Luisa looked away. Christ, please don't recognise me now, just when it's going well. She got up quickly, 'I'll get us all another drink, shall I?' she asked.

'Another decaf cappuccino for me, please, Lu,' replied Martyn

'Er, just a coke for me, please', Zach replied.

Luisa breathed a sigh of relief as she went to the counter. This situation was so bizarre. Of all the people in the world she could nearly run over, it was Martyn's son, and why on earth would he have been walking along the road from Copcut Green? Both his mum and dad lived miles away from there. And why would he not mention his connection with it when Luisa told him where she lived? Something wasn't right here; something was not right at all.

She looked at them both as she waited for her order to be prepared. They were so different to look at you wouldn't put them as father and son. Martyn's blond hair and blue eyes starkly contrasted with Zach's dark looks. But it was clear they thought the world of each other; they laughed together like best friends. She felt a tug on her insides as she thought about Lucy, her daughter who would rather spend time with her dad's girlfriend than her mother. How is Zach going to react to that? she asked herself. Even if he liked her now, he'd surely have second thoughts when he discovered that her parenting skills were about as effective as a chocolate radiator.

She grabbed the tray of drinks and carried them back to the table.

'Zach was just telling me about his girlfriend', Martyn stated.

'Yeah, she was supposed to be busy today, but she's had a change of plan, so I've asked her to pop in if that's OK?' Zach asked.

'Oooh yes, that would be lovely,' exclaimed Luisa, genuinely excited at the prospect of someone else adding to the conversation. This would now be as much of Zach wanting Martyn to like his new partner, which took the pressure off her.

'How long have you been together?' Luisa asked, glad of the new array of questions presented to her.

'A while', Zach stated.

'Really?' asked Martyn. 'So how come I've never met her then?'

Zach laughed, 'I'm allowed to have some privacy, Dad. You don't have to know everything about me. '

Luisa stirred sugar into her coffee. Maybe that's where she'd gone wrong with Lucy; maybe she was too intrusive; perhaps that's why she'd pushed Lucy away.

Zach's phone buzzed. 'Oooh, she's just outside. Hold on,

and I'll go and get her.' Zach jumped up, clearly excited, and left the shop.

Martyn looked at Luisa, 'this is OK, isn't it?' he asked her. 'I had no idea she would be joining us'.

Luisa smiled, sensing Martyn was suddenly out of his comfort zone. 'This is fine; this is normal family life', she reassured him. 'It's great that Zach feels comfortable enough to do this', she added, fully aware of the tone of her voice reflecting the sadness of her own relationships.

Martyn squeezed her hand again, sensing a shift in her mood. 'It'll all be fine Lu, I can feel it, trust me', he leant over and kissed her cheek. At that precise moment, she believed him – she believed that it would all be OK. She felt the safest she had felt in a long time, and she felt herself fall just that little bit deeper.

Chapter 25

'Martyn, Luisa, this is Lucy', said Zach, proudly introducing the raven-haired girl by his side.

Luisa spat out her coffee precisely the same time Lucy said out loud, 'What the hell?'

Martyn and Zach looked at each other, confused.

'Are you actually kidding me?' Lucy continued. 'Did you know about this?' she directed her question at Zach.

'know about what? What the hell is going on?' quizzed Zach, not knowing where to look.

Martyn stood looking at the scene unfolding in front of him. Luisa was still sitting, her face white and her mouth wide open. Zach was trying to look at everyone all at once, his arms held out in disbelief, and the new arrival stood staring at Luisa, clearly pissed off at the introduction that had just taken place.

Zach broke the tension. 'Shall we try again? Lucy, this is my dad Martyn'.

Luisa quickly interjected, 'Martyn, this is my daughter, Lucy'.

Martyn immediately cottoned on to what was unfolding

before his eyes. Although he knew it might not be appropriate, he couldn't help but laugh out loud.

'Are you serious? Lucy? Is my dad dating your Mum?' Zach asked as he desperately tried not to join in with the laughter.

'Apparently so, not that *I* was informed about it,' she replied indignantly as she sat herself down at the table, arms folded tightly, still staring intently at Luisa.

'Lucy, I've been trying to pin you down for ages; this isn't the kind of thing I wanted to tell you over the phone.' she said in a lowered tone.

'Hold on', interrupted Zach, 'I thought your mum was called Maxine?'

Luisa took a sharp and audible intake of breath.

'No, she's my step-mum, sort of, well she's my Dad's girlfriend' replied Lucy quickly.

'Ah, OK, yes, of course, it was your mum who lives at Copcut Green,' he nodded, piecing it all together.

Luisa took her chance. 'oh, you know where I live?' she asked

Zach looked at Lucy, and Lucy lowered her eyes.

'maybe we could have met sooner if I'd have got home from work a bit earlier, eh?' her passive-aggressive tone and raised eyebrow were not lost on either of them. Lucy shuffled uncomfortably in her seat, and Zach's eyes darted to Martyn to check if he'd made the connection. He hadn't; if he had, he wasn't letting on.

Martyn took control of the conversation. 'right, this is a shock for all of us. Lucy, let Zach and me go and get drinks and give you girls a minute,' he suggested as he gestured for Zach to get up and help him.

Lucy and Luisa sat in silence for what felt like an hour.

'Lucy love, listen, this is a mess. I wanted to tell you I was seeing someone face to face. I really like Martyn, but you know it must be right for you too. This isn't ideal, is it? Meeting like this?'

'Not at all,' replied Lucy. 'You just caught me off guard; I didn't want to tell you about Zach yet; I liked it being just me and him. Even Dad and Max don't know about him.'

'It's OK, Lucy; I don't know what you think I'm going to say! He seems lovely!'

'He is,' said Lucy, looking at her Mum. He is really lovely' and a smile involuntarily appeared across her face. Luisa smiled back at her. 'Well then that's OK, as long as you're happy, and he treats you well, then I'm happy too'.

'I am'. she added. And then, out of the blue, taking Luisa by surprise, Lucy asked, 'Are you happy, mum?'

Luisa smiled back at Lucy. She wasn't as happy as she could be because Lucy still wasn't back at home, but now wasn't the time or the place for that particular conversation.

'Martyn is lovely too,' Luisa assured her. 'You'll like him', she added quickly. Luisa spotted Martyn and Zach returning with a tray of freshly brewed drinks. 'But don't tell him that,' she whispered to Lucy as he set the tray on the table, 'don't want him getting a big head'; she laughed. Lucy smiled back at her. This could be what they needed, a chance meeting in unexpected circumstances. No overthinking, no planning. Yes. This is what they needed.

Martyn and Zach sat down, and the conversation started again about Lucy's vegan farmers market trip and how Zach was considering the switch. Luisa watched the three of them talking and laughing together. She studied Lucy's face. She was growing into a beautiful young lady; maybe Zach was a welcome distraction from the girls Lucy had started to hang around with. Lucy tucked a stray strand of her dark hair behind her ear and lifted her coffee cup. She took after her father in her colouring, her olive skin turning a beautiful shade of brown at the slightest hint of sun, much unlike Luisa, who had inherited her mother's pale skin that went a rather painful shade of pink before returning immediately to its almost translucent state. Her eyes switched to Zach, whose dark mop of hair hid his equally dark eyes. Sitting next to Lucy, they looked more like brother and sister than boyfriend and girlfriend.

Luisa studied them both closely. How strange, they looked somewhat similar, with the same shaped nose and build. The more she looked at them both, the more a sour taste rose from her stomach, and she felt beads of sweat on her brow. *Stop it, Luisa, stop overthinking.* But it was useless; the more she looked at them, the more she saw it. She looked at Martyn and then back at Zach. There was nothing similar about them both. Nothing.

Martyn caught her eye. 'You OK, Lu?' he asked, resting his hand on her knee. 'you look a bit peaky.'

'Mum doesn't get the vegan thing', interjected Lucy. 'She's deffo never giving up her bacon sarnies,' she laughed.

'Not sure I could either,' added Martyn. 'It's one of life's little pleasures!'

'Try telling the pig that,' scorned Lucy as she sipped her oat milk latte.

Just as Luisa thought she would either throw up or faint, Zach and Lucy stood up. 'Right, we've got to go', Zach stated. 'If that's OK?'

'Of course.' Martyn stood up and hugged Zach. Luisa shuffled out from the table and hugged Lucy, whispering in her ear, 'See you soon? Come over for your tea or something; I'll cook something vegan.'

'OK, mum', replied Lucy, 'can Zach come?'

Luisa stalled. Lucy's expression hardened.

'It's OK, mum, I get the hint', she spat at Lucy before Luisa could answer.

'No, no, sorry, yes, of course', Luisa replied. 'of course he can'.

'OK, well I'll text you soon'.

Pleasantries done with and goodbyes said, it was just Luisa and Martyn.

'Well! That was a turn-up for the books, eh? I didn't see that one coming!' Martyn stated.

'Yeah', answered Luisa, trying desperately hard to stop her mind from overthinking again.

'You sure you're OK, Lu? It must have been a shock seeing Lucy like that, without forewarning, but maybe this is what you both need: a catalyst in getting your relationship back on track?'

'Yeah, maybe', Luisa replied.

'OK, be honest with me,' he insisted, turning to face her head on. 'is it too much too soon? We had to meet them at some point, didn't we?' he said

'yes, no, yes, sorry, no, it's fine. It's just a lot, that's all she said. 'Took me by surprise.'

'As long as you're OK', he added.

'Yes, sorry, I'm fine.'

Martyn knew from experience that 'fine' often meant quite

the opposite. Had this been a step too far for them both? Zach seemed to really take to Luisa, and Lucy being her daughter wouldn't be an issue, surely? Martyn felt uneasy all of a sudden. There was a tension between him and Luisa that he couldn't quite put his finger on.

'It looks like I've been dumped from Zach time tonight though - shall we do something?' he offered, 'if you're free, that is?'

Luisa panicked. She wanted to go home and hide under the duvet for an hour or two. She was on the verge of throwing this whole thing away because of her stupid, overthinking head, putting two and two together and coming up with five. No, she wasn't going to self-sabotage it now. She would only do something once she at least had some evidence.

'Yes, that sounds nice. Do you want to come over? I'm not sure I have the emotional energy for anything else this evening,' she added.

'Sounds perfect. Shall I bring a bottle?'

'I'd bring two,' Luisa suggested. She'd need some courage to have the conversation with him later. And he would need a few drinks to take on board what Luisa was about to suggest to him.

Chapter 26

Luisa waited for Martyn to drive off, pretending to look for something in her glove compartment. She didn't want him to see where she was going. She needed to do this before seeing him later; now was her only opportunity. *Strike while the iron is hot*, she told herself. *Grab the bull by both horns. Get on with it, Luisa.* She turned the key in the ignition and drove the short distance into town, her heart in her chest the whole time. She turned down the stereo, shaking her head. Not even a familiar tune from The Courteeners couldn't even help her now, even though 'No You Didn't, No You Don't' seemed utterly appropriate. Her heart was beating out a rhythm that nothing else could match, pulsing to the ends of her fingers and making her breath fill her lungs too quickly. She needed quiet to concentrate, to gather herself together.

She parked up and took a deep breath before getting out of the car. She knocked purposefully on the battered brown front door and took another deep breath. She had a feeling there would be a lot more deep breaths over the next few hours.

'Lu, what are you doing here? Lucy isn't in,' Jon stated as he answered the door, eating something that looked suspiciously like the end of a sausage roll.

Luisa replied, 'It's not Lucy I want to talk to - is Maxine here?'

Jon shook his head as he stuffed the rest of the food in his mouth. 'Do you think I'd be allowed to eat this if she was?' he said, flecks of pastry flying from his mouth.

'Nice' Luisa said, screwing up her face. 'Well, can I come in then?' she asked.

Jon opened the door wider and beckoned her in before looking outside the front door and closing it. Luisa perched herself on the edge of the sofa, which she thought would be nice if it wasn't covered in a load of throws that looked like they needed a good wash. There was an air of stale smoke and strong-smelling incense.

'Brew?' Jon shouted from the kitchen.

'No, I don't have time. Can you come and sit down, please, Jon?' Luisa asked, surprising herself with her authoritative tone.

'Christ, what's up with you?' Jon responded as he came in and sat on the arm of the chair opposite.

'Jon, I need to ask you a question.'

'Fire away.'

'And for once in your life, will you please give me an honest answer?' she added.

'For fucks sake, Lu, ' he huffed, rolling his eyes. 'Go on then, what's up with you?'

'When we first moved to Copcut, and you worked all hours at that firm in Crosswich, did you have an affair?'

'Jesus Christ, Lu, where's this coming from?' Jon replied, clearly stalling for thinking time.

'Just answer the question, Jon', said Luisa calmly.

'What the fucking hell! What are we talking about, nearly

sixteen years ago? And you're bringing this up now?' he laughed. 'Ever likely you can't find anyone else, Lu if you're dragging the past up every five minutes'.

Luisa felt herself panicking. He always did this to her; he always made her feel like she was the one in the wrong. Megan had called him a gas lighter for years, but Luisa had it ingrained in her that she was the problem. But she wouldn't let it go this time; too much was riding on it.

'Jon, can you just answer the question?' she insisted.

'Are you being serious? You've come round to ask me this now? Ever likely Lucy wanted to move out; you're ridiculous. Move on, Lu, seriously,' he jibed.

'And yet you still haven't answered the question, Jon. Can you please, for once, give me a straight answer? I need to know.'

'Why? Why now?' he asked, still avoiding the question.

'Jon, a simple yes or no. Did you, or did you not have an affair when I was pregnant with Lucy?'. Her tone was sharp and strong.

'Right, well, you were a nightmare, Lu; you were always moody and kept banging on about needing more money. You made us buy that house that we couldn't afford and expected me to go out and earn for the both of us while you kept on about how you were going to sit under that fucking tree on a blanket. It was too much pressure. It was alright for you to stay at home on your fat arse all day!'.

Wow, thought Luisa, *if I ever needed clarification that splitting up was the right thing, then that was it right there.*

'So again, Jon, did you or did you not have an affair?' If this situation weren't so potentially damaging, she would find it rather amusing that a grown man could behave like a child caught taking the last chocolate biscuit out of the tin.

'It wasn't an affair as such,' he said indignantly.

Luisa exhaled and rolled her eyes. 'OK then, let me rephrase the question, Jon. Is there any possibility, any possibility at all, that you could have fathered a child with someone else while we were still together?' She stared at him intently. She was not going to let him bully her into ending this conversation. She was expecting another vomit of accusations to be thrown back at her, but instead, she saw the colour drain from his face. A rather white-faced Jon responded. 'How did you find out?'

'You actual piece of shit', Luisa said quietly. 'You knew - all this time you knew?!'

Jon was now visibly shaken. He had sunk to a new low here, and Luisa, although confused and angry, was also relieved that this man was no longer connected to her other than through Lucy.

'She told me she couldn't get pregnant. She'd been trying for a while with her husband.'

'Oh, so you knew she was married then?' Luisa interjected accusingly.

'Yes. She was bored, same as me,' he continued cruelly. Luisa felt her insides jar a little.

'Her husband became obsessed with her getting pregnant, and she just wanted some fun. We worked together. It just happened.'

'Clearly - carry on,' Luisa added sarcastically.

'She told me she was pregnant; I told her she needed to get rid of it. I didn't want a baby; you were already pregnant, for fucks sake,' he said as if this was his way of justifying what had happened.

How commendable of you, Luisa thought.

'And she never told you what she did about the baby?' Luisa asked.

'No, when I told her I wanted to end things, she told me she would tell her husband it was his. And as far as I know, that was that. I never contacted her again, and she never contacted me.

'And you've never wondered? Not once?' said Luisa, shaking her head in disbelief.

'Why would I? If she'd kept it, her husband would have raised it as his own, and the child would have never had reason to question.'

'Ah, right, so that's OK then', said Luisa, the sarcasm in her voice irritating him.

'What the fuck do you want me to say Lu? I don't know what your problem is; it was a lifetime ago. We had Lucy, and things went downhill for us. I have my own life going on, and she clearly just got on with it.'

Luisa looked at this man and wondered what she had seen in him. What an absolute spineless piece of shit he was. At least he was a relatively good dad to Lucy because he could have easily messed that up, given his outlook on life. He looked up at her like a helpless child. For a moment, Luisa wondered if he was going to apologise.

'So how did you find out –who else knows?' he asked her. Of course, he was panicking that someone was going to knock and ask for back pay in child maintenance or that Lucy would find him out for the shit that he was.

Luisa signed and put her head in her hands. How was she

going to begin to unpick this? What an absolute mess.

'It doesn't matter how I found out, Jon', she replied as she stood up.

'Wait, hold on, you can't leave now. Who else knows? Has she been in touch? Does she know where I live?' he panicked.

And yet again, here he was, trying to cover his own back. Luisa had heard enough.

'I need to go,' she said as she approached the front door.

'Lu?' he called after her.

Her hand paused as she reached for the latch.

'You won't tell Lucy, will you?' he pleaded.

She let herself out of the door without answering and closed it behind her.

How could she not tell Lucy? There was a very high possibility that her first boyfriend, the boy she had been spending so much time with, was also potentially her half-brother.

Chapter 27

Luisa drove home in silence, unable to tolerate even the Stone Roses. She was stunned by the revelation that had emerged over the past few hours. Her life had been thrown into a complete spin, and she wasn't sure what to do about it. She had to tell Lucy – there was no question of that. When it looked like there was hope for her own romantic relationship to flourish, she was going to break the news that could potentially break Lucy's heart. Or maybe they hadn't gotten that far in yet. They were only fifteen. It's not like they were sleeping together. Or were they? Luisa reflected on when she was fifteen and shuddered at the thought. She needed to tell Lucy before things went any further.

As soon as she got home, Luisa called Megan. She needed backup and some words of wisdom; there was too much for her to think about, her thoughts jostling for the forefront, all equally important, all equally life-shattering.

'What's up?' Megan asked as she answered the phone. 'It was meet the son day today, wasn't it? Don't tell me it's gone to shit already?'

Luisa attempted to speak but couldn't. The words clogged up in her throat, her emotions suddenly surging across her like a storm rolling in over the sea. An overwhelming sense of sadness and panic thundered through her.

'You there, Lu? Are you OK?'

Luisa managed to squeak out a 'no' before the tears started.

'I'm on my way,' replied Megan.

An hour later, there were crisis talks around the kitchen table.

'fucking hell', said Megan as she listened to the saga. 'What a mess!'.

'Understatement of the year,' replied Luisa. There is no way around this, is there? I'm going to break Lucy's heart, tear Martyn's world apart and throw Zach's life into turmoil,' she stated. 'All in one day!'

'Fucking hell' repeated Megan. 'That's some achievement, even for you!'

'Now is not the time for humour, Meg,' scolded Luisa.

'No, sorry, of course not, so hold on a minute, how old is Zach exactly?' Megan asked.

'About six months younger than Lucy,' Luisa replied.

'So you were six months pregnant with Lucy when he was sleeping with her?' she asked.

'Yep. He said he finished it with her when she found out she was pregnant,' Luisa replied.

'Wow,' Megan replied, eyes wide. 'I knew he had the potential to be a dick, but I had no idea it was this bad'.

'Don't' said Luisa, shaking her head. 'This is one huge mess, and I can't see a way out of this without upsetting a lot of people. I have toyed with the idea of emigrating to Amsterdam and leaving them all to it.'

'Why Amsterdam?' Megan asked, confused.

Luisa shrugged. 'Why not?'

'OK, so let's think about this sensibly', Megan began. 'Can you get Lucy and Zach to split up – that will solve that situation immediately. Tell her that you've seen him with someone else or something.'

'Then she'll hate me, and Zach will also hate me as he'll know I'm a liar because it isn't true. And then what if they get back together again when they realise I'm just telling a fat lie? Then, neither of them will speak to me. And that doesn't even address the Zach and Martyn situation,' Luisa cried.

'Does that need to come out, though?' said Megan. 'It's been nearly sixteen years; what's the point of rocking the boat now?' she offered, trying desperately to find something helpful to say.

'Then Martyn and I will have to split up because I can't live with a secret like that, Meg. And Lucy has to know the truth, so if I know, and Lucy knows, then it's only a matter of time. I can't do that; I can't ask Lucy to do that.'

'No, I know, I'm scraping the barrel here, Lu. I can't see a way out of this other than telling the truth. Can you hold off a couple of years until they both go off to Uni? It will fizzle out then anyway.'

'So you think from the age of sixteen to eighteen they will continue their relationship without sleeping together, Meg? Really?' Luisa asked.

'Oh fuck Lu. I hadn't even thought of that. You're right. She will be already if she's anything like the pair of us.'

Megan watched the colour drain from Luisa's face. 'But Lucy's nothing like us, Lu. Let's not worry about that.' she added quickly.

They both sat in silence.

'Fuck' said Luisa.

'Yep', agreed Megan.

'Well, I'll tell you what, Meg. I certainly didn't see my summer break panning like this,' Luisa said as she cradled the mug.

Luisa had no idea what was going to happen next. She'd been so happy in the cafe once she'd got over the shock of Lucy turning up. There were definitely positive steps taken to heal their relationship, and now it would come crashing down around them. She wanted the whole situation to disappear, but a secret can't stay a secret if people know. The truth has to come out. And there was no way around it; like it or not, Luisa would have to be the one to do it.

Luisa had practised what she was going to say a hundred times. She wouldn't go straight in; she hoped she could give enough information for Martyn to put two and two together and piece it together himself. This didn't have to end in a nuclear fallout. Slow and gentle, not going in like a steam train. She couldn't imagine how he would feel when he knew what was going on, and she really did care about him. If they could still make this work, she desperately wanted to. She had strategically placed photos of Lucy around the living room, where her resemblance to Zach was most significant. That would help. It didn't matter how she approached this; there was no good outcome; she just wanted to soften the blow as much as possible.

She had toyed with contacting Martyn's ex and asking her to come clean to speak to Martyn and Zach. She knew that was cowardly, but it took the pressure off her. Maybe she could give enough information to Martyn for him to take it back to her and ask her himself? Maybe Jon would step up as a man and tell her the secret was out? She dismissed that thought quite quickly. Jon was not a man of integrity. She doubted whether he would even share his newfound information with Maxine. What a sad little existence he must live in, wrapped up in his own little world, oblivious to what was happening around him.

She checked her watch. 18.50. Jon would be here soon. She hadn't cooked; she hadn't even thought about food since she got back. There was food in the freezer. Luisa could prepare something if need be. She had a distinct feeling that she wouldn't even get to discuss food this evening.

18.59. Luisa had paced up and down the hallway at least 50 times. 'OK, Luisa, you can do this. This is for the best; this has to happen. You have to be authentic to yourself. You would want to know over and over again to herself as she paced up and down. She was ready. She thought she was ready, but when Luisa heard his car pull up outside, she doubted she would ever be prepared to have this conversation. The plans went out of the window as she answered the front door and saw him standing there, holding two wine bottles and a single red rose between his teeth with a daft grin across his face. He was adorable; she was falling for him. Luisa also needed to tell him something that would completely shatter his whole world.

* * *

'I still can't believe it', Martyn called from the kitchen as he pulled the cork out of the wine bottle. Luisa was sitting on the sofa, her heart beating in a way that felt like she was going to pass out. Wine would help take the edge off; after a glass, she would start to sew the seeds.

'Believe what?' she asked as he passed her a large glass of Pinot Grigio. Luisa had never been more grateful.

'Zach and Lucy today', Martyn laughed. 'I can't believe it. I haven't stopped thinking about it all afternoon," he added.

'No, me neither', replied Luisa as he took a large gulp of wine.

'I'd told Zach about you, but he hadn't listened too much as he hadn't put the pieces together. Mind you, he's a teenager. Since when have they ever listened to what is going on in our lives, eh?'

Luisa nodded in agreement, her lips still attached to the edge of the wine glass.

'And I meant to ask you, what did you mean when you said you should have got home from work earlier – I meant to ask at the time, but it all escalated very quickly.'

Luisa looked at him and frowned. 'What do you mean?'

'When you told Zach about meeting if you'd got home early – the pair of them looked ever so sheepish', he said, setting his wine glass on the side table beside him.

Luisa explained about the day that she nearly ran poor Zach over. He had clearly been visiting Lucy. Luisa felt a surge of bile rise up her windpipe, the wine suddenly tasting of battery acid, and she felt the urge to throw up. How long had they been alone in the house together, unsupervised? She knew what she was like at Lucy's age, which made her worry even more. What if they had started sleeping together already? She felt hot and prickly. What an absolute fucking nightmare. The whole thing. She started wondering if the best thing to do for everyone was to end it now and forbid Lucy from seeing Zach again. Yes, that's what she was going to do. That's the answer. That was it. Right now.

'Martyn...'

He looked over at her. He sensed her anxiety. He moved over and sat right next to her, took her hands, and kissed them tenderly.

'Yes, Luisa?' He was staring right at her, directly through her eyes and into her soul.

Stop it, Luisa, stop thinking these things; he's a good man; he doesn't deserve this.

'Shall we have something to eat?' She took the easy option and diverted from the plan.

'Ooh yes, shall we? Martyn replied. 'I've not had a drink yet. Do you want me to pop into town and pick something up?'

'That would be lovely Martyn, would you mind?' aware that she was putting off the inevitable.

'Consider it done', he said as he reached for his keys. 'Chinese? Indian?'

'Whatever you fancy, I'm easy,' she said. 'But make sure there's something with black bean sauce on it.' she added.

'Chinese it is then', he laughed. He leaned over to peck Luisa on the cheek. 'I'll order it on the way; I won't be long. Don't drink all that wine without me!' he added as he left.

Luisa downed the rest of her glass and swiftly topped it up

again. She had an hour to sort herself out. *Come on, Luisa, pull yourself together. This is the right thing to do.* She got out her phone and sent Lucy a quick text.

'Hi Luce, I hope you're OK. It was lovely to see you earlier. X'

Right, that would have interrupted whatever they were doing.

She was relieved that Lucy was online and had read the message. *If she's on her phone, then she's not having sex.*

By the time Martyn returned, they were one bottle down, and Luisa was feeling much more relaxed, partly due to the wine but primarily because Lucy wasn't too preoccupied to use her phone.

'Ohh, good choice', she exclaimed, and she helped him unpack the food. 'Ooh, what have you had?'

'Help yourself, dear,' Martyn laughed as he watched Luisa stabbing at the contents of the plastic tubs with a fork. She wiped some stray chow mein sauce from her chin. 'Sorry, I didn't realise I was so hungry,' she said.

By the time the food was eaten, both bottles of wine were empty, and they lay on the sofa, stuffed. Martyn was stroking Luisa's hair as her head rested on his lap. If it weren't for the fuck off secret she was keeping, she would have felt positively content at this precise moment.

Luisa *had* toyed with telling him but, selfishly, didn't want to ruin the evening. It's not like anything would change in one night. She'd tell him in the morning; he was going to stay the night again; he'd been drinking as much as she had—just one night, in someone's arms, someone who loved her and who she loved back. Just one night before, it all fell apart. That's all she wanted.

Chapter 28

Luisa was woken up by a pounding on her front door. Either war had broken out, or she'd won the lottery. Either way, whoever was hammering that hard at the house at the end of the street at this ungodly hour wanted attention. She sat up and rubbed her eyes, reaching for her phone to check the time. Flat battery. That's what happens when you drink too much before bed; you forget to charge your phone. She pressed the button on the side of her Samsung and put it on the bedside table to come to life.

'Jesus Christ, what's going on?' Martyn muttered, stirring next to her.

'There's someone at the bloody door' stated Luisa.

'Lucy?' asked Martyn.

'Oh shit. Yes. Obviously. I bet she's not got her key,' Luisa said as she leapt up to grab her dressing gown from the back of the bedroom door. Luisa made her way down the stairs, desperately trying to understand how Lucy could have gotten over to Copcut at this time of night whilst desperately trying to tie the belt on her dressing gown.

She flung the front door open.

'What the fucking hell are you doing here?!' she exclaimed

as a wide-eyed Megan stood before her.

'Why haven't you answered your phone, Lu? Nobody has been able to get hold of you!'

'It's flat, Megan,' she replied, panicking. Megan had a look in her eye that was making her feel anxious.

'Oh god, Luisa, you need to come quick. It's Lucy. There's been an accident.'

Luisa saw black flashes in her eyes, and her stomach contracted so hard that she felt her insides rising up inside of her. A thick, sharp liquid came up her windpipe, and she struggled to catch her breath.

'Lu, listen to me, she's OK, but you need to come, she's asking for you. I've got my car, Lu. Grab some clothes quickly, I'll take you.'

'Right, yes, OK, hold on', Luisa stammered as she turned to run up the stairs.

'Is Martyn here?' Megan shouted after her.

'Yes, why?' she shouted back.

'Then you better get him too; it's both of them, Lu, they're both in there.

Martyn was already up and was pulling his clothes on.

'What's happened, Lu?' he questioned, reaching for his phone. 'Shit, shit, shit. I've got dozens of missed calls from Claire.' His phone had been on silent.

Luisa pulled on some leggings and a hoodie that was hanging on the bannister and reached for her phone, which had sprung to life.

'Fuck Martyn, me too, Jon's been trying to contact me'

They both hurtled down the stairs. Luisa jumped into the passenger seat, and Martyn climbed into the back.

'Meg, what's happened? Are they OK?' Martyn asked from the back.

'Right, all I know is there's been an accident involving a car; they were crossing the road, and the car didn't stop'.

'Jesus Christ!' cried Martyn, putting his head in his hands.

'Where? Where were they crossing the road?' asked Luisa. She had no idea why that was important at this moment in time.

'Down from the pizza place in town, they were on a crossing Lu, the car just didn't stop'.

'Have they got them?' Martyn Asked.

'Got who?' asked Luisa, annoyed with Martyn for asking a stupid question at a time like this.

'The driver,' he affirmed. 'I'll fucking kill him'.

'I don't care about the fucking driver at this point, Martyn, I just need to know if Lucy is OK.'

Martyn sat back in his seat, a rage inside him that he didn't know what to do with.

'It was a woman,' Megan replied. 'and yes, they got her, she ran into a lamppost further down.'

'What the hell?' Martyn shrieked. 'Was she fucking pissed?'

Megan looked at him in the rearview mirror. Martyn was rocking back and forth with his head in his hands. Now was not the time to tell him that yes, she was; she was actually three times over the limit. Martyn didn't need to know that right now. She looked over at Luisa, who was scrolling through her phone's missed calls and messages. No, Martyn didn't need to know that the driver was drunk, and Luisa definitely didn't need to know that she knew the driver; she knew the driver very well.

'Jon and Maxine are at the hospital; Jon called me when he

couldn't reach you.' Megan said.

'And Claire? Is she there?' Martyn asked.

'I don't know,' replied Megan. 'Jon didn't say'.

'No, I don't suppose he'd know who she was anyway', suggested Martyn. Meg glanced at the passenger seat, but Luisa was too preoccupied with her phone to realise the statement's implication.

'She's on her way; Martyn offered. She's just messaged me. 'Christ, why did I put my phone on silent... I never do that,' he said, shaking his head.

They drove in silence for the rest of the journey. Luisa watched the world flit past the car window; strangely, she could only think about seeing Jon. Jon would know what to do; she's his daughter, too. He'd make it OK. He was fucking useless at everything else, but he would know what to do, she tried to convince herself. Still with his head in his hands, Martyn was fixated on his phone being silent, like he could have somehow stopped the accident by turning his ringer on. It's all he had. Martyn had spent his life protecting his little boy; he'd dedicated his whole life to him. The one night that he throws caution to the wind and does something completely selfish, this happens. This was a sign that he shouldn't be looking for a life of his own. Zach was his life, and he should have always put him first. He's a dad first; everything else has to come second. No more; from now on, it's just him and Zach; yes, that's what he'd do. Martyn had the same conversation with himself all the way to the hospital, which would only work, obviously, if Zach was OK.

Megan dropped them off at the emergency ward entrance and

drove off to find a car parking space, which, given the time of night, should have been relatively easy, but not at a hospital, apparently. They both rushed to the help desk and spoke at the same time.

'Zach Woodhouse'

'Lucy Middleton'

The receptionist was highly efficient, if not a little stony-faced.

'And you are?'

'I'm his dad'

'I'm her mum'

The receptionist tapped her fingers on the keyboard on her desk and told them they could find Lucy on Ward Thee, following the yellow lines on the floor. Zach was still in A&E, and Martyn was directed in the opposite direction. He turned to speak to Luisa, but she was already gone.

Luisa followed the yellow lines on the floor around the maze of corridors. She couldn't help but think about the Wizard of Oz. Lucy loved that film. She would sit with a cushion in front of her eyes until the black-and-white part was over; it was the old woman on the bicycle that scared the shit out of her. When Lucy was out of hospital, she'd put it on, and they'd sit under a blanket together with hot chocolate. That's what she'll do. Just the two of them, Obviously, if Lucy was OK.

As they reached the end of the corridor, Luisa could see Jon sitting with his head in his hands and Maxine beside him with her arm on his back. Jon immediately got up and ran toward Luisa, who burst into tears.

'Jon, is she OK? Where is she? Can I see her?'

Jon held her tight. 'It's OK Lu, it's OK, she's OK, she's going to be OK.'

'Can I see her? Where is she? I need to see her?' Luisa cried.

'You can in a minute; they're just doing some observations. She's OK, honestly, just a bit battered and bruised. They've taken some x-rays of her arm; they don't think it's broken, but they just need to see what's going on.'

'Oh god, my phone was flat; I'm so sorry, Jon, I should have been here sooner.'

'I'll get some tea, shall I?' offered Maxine, and she made her way through the swinging doors.

Jon felt Luisa's body become a dead weight in his arms, and he used all his strength to keep her upright, supporting her to stop her from falling into a heap.

'it's OK, It's OK, Lu, I'm here, she's going to be OK,' he whispered into her hair.

'So, can I see her? Where is she?' Luisa managed to ask through her sobs.

'We can in a minute; someone will be out to us,' he answered.

'So we just wait here?'

'we just wait here.'

* * *

'Where have you been, Martyn? I've been calling all night,' Claire hissed audibly.

'My phone was on silent, Claire. Where is he? Can I see him?'

'He's OK, he will be OK, he's lost a bit of blood, they've had to operate', she told him a matter of factly.

'Jesus,' Martyn exclaimed, fighting back the tears. 'Tell me what's happened, what's happened to my boy?'

Claire sat down and patted the seat next to her. Sit down, for god's sake,' she directed.

Martyn sat heavily next to her, his eyes searching her face for any hint of emotion that would tell him how serious this was.

'He was at the crossing in town; apparently, the traffic lights were on red. The car tried to stop but left it too late to brake. It just hit him. She didn't even stop Martyn; she carried on driving.' Claire's eyes told him that although she was trying desperately hard not to show emotion on her face, she was close to falling apart.

'Fuck fuck fuck', Martyn shouted while pulling at his hair.

'It's his leg. His leg took the impact. They said if she hadn't attempted to brake he may not be here at all'. This was it. This was the moment she couldn't pretend to be strong. Big fat tears collected in her eyes, and as she blinked, she released them like a stream down her cheeks. She wiped them away angrily. She was never any good at showing her vulnerable side. Martyn had always said she had her walls up, and there was no way of getting in.

'Is it broken?' Martyn looked up

'Fractured. But there was a deep cut that they couldn't stop bleeding. He's lost a lot of blood, Martyn'. Her face told him that this was a problem.

'Can I see him? Where is he?'

'He's still in theatre. They said they'd be finishing up soon; someone will be out to us.'.

'OK, OK, so we just wait here?'

'We just wait here.'

Chapter 29

A nurse came through the doors and smiled at Jon and Luisa. 'Lucy's mum and dad? she enquired.

Jon and Luisa nodded.

'I'm Mary; I've been looking after Lucy this evening,' she introduced herself as she sat beside them.

'Is she OK? Please say she's OK!' Luisa asked.

'She is fine - don't worry, she will be absolutely fine. Do you want to come and see her now?'

'oh my god, yes' Luisa exhaled.

'Yes, please, thank you', added Jon.

'OK, but before we go in, she's a little bruised. There are monitors attached to her - we're just keeping our eye on her. She's a bit woozy, but she's awake. The consultant will be along to talk you through everything.'

Luisa liked Mary. She liked her a lot. Luisa wanted to be her friend. She would have done anything for Mary at this precise moment.

'Thank you, thank you', she said through her tears.

'Now, no more tears; your baby girl is fine', she confirmed as she put her arm on Luisa.

Luisa didn't notice the beeping monitors or the wire attached to Lucy's finger. She saw her baby girl lying in a bed with crisp white linen and a pale blue blanket over her. Her hair was matted with what looked like blood, and there was a graze down one side of her face. Her left arm was in a support. But she was OK. She was awake, and when she saw them both, she cried, 'I'm so sorry, I'm so sorry.'

'Lucy, sweetheart, no, no, no', Luisa ran to her. 'You've nothing to be sorry about. Nothing at all.'

'We looked, we did; you always told me, mum, to wait for the green man, even when there's no traffic. I always wait. We waited,' she insisted.

'Shhhhhh, Lucy, shhh, it's not important. You're OK, that's all that matters.'

Jon stood beside them both and put his hand on the edge of the bed.

'Hey Lucyloo', he said quietly.

"Hey, Dad," she replied with a smile.

Maxine appeared at the door with two plastic cups of tea.

'Not sure if these are going to be drinkable guys, but they're warm and sweet', she offered.

Luisa smiled back, gratefully taking one of the flimsy plastic cups from her. She was surprised that Maxine had added sugar. 'The world's most addictive drug', Maxine told Lucy once when she'd asked for it in her coffee. Nevertheless, she was grateful for the drink. Her mouth felt like the bottom of a flip-flop. She could have really done with a couple of paracetamol, too, for the after-effect of the amount of wine she had drunk. The irony of being in a hospital, surrounded by drugs, and not being able to have any of them.

The consultant appeared soon after to speak to them both

and called them to the side of the room. At the same time, Mary made more observations, and Maxine waited out in the corridor. He explained that the x-ray showed a minor fracture in Lucy's left arm, hence the support, but other than that, she was OK. It should heal itself within a few weeks with rest.

'They were very lucky,' he added as he left the room.

'Who was he?' asked Jon.

'What?' asked Luisa.

'The boy she was with, there were two of them. Lu, who was she with?'

Luisa felt the stabbing pain in her chest again. She had put the situation to the back of her mind. Now was definitely not the time to have this conversation.

'I don't know Jon. It's not really important right now, is it?' she said as she returned to the bedside.

It was important though. It was probably the second most important thing of all, behind Lucy. But now wasn't the time or the place. She hadn't even thought about Martyn and Zach. Her concern was for Lucy; that was all she had room to think about right now.

She sat back beside her battered and bruised little girl. 'How are you feeling, sweetheart?' she asked, wiping her hair off her face.

'I'm tired, mum,' she replied.

'That'll be the painkillers, ' interjected Mary, and she dropped the clipboard back in the slot at the end of the bed. 'She'll be sleepy while they do their thing. Might it be best to let her sleep for a while? Why don't you go and get some rest and come back later - I reckon she'll be able to come home later today as long as her obs are OK over the next few hours'.

Luisa looked at Lucy, who was already asleep, her long dark eyelashes meeting her cheeks. She looked so beautiful. Luisa felt her eyes filling again.

'We'll get off then, shall we? Jon offered. 'Do you need a lift home? We have the camper outside.'

Luisa shook her head. 'Megan's here somewhere. I'll get a lift with her - and Jon? I think she should come home to me. I'm off work for a few weeks now, so I can look after her.'

Jon didn't speak; he just nodded his head. He knew that Luisa would do everything possible to care for Lucy, which she needed right now. And if he was honest, Jon couldn't help but feel that she probably needed more than plant-based food in her system. And although he was entirely on board with natural remedies, he wasn't sure Maxine's unorthodox approach to pain relief would go down well with Luisa right now. There would be no resistance from him; Lucy needed to go home.

Chapter 30

Martyn had walked up and down the corridor so many times that he knew it was one hundred and sixteen steps to the next set of doors and back again.

'Can you stop walking up and down Martyn?' Claire instructed, exasperated by the incessant tapping of his shoes on the flooring.

'I can't just sit there, Claire. It's making me anxious.'

'Can't you read a magazine or something?'

'No, I can't read a fucking magazine Claire, our son is lying on an operating table. Now is not the time to read about what fucking bulbs to plant at this time of year.'

Claire shook her head. Now that Zach was older, they had less and less to do with one another. She had nothing in common with Martyn; if she was honest, she never really did. They married because Claire thought she wanted to settle down, but she was quickly bored. She always said she took after her mum; she was a 'free spirit', not one to be tied down. Claire should have called the wedding off, but it had cost so much money, and she really liked the idea of wearing a white dress and feeling like a princess once in her life. And Martyn was a good husband; he was just so, so dull. She would never be a perfect housewife stuck in the home all day looking after a baby.

Claire never even wanted a baby, not really; it was such a responsibility. She and Martyn had been trying for a while, and every month, she took it as a sign that it wasn't to be. It wasn't the right time. And then she became pregnant. And that really wasn't the right time or the right person. She really should have got rid of it, she thought to herself. She came very close. But Martyn, although boring, was a good man. And all he wanted was a child. He wanted to be a hands-on dad. Having a baby would answer all of his prayers and take the pressure off her. And the baby's father didn't want anything to do with her; he was busy with his own life. Their relationship was built on thrills and excitement, not nappies and domesticity. No, she would go back to Martyn and make it work. There wouldn't be any questions; it was the easy option.

Claire shook her head hard to remove the thoughts from her mind. How could she think about that time now, about how close she came to aborting Zach when he was lying in an operating theatre. She looked upwards. Claire wasn't at all religious, not in the slightest, but if ever she needed a prayer answered, this was the time.

'I deserved to be unhappy', she said quietly, 'but not Zach, please don't punish me by taking Zach'.

'Huh?' responded Martyn

Claire looked at him. She studied his face that was so familiar yet so unrecognisable. His grey stubble reminded her that they weren't kids anymore; they were adults, and they needed to deal with important shit. She could just tell him now; she could come clean, get it all out in the open, and be done with it. It's not like she and Martyn had a relationship anymore. She was a terrible person; everyone should know how awful she was. At least then, she could die knowing that the truth was out.

'Nothing', she replied. 'How much longer do you think it will be ?' she averted her thoughts briefly

Martyn shrugged. 'Soon, I hope', he said, his elbows on his knees going up and down as his foot tapped on the floor.

Fuck I'm a selfish bitch, she thought, mindful to keep her thoughts concealed. *Telling the truth would get it all out in the open, but for what gain? So I can have a clear conscience? What about Zach? What would this do to him?* She shook her head. *What the fuck was I thinking?* She shook her head once more to try and move her thoughts right to the back of her mind. No, now was not the time or the place.

'Zach's parents?' a man wearing brown cords and a checked shirt, undone at the collar, asked.

Claire and Martyn both stood up and said yes.

'Mr Postraski, Senior Consultant, I've been looking after your son this evening. I have to say, he's an extremely lucky young man.,' he added, pushing his glasses to the top of his head.

'How is he?' Martyn questioned desperately.

'So he's had a rather nasty knock to the leg, but it is a clean break, so I am very confident it will heal without any complications. With some time and rest, he'll make a complete recovery.'

'Thank god', Claire exhaled. 'So he's going to be OK?'

'He should be, yes. However...'

'No, no, no', thought Claire, ' stop talking now. She didn't want to hear a however or a but.

'As you will be aware, he has lost a lot of blood. He has an extremely rare blood type, but we should have sufficient stocks here to complete his transfusion. We have ordered more, but there is a shortage.

'Could we donate some?' offered Martyn. 'We're his parents; surely, one of us will have the same group?'

Claire felt her insides contract, and she suddenly felt very hot and faint.

'Unfortunately not, it's not advisable to donate blood from a direct donor because of the increased risk of rejection,' Mr Postraski explained. 'Don't worry, we have enough for now; he's in good hands. We'll move him up to Ward Three shortly; he'll be more comfortable there; you might want to go up and wait there for him? We'll get him settled, then you can see him, OK? Any questions?'

The pair had a million questions, but neither could articulate what they wanted to say.

'No, thank you so much for everything' said Martyn. Mr Postraski had already made the hundred and sixteen steps to the door and was on his way to his next emergency. Claire and Martyn stood for a moment. Martyn broke the silence. 'What ward was it? Three? Shall we make our way there then?' he suggested.

'Yes, we should, we'll go up. Shall I get us a coffee?' Claire offered, grateful to go outside for a vape and escape the scent of bleach and blood.

Martyn nodded. 'Yes, that would be good,' he said, suddenly feeling very dehydrated.

And with that, they headed off in opposite directions, Martyn following the yellow line and Claire heading toward the exit.

Chapter 31

Jon and Luisa left the room and went back into the corridor to find Maxine chatting with Megan about how fenugreek could work wonders for inflammation and how she should try Black Okosh when her menopause symptoms start. Megan nodded politely, her eyes darted to Luisa as she entered the corridor.

'Lu! How is she?' she asked.

'She's going to be OK, Meg, Luisa replied, emotionally worn out. 'Would you give me a lift home so I can freshen up? I'll need to come back later; they say she can come home.'

'Oh, thank god,' replied Megan. 'Of course, yes, obviously – you want to go now?'

Luisa nodded, the exhaustion taking its toll.

'Err, what about, you know?' Megan asked, trying to be as discreet as possible, conscious that Martyn's car was still at Luisa's house.

Jon looked at Luisa, trying to gain a clue from her expression. Luisa sighed. She didn't want to see Martyn right now; she wanted to go home, shower, get Lucy's room ready, change the sheets, run the hoover round, tidy up from last night's Chinese, and clear the empty bottles away. She needed to get the nest ready for her baby girl.

She was just about to tell Megan they should get going when Martyn appeared at the end of the corridor.

'Lu! Thank God, how is she?' he asked as he strode over to her, arms open.

Luisa backed away. 'She's OK, Martyn. She's fine.' she told him, avoiding eye contact. Martyn looked hurt and confused.

'How's Zach?' Megan asked quickly, desperate to ease the awkwardness. Luisa felt like retching.

'Not too good, but he's going to be OK', he replied, searching for a sign from Luisa that things were OK between them. 'Lu?'

'Sorry Martyn, I'm tired. I need to go home. Are you coming to get your car? We're leaving now.'

Martyn shook his head. 'Zach's being transferred soon; we're going to wait; we haven't been able to see him yet', he replied, tears forming in his eyes.

'Oh Martyn', signed Megan; she went over and put his arms around him. Luisa could only watch. She had nothing left to give him, not even a hug or smile. She was also very conscious that Jon was standing behind them.

'Don't think we've met', she heard him say. 'I'm Jon, Lucy's Dad.'

'Ah yes, Jon, Luisa mentioned you and Maxine.' Maxine nodded and smiled, her blond curls bouncing up and down enthusiastically.

'Martyn, err, Luisa's friend', he stated, looking at Luisa. She cast her eyes to the floor. She couldn't do this now.

'Pleased to meet you', continued Jon. 'So, Zach, he's your son?'

Luisa felt the colour drain from her face. Megan was trying to keep up with what was happening. This couldn't happen here, not now.

'Zach was with Lucy, Jon', Megan explained. 'He took the brunt of the impact.'

'Oh shit mate, sorry to hear that, is he OK?'

Martyn nodded. 'Yeah, he should be; we haven't seen him yet. He's on his way up here.'

Luisa could feel herself losing a grip of her thoughts; the room was spinning, and she felt a prickly heat moving up her neck. 'Meg. I need to sit down,'. she wheezed and grabbed Megan's arm.

'Any word on the fucking animal that did this?' Jon continued. 'I swear when I find out who it was', his fists clenched by his side, and Maxine put her arm on his shoulder.

'No, I don't suppose we will either until it comes out, if it comes out, in the press', stated Martyn. 'The family support officer is supposed to be contacting us.'

'I don't need fucking support', added Jon, 'I need to know who did it'.

'Not now, Jon, ' Maxine whispered behind him. 'Not now.'

'Not now? Not now? Oh, I think now is the perfect time when our kids are lying in fucking hospital. I swear if anything had happened to Lucy, I would fucking kill them.'

Luisa put her head in her hands.

'JUST STOP!' she shouted. 'JUST STOP IT'.

A veil of silence fell over the corridor, only shattered by the opening of the doors at the end of the corridor by a woman carrying two coffees.

They all looked towards her as she approached, concentrating hard not to spill the thick black liquid in the flimsy cups. Luisa threw her eyes at Megan, and they both spun their heads around to watch Jon, whose face had turned a rather sickening shade of grey.

Martyn broke the silence. 'This is Zach's mum, Claire'.

Claire stood with the cups in her hand, and briefly, you could hear a pin drop in the corridor of Ward Three. Martyn took one of the flimsy cups from her and took a sip. Luisa looked at Claire, then at Jon, who was beyond pale and looked like he would pass out.

'Jon, are you OK? Do you need to sit down?' offered Maxine, who was entirely used to people whiting out.

'Err, no, no, but we should be getting off. Sorry, we need to go. Come on, Max, we need to get freshened up; we'll be off, Lu. I'll call in a bit, and the pair hurriedly retraced the yellow line out of the doors.

Luisa watched Claire's face change from a waxy pale to crimson, the colour creeping up her neck like a disease. Megan broke the silence, 'Hi Claire, Megan, Luisa's friend. Lucy's godmother.'

'And I'm Lucy's mum,' Luisa said quite defiantly. 'And that was Jon, Lucy's dad,' she added savagely.

Claire stared at Luisa, her eyes flashing with panic. She knew the connection. She knew that Luisa knew, too.

Martyn, who knew nothing and being the gentle soul that he was, did his best to keep the conversation flowing.

'Lucy was with Zach at the accident, Claire. Luisa and I are dating,' he explained. Luisa suddenly felt quite embarrassed. Dating at her age, why did he say it like that? She threw him a look, and he shrugged his shoulders. There were no guidebooks on how to behave when you and your partner's respective children have nearly been taken out by a drunk driver, and you introduce your ex-wife to the mix. Add to that a night of no sleep, and things seemed all the more surreal.

Again, Megan came to the rescue. 'OK, well, we have to get going, so shall we just crack on?' she directed this at Martyn, who nodded. 'Yeah, don't worry about me; I'll get a taxi over later to get my car or something', he said.

Luisa felt her insides contract again. Worry about him? Was he being serious? As if she didn't have enough to worry about right now. She left without saying goodbye.

'So that was intense,' Megan said after they had left the car park. Luisa didn't reply. 'Lu?'

'Yeah?'

'That was intense. That whole situation,' Megan repeated.

'Yeah, I guess', Luisa said distantly, her eyes fixed on the world outside the passenger window.

'Look, Lu, I know it's been a crazy night, but don't be too hard on Martyn, eh? He's a good man. He's also been through it. And he has no idea what's coming, does he - just be gentle.'

Luisa sighed. She knew Megan was right; she just didn't have the energy right now for him. Lucy needed her. She'd got her back. She was coming home and going to spend every minute with her; she wasn't going to lose her again. And if that meant her never seeing Martyn, then so be it.

'I know Meg, I'm tired. I need a shower, and I need to get back to the hospital.

Megan gave in. She knew there was no point talking to her about this now. But Luisa couldn't avoid it forever. Even if things with her and Martyn didn't work out, she still had to deal with the Lucy and Zach relationship. And Luisa still didn't know about the driver. Shutting herself in her house, playing nurse to Lucy, could work for a while, but she couldn't avoid the truth for long.

Chapter 32

Claire and Martyn sat silently, drinking the brown liquid masquerading as tea from flimsy plastic cups. Martyn looked at his ex-wife. She still had the dark hair he'd first noticed about her years ago, although there were now silver highlights hinting at her age. Claire had always been attractive to Martyn, but it was more than her looks; She was fiery, like a hot coal, burning holes and setting fire wherever she went. Claire was too hot to handle, and he'd loved that about her. He was the opposite; he sat back and watched her spark. He was happy to do that; he was happy to take a back seat.

Claire was still attractive now, and he was glad Zach had inherited her looks. Claire's hair was raven black, starkly contrasting her pale Irish skin and blue eyes. It was a surprise when the midwife handed him a little wailing bundle of black hair and dark eyes. Martyn always believed that all babies were born with blue eyes, but that was 'poppycock', according to the midwife. Although she had said it was very unusual for a baby to have dark eyes when both parents' eyes are blue, it was very unusual indeed.

'One in a million,' Claire had said. He certainly was a special little boy right from day one.

He thought back to that day when Zach was born. He always thought he would get this overwhelming sense of love, and everything would be right in the world when he saw his own child, but when Martyn looked down at this tiny bundle, he didn't feel anything like that. He felt a bit awkward, if truth be told. 'Here you are, Dad,' the midwife had said. 'you hold your son while we sort mum out.' And that was it; he was handed a bundle of blankets, dark hair, and wailing. Zach had cried for what felt like forever. Martyn had never held a baby, let alone stopped one crying, and he wasn't sure what to do.

They didn't tell you about this bit. They told you what to expect during labour and how to help if allowed. Martyn knew all about this third stage but hadn't been told what he was supposed to do afterwards. He'd felt a bit of a fraud. He hadn't been much help during the actual labour; he'd just sat there as it happened around him. He'd tried to be helpful, he'd offered to rub Claire's back and stroke her hair, but she'd got agitated and told him to 'fuck off'.

He actually wanted to go over and hug her and tell her he loved her, but she was being looked after by the midwife, and he'd been given an important job; he'd been left holding the baby. Zach eventually stopped crying, making Martyn feel better about the whole situation.

Martyn was suddenly jolted from his thoughts by the doors crashing open and a bed being wheeled down the corridor.

'Zach!' Martyn exclaimed as he stood up.

An efficient-looking nurse in NHS blue scrubs who was supervising the delivery intercepted them both before they had a chance to get too close to the bed, and before they knew it, it had disappeared through the ward doors.

'Can we see him now? Can we go in?' Claire asked, exasperated. 'We've been waiting forever.'

'We just need to get him settled first, but then yes, of course, I'll come out and get you, OK?' she informed them. It wasn't really a question.

'OK, yes, thank you', Martyn replied compliantly, and Claire sighed audibly beside him. They both sat back down despondently. Martyn reached over to put his hand on Claire's shoulder. She shrugged it off aggressively.

'Come on, Claire, he's my son too.' pleaded Martyn, desperate to share his anxiety with someone.

'Not now, Martyn, please', she scolded, not even turning her head to look at him.

He sighed. She was always like this, never letting him get close. Ironically, that's how they had worked in the early days; she'd spend time building walls around herself, and Martyn spent his time trying to knock them down. It worked; it was unconventional, but it worked for them both until it didn't. She had become withdrawn; she'd complain about the noise he made when he ate, he breathed too heavily, and she couldn't stand his snoring. They hadn't shared a bed since Zach was born. It was more than the baby blues; it was angrier than that, more of the resentful reds. Then, one day, out of nowhere, Claire told him to leave.

'I can't do this anymore, Martyn. You need to leave.' Just like that, matter of fact, there was no emotion, no shouting, no explanation.

'Leave?' Martyn asked. 'Where do you suggest I go?'

'I don't give a flying fuck where you go Martyn, anywhere but here'. She hadn't even looked at him as she'd said it.

He left that evening, packing his clothes into an old gym bag. He went upstairs to Zach's room and kissed his dark mop of hair as he slept. 'See you soon, son, I love you', he whispered – and he meant it.

After a couple of uncomfortable nights sleeping on the back seat of his car, he'd managed to sleep on a mate's sofa until he'd secured a flat. He'd returned to the house every other night and taken Zach out in his pushchair, and as soon as he was settled, he had him three nights a week, sometimes more, Zach's room fully furnished while Martyn slept on an air bed. That's what Martyn did: put others before himself. That's what drove them apart, Claire told him later; you just never had anything about you, too soft – too nice. He'd take that; he didn't care what she called him as long as he still had his son.

It was touch and go in the delivery room for a moment, a lot of rushing around by the midwife. She'd called for backup, something about the placenta not coming away correctly. It all happened a bit quickly. They were prepping her for theatre, where they would remove it. They were asking him something, what was it? He could remember the midwife saying it was important, and could he recall what it was?

The door opened and jolted him back, but it was just the porters going back down the corridor. It wouldn't be long now; he'd see him soon. Now, what was that question they kept asking him? Ah, that was it; they were asking about her blood group. He remembered now. The midwife had got Claire's notes out.

He remembered it because the midwife had said, 'Excellent, it's a common one', and although he hadn't known what that meant, he'd been relieved that she saw it as a positive. They hadn't needed it in the end; someone senior had come in, gloved up, and removed it by hand. It was genuinely a work of art. If he hadn't been holding Zach at the time, he'd have stood up and applauded her. They hadn't needed to take her to the theatre or get reserves of Type A blood ready. They just took Zach off him, passed him to Claire, and wheeled them both off to the ward. He'd asked to stay, but Claire had asked for some time to rest. She needed to stay in to be kept an eye on overnight. So he'd gone home empty-handed to an empty house, unsure what he was supposed to do. So he cleaned the house and changed the beds. She'd appreciate that when she came home.

'OK, he's settled. Do you want to come in now?'

They both jumped up and made their way through the door, Martyn letting Claire through first, of course.

Chapter 33

'Shall I make us a decent brew?' shouted Megan up the stairs to Luisa, who had just got out of a long-awaited shower.

'Have I got time?' replied Luisa, rubbing her hair with a towel. She wanted to get back to the hospital as soon as possible. She would drive herself back to the hospital, and Megan would wait at the house in case Martyn came for his car keys.

'There's always time for a decent brew, Luisa. And Christ knows when you'll get another one, given that gnat piss we had from the machine,' she laughed as she poured the boiling water into the mugs. Luisa appeared in the doorway with her hair still damp.

'Does that feel better, Lu?' she asked as she poured the milk. 'You certainly look better than you did half an hour ago'.

'Yes, much', replied Luisa as she sat at the table. 'What a night!'

'You're telling me,' agreed Megan. 'I nearly shit myself when Zach's mum appeared through those doors.'

'I think Jon actually did,' added Luisa, shaking her head.

'Poor Martyn, he's got no idea, has he?' Megan added.

'Don't, Meg, I can't even think about that right now. I don't even want to see him; I have no idea what to say to him.'

'Why though Lu? He's still the same Martyn he was twelve hours ago. He still thinks the world of you, nothing has changed,' she added.

'I know, it's not that Meg; I don't want to have the conversation with him, especially not now, not after all this.'

Megan shook her head. 'He has a right to know Lu. And Lucy still needs to know; you can't keep a secret like this.'

Luisa signed. She knew this. Luisa knew this had to come out sooner rather than later, but right now, she just wanted her little girl back so that she could look after her. She wanted to wrap Lucy up in a bundle and keep her safe, just the two of them, just for a while. She had some making up to do, and she wasn't going to ruin it by completely pissing her off. Not yet, anyway.

'I get that' said Megan.

The Top Gun ringtone interrupted them, and Luisa looked down at her phone.

It's Jon - again,' she said, rolling her eyes and cutting off the call.

'You don't want to speak to him either?'

'not really', she said, her eyes showing her tiredness. 'I have nothing to say to him'.

The phone rang again. 'He'll just keep calling until you answer; you know what he's like,' Megan said, shaking her head.

Luisa frowned. Megan was right; Luisa would rather have this conversation with Megan here as a backup. She picked up the handset.

'Hi,' she said flatly.

'Lu, it's me. Look, I just need you to promise you won't say anything,' a panicked Jon gabbled.

'To who?' Luisa replied, knowing exactly who he meant but wanting to make this as difficult for him as she possibly could.

'To anyone. To Lucy, to Max, I can't deal with this now, Lu, there's no reason to tell anyone. I'll deal with Lucy and Zach. I just need you to promise you won't say anything.'

And that was why she didn't want to answer the phone. She sat shaking her head in silence.

'Lu! LU! You there?'

'Jon, you know I can't do that; Martyn has a right to know.'

'You can't do this to Lucy, not now; you don't want her moving back out again, do you? That's what will happen. She's just been in an accident; she doesn't need this from you right now.'

Luisa felt herself break a little.

'And how do you think she will feel when she finds out you've put your boyfriend before her? You've only known him five minutes,' he continued.

This was Jon's way. He always did this to her, making her feel like she was silly, her decisions were stupid, and she hadn't thought things through properly.

'I can't talk right now, Jon; Luisa said, 'I'll get Lucy to call you later when she's settled,' and she hung up.

'Maybe he's right, Meg; maybe I should keep quiet until Lucy's back on her feet. She's my daughter; she's my priority. It's not like she can see Zach for a while anyway; he can't even walk at the moment.

Megan shook her head. One call from Jon and she was again reduced to someone who questions themselves at every turn.

'It's your call, Lu, but you know you can't avoid this forever, right?'

Luisa put her cup down on the table and picked up her keys.

'I'm going to make my way back over. Thanks for this, Meg, honestly, thanks for everything.'

Megan got up and hugged Luisa. 'Always,' she said. 'Now you get yourself off, and I'll get the house ready for the royal highness', she said, laughing.

Chapter 34

There had been a change of staff on Ward 3 and Zach was being looked after by a rather jolly nurse called Fran, who had taken quite a shine to Zach. 'Ooh, if I was twenty years younger,' she laughed as she checked Zach's monitors. 'You'd have to have kept your eye on me', she winked at Martyn and Claire. Martyn smiled at her, grateful for her humour and spirit. Claire did not acknowledge her; she just held Zach's hand in silence.

'Oh, hark at me, sorry, I shouldn't say things like that, should I? I'll be getting myself into trouble. You can't say anything nowadays, can you? Sorry, just ignore me,' Fran rambled on. Martyn laughed, 'You're OK, Fran, you carry on; it's nice to have someone to talk to who isn't reading from a script'. Fran smiled at him kindly.

'So you're not in too much pain, Zach?' Fran asked, you just buzz me if you need some more painkillers, OK?' She popped the chart back in the slot at the end of the bed.

'Just give me a shout if you need anything,' she added as she swished the curtain back around.

'Thank you', replied Martyn.

Zach smiled over at his parents. If it weren't for the plaster and winch holding his leg at an angle, you wouldn't have known anything was wrong with him.

'Have you brought me any food?' Zach asked. Martyn laughed. 'As if the first thing you want is something to eat, I should have known'.

'Are you in much pain?' Claire asked.

'Not so much now', Zach replied. 'It actually feels OK at the moment. Have either of you heard how Lucy is?' he asked, his face showing concern.

'she's OK, son', replied Martyn, 'she'll be going home later'.

He watched Claire's lips purse.

'Oh, that's great', smiled Zach.

Well, now isn't the time to think about her' injected Claire. 'You need to concentrate on getting better, not thinking about girls'.

'What's got into you?' Zach asked, taken back by his mum's harsh tone.

'Come on, Claire,' Martyn said, 'Give him a break'.

'Ha! I see what you did there, Dad,' Zach laughed.

'Too soon?' laughed Martyn.

Claire didn't share their humour and didn't like feeling left out. And she certainly didn't like the idea of Zach seeing Lucy again. Not now, not now she knew who she was.

Martyn couldn't help but feel a sense of relief as he stood up and stretched his back. Hospital chairs were notoriously uncomfortable, and after spending twelve hours on one, his body began to feel the strain. He reached for Zach's chart, a document filled with numbers and medical jargon he didn't understand. He flipped through the pages, trying to make sense of the notes. His attention shifted to Zach, who was conversing with Claire. Martyn couldn't help but smile as he watched his son, appreciating the sense of humour that Zach had inherited. He knew Zach had a lot going for him, and the thought of anything happening to him was unbearable.

Martyn recalled Jon's angry outburst about the driver responsible for the accident as his mind wandered. He could understand Jon's rage, even though he didn't share the same fiery temperament. Martyn was more reserved and calm by nature. He looked at Claire, who was known for her fiery personality, and he couldn't help but notice that Zach had inherited some of those traits. However, unlike Claire, Zach wasn't prone to violence when he lost his temper. It was another point of contention in Claire and Martyn's relationship.

The police had apparently arrested someone at the scene. Martyn shook his head. So many lives were affected by one person's stupid decision, he thought.

Claire stood up and looked over at Martyn. 'He says he's cold," she said, "Can we get him a blanket?'

'I'll go,' offered Martyn, grateful to be able to do something useful at last. He had a history of feeling helpless at hospitals.

'Hi Fran? Sorry to disturb you, but can we have an extra blanket for Zach? He says he's a bit chilly,' Martyn asked at the nurse's station.

'Ooh yes, of course, my love', Fran said. 'It's quite normal to feel cold after a blood transfusion', she added. 'Nothing to worry about'.

'Ah, OK', Martyn said, grateful to speak to someone who didn't shut him down with one-word answers. He'd been surrounded by people all night but not actually had a conversation with anyone.

'I'll bring it over, love', she said, 'you go and sit yourself down'.

'It's OK, I'll wait; I've been sitting all night,' he said. 'it's nice to stretch my legs.'

'Right, well, if you're offering, come for a walk to the store with me, then you can bring it back,' Fran said.

They walked along the corridor together; Fran told Martyn about her most recent grandchild, Jasmine, who was only a few weeks old. 'Squealed like a little pig she did', laughed Fran. 'Looked like one too poor thing'.

Martyn laughed, 'You can't say that, Fran!'

'I can, she's one of my own, plus it's the truth.'

'Well, let's hope it's an ugly duckling situation and she blossoms into a swan', added Martyn.

'Let's hope so,' said Fran, still laughing. 'Was your boy handsome when he was born?' she asked.

'He's always been beautiful,' said Martyn wistfully. 'From the day he was born.'

'Aw, there's a proud dad if ever I saw one', said Fran, smiling. 'Were you there at the birth?'

'I was. Claire, my wife, ex-wife, Zach's mum, had some complications immediately after he was born, so I was left holding him for a while. I kept staring at him, wondering how on earth I would manage with something so tiny,' Martyn recalled.

'And now look at him!' said Fran, handing Martyn a blanket as she took some down from the store cupboard.

'Yea, he's a good lad. He was knocked over, did you know? Drunk driver,' he added, rolling his eyes.

'Aye, I had been told,' Fran added. 'He's been very lucky, hasn't he - and he's drained us of Type B! It's rare that you know, we don't see it very often; he's lucky we had our stocks up.'

Martyn looked at Fran, confused.

'Sorry, blood type B, it's very rare'.

'Oh yes, sorry', said Martyn, frowning. 'How rare is it?'.

'Well, I don't know the exact numbers, but only about ten per cent of people have it.'

Martyn pondered this for a moment. 'Fran, can I ask a question?' he asked.

'Crack on sweetheart'

'Can you have type B blood if both parents are type A?'

'Absolutely not. No. The only way you can get blood type B is from a parent. A and B, yes, but not A and A. Now you go and get that blanket on and warm that lad of yours up,' she directed.

Martyn went back to the bed and lay the blanket over Zach, who was now fast asleep.

'Claire, what blood type are you?' he asked.

Claire looked at him, her insides falling like a plane hitting an air pocket.

'What? Martyn, why do you always ask the most stupid questions?' she spat as she busied herself tucking in the blanket.

'Claire. I asked you what blood type you are; can you at least answer me that?'

She looked him in the eye, refusing to answer, desperately trying to contain the breath that was trying to escape from her chest.

'Do you know what blood type I am, Claire?' he asked her, his eyes fixed on hers, his voice calm despite his heart pounding so hard in his chest he feared he would wake Zach.

'I'll tell you, shall I? I'm type A'.

'Shit, he knows', she thought. 'Shit shit shit.'

'So I'll ask again, Claire, what blood type are you?'

She stood up and matched his eye line, her voice also calm despite the sour liquid rising at the back of her throat and the sweat trickling down her cleavage.

'A Martyn, I'm type A'.

The curtain swished open, and Fran bowled in between them both. 'Everything OK here now? Oh bless him, he's asleep, he's warmer now, yes?' she asked.

'He is, thank you,' replied Martyn, his eyes not breaking contact with Claire's. 'We're going to leave him to rest for a bit now, Fran', he told her.

Claire picked up her handbag and started to walk out.

'Yes, good idea', Fran said, frowning as she watched Claire leave the room. 'No point in you being here when he's sleeping; he'll need you when he's awake,' she added knowingly.

Martyn followed Claire out of the door. He had more questions, and he wouldn't let her fob him off with one-word answers. Not this time. Not now he knew that he wasn't Zach's father.

Chapter 35

'So we're going to do this here are we?' Claire asked as she stood in the hospital car park. It was the middle of the day, but the sky was grey and cold despite it being the end of July. She pulled her denim jacket around her tightly.

'We are', replied Martyn coldly. 'Care to start?'

Claire's eyes were fixed on the ground. She knew she would have to confess, but she was desperately trying to work out how much she should say. She could admit that Martyn wasn't Zach's father and keep his identity secret. But that wouldn't solve the problem of Zach and Lucy. *Fucking hell, how has this happened?* It had been fifteen years, and no one had ever questioned it. Claire hadn't even seen Jon since, not once; how has Zach managed to find the one girl whom he couldn't have a relationship with out of all the girls he knew? Why Lucy? Why now?

'I'm waiting, Claire', stated Martyn, his calm tone making Claire feel sick. Even now, he couldn't shout or lose his temper; she would have preferred that; she knew what she was dealing with when people shouted. She couldn't cope with this passive aggressiveness. He couldn't even do angry correctly.

'We couldn't have kids,' she started. 'You said it's all you wanted.'

'No, Claire, from the beginning, please.'

She cast him a look. *He wasn't enjoying this, surely?*

'OK, OK. I was bored. I was bored of trying for a baby every month, and it not working. All you wanted to do was settle down; I wasn't ready. I still wanted to go out, but you never wanted to. You wanted to stay in on the weekends and watch Red Dwarf. I hated Red Dwarf; I wanted to go dancing. I felt trapped'.

Martyn held his stare; he knew she was right. He never wanted to go out drinking and dancing, but that wasn't an excuse. Martyn could have done the same thing and said that she didn't want to do what he wanted. It wasn't an excuse; he wouldn't take the blame this time.

'Go on,' he pressed.

'I don't know what you want me to say. I met someone else, we had fun, there was no pressure, we had things in common, neither of us wanted to settle down or have kids,' she explained.

'So hang on. You didn't want to be with me, to have a baby and settle down, yet you went out and got pregnant, had a baby and settled down? Can you see how that doesn't make much sense to me, Claire? he questioned.

'No, it wasn't like that. I knew how much you wanted a baby,' she said. 'it made me think it would be the answer, to make us happy again.'

'So you did it for me, nice, how thoughtful', Martyn said. 'And at what point did you decide to come home to me and pass the baby off as mine?.'

'He didn't want a baby; he wanted me to get rid of it. We'd had so many failed efforts that I thought it may be our only chance.'

'Right, so let me get this straight: you told him you were pregnant, he told you to get rid of it, you didn't want to, so you came home and told me it was mine.'

'You're making it sound so callous,' sneered Claire.

'Oh, I'm sorry, Claire, do forgive me', he uttered sarcastically.

It had started to rain, the icing sugar rain that was so fine you couldn't see it, but that fell like a blanket, leaving a shimmery wet veil over everything. Martyn didn't care. He wasn't leaving until he'd heard everything.

'We were happy, Martyn, weren't we? You wanted a baby, and I wanted a baby too once I was pregnant; I wanted to settle down and be a mum, and we were happy for a while, Martyn, weren't we?' Claire said desperately.

'I was, Claire, because I thought I had a baby on the way. I thought I was going to be a dad. And when Zach came along, I threw myself into being the best dad I could be. But It wasn't enough for you, was it? You still wanted more; you didn't want me; you just didn't want to be left alone with a baby you didn't want.' Martyn spat angrily.

'How dare you say that! I love Zach. I've always loved Zach,' Claire stated defiantly, the rain dripping down her face, conveniently concealing her tears.

Martyn couldn't argue with that; she's been a good mum. Zach was happy, which was the important thing.

'So who was he?' he asked finally. Claire looked him in the eye

'You don't know him; it's not important', she said quietly.

'Oh, but it is, isn't it? It is important, Claire. It's important to me. WHO WAS IT?' Martyn demanded.

She couldn't tell him. Not now, not like this. She'd give him time to get his head around this, and then she would tell him. She would, just not now.

'Someone I worked with, he left town after I got pregnant', she said, which wasn't entirely untrue, making her feel slightly better about it.

'You are unbelievable, Claire, you know that, don't you?' he sneered. 'Now I am going to go back into that hospital and sit with my son until he wakes up, and you're going to go home.'

'No, no, Martyn. I need to see my son. And you don't tell him this, not one word of it,' she cried out, finally releasing the tears freely down her face.

'You can see him, Claire, but not yet. I need to spend some time getting my head around this. I'll call you later,' he said as he turned his back and walked back across the car park towards the hospital entrance.

Claire stood in the rain, her hair flattened to her head, her clothes soaked through, and she cried like she had never cried before. She cried for her son, she cried for herself, her marriage and her fear of having to confess the rest of the story.

Chapter 36

Luisa had lost herself in Shed Seven's 'Chasing Rainbows' that was blaring out of her car stereo. She was excited to get back to the hospital and to see Lucy, excited to get her back home again. The relief that Lucy would be OK filled her with renewed optimism. A cup of Yorkshire tea and a chat with her best friend had helped her regain her focus and determination. She'd get Lucy back, get her comfortable, and then think about Martyn and Zach. Luisa told herself to take one step at a time; you can't solve all the problems in one go.

As she drove back around the corner where she nearly killed her daughter's boyfriend and her partner's son, it suddenly dawned on her just how close she had come to losing Lucy. A fucking drunk driver, they didn't stand a chance. At least if she'd have run Zach over that night, it would have been a terrible accident, and no one really to blame; she was sober, she wasn't even driving too fast, so she may have taken her eyes off the road for a split second as she reached for her sunglasses, but she wasn't drunk. No, the drunk driver must pay for what they did. It didn't matter that Lucy and Zach were OK; it was the principle. Once Lucy was settled, she would start a campaign or something, and then after that, she'd tackle the Martyn and

Zach situation; yes, that's what she'd do. First things first.

She could smell the petrichor through the car window. At least she could get Lucy all cosy and safe in the house, shut the world out, and keep her safe and warm. That's what she'd do; she'd wrap her baby up warm, keep her safe and make her something to eat. Chicken nuggets if that is what she wanted, or Quorn, or salad, whatever she wanted. Take her mind off everything: boys, school, everything. Just her and Lucy for the rest of the holidays. She'd keep her safe at home, and then, once term started again, she'd be OK to go back to school, and this would have all blown over.

She pulled up in the hospital car park and looked for a space. There were never any spaces here; it was a nightmare for parking. *Good job it's not an emergency.* It would be awful if she were in a rush. As she drove up and down the rows of cars, she saw various people milling around. There was a couple walking slowly along the rows, a young couple, the girl heavily pregnant. Luisa thought back to when that was her with Lucy, waddling along at a snail's pace, unable to bend down and put on her socks. It seemed like yesterday.

An elderly couple were shuffling along together. The man was wearing a full suit and was holding the umbrella over an elderly lady stooped over a Zimmer frame. He was getting wet, but he didn't seem to mind. Luisa couldn't help but smile. She could see a lady standing at the end of the row in the rain, her face in her hands. 'How awful', Luisa thought; she must have had some bad news. She was soaked, her denim jacket useless in the persistent rainfall.

Luisa spotted a space and reversed her car into it. She'd come out and move it to the pickup point later when it was time to leave, save Lucy walking across the car park. She'd do what she could to protect her. Anything.

As Lucy followed the yellow line to Ward 3, thoughts of Martyn entered her head. She couldn't deny that she had been harsh and hurtful to him the night before, and since leaving the hospital, they hadn't exchanged any messages or calls. The silence between them felt heavy and unsettling. Maybe it was for the best; maybe things would come to a natural end now. It would inevitably end anyway once Luisa told Martyn what she knew. She should text him, though, to check in on him. He hadn't done anything wrong, and she wanted to know how Zach was.

Luisa opened the corridor doors while rooting for her phone in her bag. She'd text him before she went in, then she could concentrate on Lucy for the rest of the day, knowing she'd done the right thing.

'Luisa?'

Luisa looked up, surprised to hear her name. Seeing Martyn sitting on the chairs outside the ward doors, her heart sank. He appeared drenched, his face worn and paler than usual. The worry immediately consumed her.

'Oh god, Martyn; she went over to him and squatted beside him to see his eyes. "What's happened? Is it Zach? Is he OK?' she asked.

He nodded slowly, his expression reflecting the weight of the situation.

'Oh shit Martyn, shit, where is he? What's happened?

Where's Claire?' she asked, her concern evident as she tried to make sense of the situation.

But Martyn didn't respond with words. Instead, he rested his face in his hands and began to sob, his emotions overwhelming him. Lucy immediately moved to sit beside him and wrapped her arms around him.

'Martyn, talk to me,' she insisted.

'It's Zach Lu, she told me; he isn't mine. He's not my son'.

Luisa did her best to keep in the vomit that had risen at the back of her throat. *Fuck. Fuck Fuck.*

She continued to hide her face in the crook of his neck, desperately trying to find the right thing to say. It was no use; she couldn't pretend; he would find out; it was too late; she was too late.

'Oh Martyn I am so sorry.'

He pulled away from her, his furrowed brow nearly hiding his eyes.

'What the fuck' he whispered. 'You knew?' he held Luisa at arm's length. Luisa suddenly felt very vulnerable. She had never seen him like this, his face contorted with anger and disbelief, his breathing heavy.

'You fucking knew!' he hissed.

'I'm sorry, I'm so sorry, I only found out yesterday. I was going to tell you last night, but then the accident and everything didn't seem right,' Luisa struggled desperately to find the right words.

Martyn stood up and paced up and down.

'What? What the actual fuck, Lu? How? How did you know?'

Luisa sat back in the chair.

'Not here, Martyn, not like this.'

'Oh yes, here', spat Martyn. 'I have spent my whole life

doing what everyone tells me. No more Luisa. No more. You tell me right now how you knew about this and didn't tell me,' he instructed.

She took a deep breath. 'It was in the coffee shop when I saw the two of you together', she explained. 'Zach's dark hair was more Lucy's colouring than yours; it was so dark, and you are so fair. '

'What the fuck has Lucy got to do with it?' he asked, confused.

'Let me finish, Martyn,' she pleaded.

'You don't question someone's paternity given the colour of their hair, Luisa', he stated.

'No, but it was eyes too, Martyn. You have blue eyes; Zach's are dark brown.'

'Again, that's not unheard of,' Martyn added.

'It is when your parents both have blue eyes, Luisa added quietly.

'No, but you hadn't even seen Claire at that point;

'No, I know, that just confirmed it for me'.

'So how could you be so sure? You said you knew; you hadn't guessed, so how can you be sure. You can't make a claim like that based on hair and eye colour alone.'

Luisa could feel herself getting into a muddle. How was she going to explain this? *Honesty is the only policy,* she reminded herself. Is it, though, is it actually, when it's going to hurt people. Is it still the only policy?

'Did you not notice how similar Lucy and Zach are, Martyn? Their colouring, their facial structure.'

Martyn didn't respond. Luisa took that as a go-ahead to continue.

'I had this feeling, Martyn, I needed to be sure. Lucy's my

daughter, Zach is your son.'

Martyn stared at her, ;he IS my son;,

'Yes, yes, you know what I meant.

'you told me on our first date that Claire lived in Crosswich. I know Crosswich well. Nearly sixteen years ago, when I was pregnant with Lucy, Jon worked at an insurance company there.'

Martyn was listening intently, his face becoming stonier by the minute. . 'insurance?' he repeated. 'What was it called?'

'Seagull Insurance? No, Beagle?'

'Regal' interrupted Martyn, 'Regal Insurance'

Luisa looked at him. He hadn't made the connection. 'Yes, that's it, Regal Insurance.'

'Martyn shook his head. OK, carry on.

Before I carry on, I just need to let you know that I had no idea about this until yesterday, I promise.

'Just get to the point, Luisa, please. Surely, it can't get any worse than what I've already been told.'

'I wouldn't be so sure; she said, taking a deep breath.

'I went to see Jon after you left the coffee shop yesterday. I had to ask him for my own piece of mind.

'Ask what?'

Martyn, please, you're not making this very easy for me

'Damn right, I'm not, he replied; you've still not answered the question; how did you know?' His patience was wearing thin.

'I asked him if there was any chance he'd had an affair while he was working there.'

Martyn was still confused; he shrugged his shoulders and shook his head at her, insisting she continue.

'And I asked him if there was any chance it could have

resulted in a baby.'

She stopped at this point, allowing time for Martyn to process the information. His face shifted from confusion to realisation as the puzzle pieces fell into place. He understood the implication of Luisa's questions, and his expression grew stony. Luisa could see the tension building in him.

'You have got to be fucking kidding me', he said, his voice unnaturally calm and controlled.

'Please tell me this is some sort of sick joke, Luisa,' he finally whispered.

She shook her head. 'I'm sorry, Martyn, I was going to tell you last night, but we'd had a drink, and it didn't seem like the right time.'

'Didn't seem like the right time!?'

'I was going to tell you, I honestly was. I was worried about Lucy and Zach too; they're half-brother and sister; they can't be together,' she pleaded.

'Jesus fucking Christ', Martyn said, his head in his hands.

'It's such a mess'

'Fuck fuck fuck.' Martyn started pounding his head with his hands; his calm facade shattered.

'Martyn, please, don't, this isn't going to help', she pleaded; we need to be strong. You need to be strong for Zach. Lucy's coming home.'

He looked at her and pursed his lips. I'm going through those doors, and I'm going to see my son Luisa.'

Luisa nodded.

'And when I leave, I'm going to go and pay your ex a visit.'

Luisa's face crumpled. 'No Martyn, please, there's nothing to be gained from that'.

Martyn ignored her and pushed the ward door open, leaving

Luisa alone in the corridor.

Chapter 37

By the time Luisa had collected Lucy's painkillers from the hospital pharmacy, it was getting on for 6 pm. Luisa's stomach grumbled, reminding her that she hadn't eaten all day, her body fuelled only by shit hospital machine tea and the previous night's Chinese. The nurse on the ward was lovely and spent some time with Lucy, asking about her plans for Uni. She'd asked her if she'd got a boyfriend, and Lucy had blushed. Luisa had felt her insides collapse a little.

'Ooh, we've got a lovely young man further across the ward, Lucy; he's a bit of a looker! Unfortunately, his leg's hanging from the ceiling at the moment,' she'd told her. 'Shame though, you'd have made a lovely couple', she added, winking at Lucy.

Lucy blushed, looking visibly uncomfortable with the conversation.

'How long before I can take her home?' Luisa had interrupted.

'Just waiting for the discharge papers to be signed, then you can get on your way; the nurse told them.

'You're coming back to mine, Lucy; me and your dad have discussed it.' Luisa said.

Lucy nodded in agreement, 'Yes, I know, just till I'm feeling better.'

Luisa put her hand on hers, 'for however long you want,' she said, reassuringly squeezing her hand.

* * *

Back in the car, they sat in silence all the way back to Copcut. Luisa noted that Martyn's car was still outside; he'd not left the hospital since last night. She helped Lucy from the passenger side and up the steps to the front door. Megan flung the door open. 'Here she is! The invalid', she declared as she threw her arms around Lucy.

'Ow,' Lucy winced. 'Careful, Meg!'

'Oh god, sorry Luce, I forgot, I'm just so pleased to see you', Megan laughed.

Lucy let a guarded smile appear on her lips, 'It's OK, Meg, I'm just still a bit sore'.

'Come on, in you come, kettle's on, and there's a cottage pie in the oven. Not sure what is going to taste like, Izzy says my cottage pie tastes like dog shit, but it's all you had in Lu' Megan gabbled.

'Lucy doesn't eat meat, Meg, remember?' Luisa reminded her.

'Oh shit, I forgot. Oh, fucking hell; sorry, Luce,' she apologised. 'Shall I go out and get something else?'

'It's fine, Megan, honestly,' replied Lucy. 'I'll be honest with you, I was getting fed up with tofu and beans.' She pulled her bottom lip down.

'Thank fuck for that,' said Megan as they all laughed, guiding Lucy through to the kitchen.

The three sat cradling their mugs of hot Yorkshire tea, and Megan filled them in on Izzy's plans for Uni.

'Honestly, it's costing a bloody fortune for her accommodation. She's insisting on an en-suite -she doesn't have one at home, so I have no idea why she feels the need to have one there,' she rambled on. Lucy giggled. Luisa smiled as she watched her listening to Megan, wide-eyed, taking it all in. It wouldn't be long before she, too, would be making plans for Uni if that's still what she wanted to do. How soon they grow up. Tears started forming, and she got up before anyone noticed, feigning needing the loo. This wasn't about her, this was about Lucy, she needed everything to focus on her now. As she left the kitchen, she turned to look at her best friend and daughter chatting away at the table, just like they all did a few months ago before things got crazy. It was so good to have her home, if you forgot that she had to get run over to get there. And for a moment, Luisa forgot about the devastating news she would have to tell her. Not now, though, for now, she would enjoy having her daughter back, enjoying taking care of her.

'When were you going to tell me mum?' Lucy demanded as Luisa returned from the bathroom. Luisa stopped and held on to the kitchen work surface, her eyes darting across to Megan, looking intently at her mug. Lucy's mouth was wide open, matched by her eyes popping out on stalks.

Luisa scrunched her face up, wondering where this conversation was going. Surely Megan hadn't told her, not like this, not without any warning.

'that you've been internet dating!? Oh my god, mum, I didn't even know you knew what Tinder was!' she laughed.

Luisa felt her insides relax. 'Call yourself a friend!' she giggled at Megan, who was clearly enjoying her embarrassment.

'Well, it was just a bit of fun, but then obviously Martyn came along, and that was that', she shrugged.

'You met Martyn online????' Lucy asked, her eyes even wider.

'Well, where do you think I met him? In the supermarket?'

'He just seems so, you know, normal,' she said. 'although, to be fair, mum, he is dishy for an older man, I'll give you that.' she stated as she dunked another biscuit in her tea.

'Are we not wanting this cottage pie tonight, then?' Megan interrupted, reading the signs on Luisa's face that she wanted to steer the conversation in another direction. 'It'll keep for tomorrow; if so, you just need to bung it in the oven. '

'What do you reckon, Luce?'

'Yeah, maybe; I'm actually exhausted, mum. Would you mind if I went up to bed?'

Luisa smiled at her. 'of course not, you get yourself on up.

'Have you got my phone, mum? The nurse said it should be with my things from the ambulance.'

Luisa shot a look over to Megan.

'No love, not that saw. Are you sure they had it? I'll call the hospital if you want, see if we can track it down?'

'OK, thanks. Will you do that now?' Lucy persisted.

'Yes, I'll just sort out this pie, then I'll call; you get yourself up to bed'. Luisa planted a kiss on Lucy's forehead.

'Thanks, mum.'

'I'd better be off too, Luisa. Are you going to be OK?' Megan asked, sensing Luisa's tiredness.

'Yes, yes, of course. Thank you, Meg, for everything; you've been an absolute star, as usual. What would I do without you, eh?' Luisa smiled.

'No need to thank me. I'm just glad you're all OK. Do me a

favour, Lu? Just chill out for a bit. You've got her home; you don't need to tell Lucy anything yet. Let her settle in a bit first, eh?'

Luisa nodded as she bit her bottom lip.

'It's probably a good job they haven't found her phone; she can't contact Zach, can she? That gives you a bit of time.'

Luisa looked Megan in the eye and scrunched her face up.

'What? What's that look for? She enquired suspiciously.

'Luisa reached into her hoodie pocket and pulled out a rather scratched and battered phone.

'Oh shit, that's Lucy's, isn't it?' Megan whispered quietly. Luisa nodded. 'The nurse gave it to me when I got her discharge papers'.

'I didn't see anything,' Megan said, shaking her head. 'Do me a favour, though, Lu, don't turn it on.'

Luisa rolled her eyes. 'I won't' she stated. You get yourself back home to gorgeous Izzy before she sends out the search party. Luisa opened the front door to let Megan out. Her stomach dropped as she saw Martyn's car still parked outside.

'You're going to have to see him at some point,' Megan said as she walked down the drive. 'His keys are on the hallway table.'

Luisa rested her head against the edge of the door. 'I know, I know - see you soon. Love you.'

'Love you too, Lu. Speak tomorrow,' Megan waved as she got into her car.

Luisa shut the front door quietly and padded back into the kitchen. It had been a while since she had to clear more than two mugs away.

The battered mobile in her pocket started to feel like a lead weight. She had told Lucy a lie, she'd promised herself she'd never be dishonest again, and the second Lucy was home, she had already done it. She'd lied to Lucy, she still had to tell her some awful news, and she still had to deal with Martyn; all this on top of the day she had already had. Her chai latte in the coffee shop seemed like an eternity ago, let alone eighteen hours. How quickly things can change.

Luisa must have fallen asleep on the sofa as the Top Gun theme jolted her awake. She answered without thinking, her head in a haze of sleepiness, confusion and panic.

'Hello?'

'It's me.'

Chapter 38

Luisa sat up urgently.

'Jon?'

'Yea, is Lucy there? Is she OK? I've tried to call her, but her phone's off.'

'She's asleep, Jon, she was tired, she's fine.'

'OK, well, can you wake her up? I need to speak to her.'

'No, Jon, I'm not going to do that; she's had a rough night; shall I get her to call you in the morning?' Luisa asked, her eyes adjusting to the bright light that her screen threw into the darkness.

'I need to talk to her, Lu.'

'What, now?' Luisa questioned. 'Right now?'

'I need to tell her. I need to tell her about Zach, about what I've done. I have to tell her right now; I'm going to come over and tell her.

Luisa was thrust into being suddenly very alert.

'Jon? Are you OK? Think about what you're saying. Have you been drinking?'

'I've fucked it all up, Lu. All of it. I'm a fucking loser. I don't deserve to be happy any more; I'm going to tell her what a fucking loser I am. She needs to know what a fucking loser her dad is.'

Luisa sighed. Another reason she was glad she wasn't with him anymore was this incessant self-loathing when he'd had a drink. It used to drive her insane, always coming in worse for wear, telling her how shit everything was. As if she needed reminding.

'Jon, not now. Now really isn't the time. You need to go to bed, sleep it off; things will seem better in the morning'.

Silence on the end of the phone.

'Jon? Are you still there?'

'Yep. Still here, where else would I be?' Jon responded petulantly.

'Is Maxine there?' Luisa asked. Maybe Maxine would talk some sense into him.

'Nope, she's gone.'

'What do you mean she's gone? Where's she gone?'

'Fuck knows, took the camper, told me she was done with all the negative vibes and left. Took her stuff. Took her crystals and all her hippy shit and left.'

Luisa sat back on the sofa. *Shit.* At least when Maxine was there, she kept him calm and out of the way. Even though she was a bit strange. His only focus now would be Lucy, just when she could do with him keeping out of her way, just when things were getting back on track.

'Shit Jon' was all she could offer.

'I'll come over in the morning then, shall I?' he told her. He clearly hadn't put two and two together and realised he wouldn't be going anywhere if Maxine had taken his camper van.

'I'll call you when she's awake,' Luisa told him.

'OK, tell her I love her though, will you? Tell her that her old dad loves her more than anything,' he said pathetically, and the line went dead.

'Anything else?' Luisa asked, her eyes looking upwards. 'Want to throw anything else my way?' she said out loud to the empty room. Someone or something must have been listening as she heard the slamming of a car door, the telltale sound of an engine pulling away and a gentle tapping on her front door.

Luisa's heart started beating hard. It had to be Martyn. She toyed with the idea of pretending she wasn't in, but given her location in the middle of nowhere, there wasn't anywhere for him to go. He couldn't even sit in his car as his keys were currently sitting on her hallway table. 'Come on, Luisa, be a big girl; twenty-four hours ago, you were sharing a bed with this man', she said to herself.

She got up, outwardly groaning at the pain in her shoulder where she'd fallen asleep with her head propped up on the arm of the sofa. She opened the door carefully so as not to wake Lucy. As Martyn stood on the doorstep, raindrops clinging to his eyelashes, Luisa felt a complex mix of emotions welling inside her. She longed to reach out, hold him close, and seek solace in his arms, yet, at the same time, she also yearned for some space and time to process everything.

The silence between them seemed to stretch on endlessly. Martyn's gaze remained fixed on the damp doormat, and Luisa couldn't tear her eyes away from the rain dripping from his blonde hair and collecting on the end of his nose. The yellow light from the hallway spread across his face, highlighting the weariness in his eyes. Rain continued to fall, and Luisa could see the frustration in Martyn's movements as he angrily wiped away the raindrops from his lashes. It was a moment suspended in time, filled with unspoken words and the weight of the night before.

'Can I come in?' Martyn broke the silence, his voice soft and weary, his body language reflecting his vulnerability. His hunched posture and how he kept his hands in his pockets conveyed a sense of defeat, a far cry from the lively and vibrant man Luisa had first met. Luisa hesitated momentarily, her gaze flicking up the stairs to where Lucy was asleep. Then, she whispered, 'Lucy's asleep, but yes, come in out of the rain. You're soaked through.'

She opened the front door wider to welcome him, and Martyn lifted his eyes to meet hers. Luisa couldn't help but notice the profound change in him. The sparkle that had once danced in his blue eyes was dimmed, replaced by a cold weariness. They were still blue, but it was as if they had weathered the storm, their brilliance subdued by the debris and turmoil that had tormented their lives.

Luisa felt herself filling up and turned her head quickly to avoid Martyn seeing. This was all her doing. She was to blame. If she hadn't insisted on moving to this bloody village, if they'd stayed somewhere more affordable, then bloody Jon would never have worked all those hours, if she'd paid him more attention, maybe. If she'd kept Lucy at home instead of letting her move to Jon's too easily, had she even put up a fight? God, she'd made such a mess of everything. And here was Martyn, lovely, kind, gentle Martyn, the man who would do anything for anyone, who made her feel special, gave her a bit of spark back, made her laugh, held her like she was the most precious item in the world, here he was, stood in her doorway, broken.

She filled the kettle instinctively and reached for two clean mugs. She could hear Martyn removing and shaking his jacket before hanging it up. She wished she could just hold him, tell him everything would be OK, but she couldn't. She didn't know if anything was going to be OK ever again.

In all honesty, Luisa needed more than anything else in the world right now was someone to do exactly that to her, but the secrets that had emerged over the last few hours meant that no-one was left to console her. She was carrying the weight of too-heavy secrets and was on the verge of snapping. She rolled her eyes. F*or fucks sake, Luisa, this isn't about you,* she reminded herself, took a deep breath and turned to take Martyn his drink.

'It's a lot, Lu, it's just a lot'. That's all she could get out of him as he cradled his tea. There was nothing she could say. Her gut instinct was to protect Lucy, who was still unaware that her boyfriend was her half-brother. That didn't even touch the issue of Martyn raising a child he thought was his flesh and blood. Add to that the affair and the deceit. He was right; it was a lot. His shoulders were hunched up, and his face resembled the colour of a weak cup of tea.

'I don't know what to say,' Lu offered honestly. 'it's certainly a mess'. She didn't look up at him. She didn't want to connect with him; she wanted a void between them to soften the burden; she couldn't deal with her feelings for him just now.

'What am I going to do?' he asked. 'How am I going to tell

him?'

Luisa looked up, panicked.

'What do you mean?'

'How am I going to tell Zach that I'm not his dad?' she could hear the despair, the wobble in his voice giving away his emotions.

Luisa sighed. She was more concerned about him telling Zach he couldn't see Lucy anymore. She needed to protect her baby girl.

'Maybe that's Claire's responsibility? Luisa was aware of how sharp her voice sounded. 'Maybe she needs to tell him. After all, this is all her doing.' she stated bluntly, surprising herself at the venom she spat out.

'Takes two'

'I'm fully aware of that, Martyn, thank you.'

'I mean, all I am saying is, it isn't all Claire's fault.'

'Oh, so you're defending her now? Really? Really Martyn?'

Martyn took a deep breath and let out a long sigh. 'Not now, Luisa; I can't cope with falling out with you as well; I'm clinging on as it is; please, can we not fight?'

Luisa put her mug down on the side. She was still standing, not wanting to sit too close to him.

'We've both got a lot to deal with, Martyn, maybe we should...' she tailed off, hoping he would catch on.

'We should do what?'

'I'm just saying, maybe we need to concentrate on our own lives for a bit,' Luisa confirmed.

Martyn shook his head. 'Do you mean that?' he asked.

Luisa didn't reply. She stared at the contents of her cup, the tea a familiar friend, the only comfort she had right now.

'You really mean that, Luisa? You want me to walk out of the door and not come back?'

'I didn't say that; I just think we need to concentrate on our kids', she stopped immediately, regretting her choice of words.

Martyn let out a sharp breath and nodded his head.

'Your keys are on the hall table'' she added, her gaze still fixed on the mug before her.

Martyn got up and left. Luisa heard the front door close and the hum of an engine and then nothing, silence, just the beating of her heart thumping in her ears. Silence. The one thing she spent so long craving, and right now, it was the last thing she wanted.

Chapter 39

'Mum, for god's sake, will you stop fussing?' groaned Lucy as Luisa started plumping the sofa cushions behind her. 'You are driving me insane!'

Luisa laughed. 'If I can't look after my own daughter after she's been knocked over by a car, then it's a pretty poor show', she replied. 'Now, can I get you anything else before we put this film on?'.

'No, at this rate, it'll be time for bed before we get a chance to watch it.'

The familiar sounds of Dorothy talking to her dog began, and Luisa sat back and smiled. Maybe things weren't so bad after all. Luisa still hadn't told Lucy about Zach, she still hadn't given Lucy her phone back, Jon had been AWOL, and she hadn't heard from Martyn, but other than that, things were fine. She let her mind wander back to Janet. Luisa was actually looking forward to getting back to work to get some structure back in her life. She hadn't put much thought into the Vodka situation, but as Janet was returning in September, she figured the misunderstanding would be explained.

'Are you looking forward to getting back to school, Lucy?'

Luisa asked.

'Not unless I get my bloody phone back – any news on that mum? They better not have bloody lost it. I haven't been able to speak to anyone.'

Luisa felt a surge of panic shoot through her. The phone was still stashed away upstairs in her knicker drawer. She couldn't hide it forever; maybe now was the time for the conversation. They had been getting on well, talking about plans for the future; she hadn't actually mentioned Zach since the police had come and taken a statement. Maybe there had been enough space between them for her to realise that it wasn't meant to be anyway. She looked at her daughter, her long eyelashes, her raven hair falling around her shoulders. All she had ever wanted to do was protect her, help her find her way in the world, share experiences with her, and love her. Lucy giggled, as she always did when the munchkins appeared out of the bushes, her nose creasing, pushing her cheeks up to her eyes. Would it be so bad to tell her now? A bit of distance may have been the green light she needed for the conversation.

'Mum?'

'Hmmmmm?'

'My phone? Can you call them again, please?'

'What right now?'

'If you don't mind. I can pause the film. Please, mum, please, please, please!'

'OK, hold on, I'll go to the kitchen.'

'Put the kettle on while you're there.' Lucy instructed.

Luisa shut the kitchen door behind her. *Deep breath, Luisa Mulligan; you can do this. Once it's said, then you can deal with the aftermath.* She reached for her phone. If she was going to make a fake call to the hospital, it needed to be realistic. She could act better when she had a prop. She had set it to silent - she didn't want anything interrupting her time with Lucy.

To her relief, there was just one message from Megan. Nothing from Jon. She was taking that as a good sign, although she couldn't help but feel a little disappointed that there was, yet again, no contact with Martyn. She wondered if that was it for them. It had to be. She couldn't see it working out for them; being together would mean Lucy and Zach spending time together - that would be cruel.

She clicked on the Whatsapp from Megan.

'MUM! What are you doing???' Lucy shouted from the living room.

'Just hold on a minute Luce!' Luisa laughed. 'I can't make a phone call and make tea simultaneously!'

She let the message open as she lifted the kettle to the sink. She didn't need a man in her life, did she? She had Lucy, and she had Megan. Lovely, lovely Megan, who was always there for her. She picked up the phone and read the message.

'Luisa, I need to come and see you. Are you in?'

There was no kiss. Something was wrong. Luisa could sense it. She dialled Megan's number immediately.

'Meg? It's me. Is everything OK?'

'Can I come round Lu, please? I need to see you.'

Luisa was sure she could hear the telltale sign of someone crying.

'Yes, yes, of course, I'm here.'

'OK, see you in a minute', Megan replied before the line went dead.

'MUM!!!'

'There's no answer, Lucy. I'll try again later. They're probably busy saving lives.'

Megan knocked on the door shortly after; she must have been in the area. When Luisa opened the front door, she immediately knew something was wrong. If the red rims of Megan's eyes and the pale complexion didn't give it away, the oversize jumper and out-of-shape leggings did. She set the two mugs on the table beside an unusually quiet Megan.

'Meg, you're worrying me, what's up?'

'I found a lump Lu, in my boob.'

Luisa felt her heart stop momentarily, her pulse kicking back and sending sharp tingles across her body. She reached across and put her hands over Megan's.

'OK, OK, have you seen anyone about it? The Doctor?'

Megan nodded. 'I've had a biopsy taken. I'm waiting for the results. I just can't keep it to myself any longer. I've tried so hard to keep it in.'

'Any longer? When did you find it?'

'Last week. You've had enough going on, Lu.'

'Megan, I'm so sorry.'

'I'm just so scared. I can't tell Izzy; I can't worry her. I haven't got anyone else to talk to; I thought I could do this waiting, but I can't. I don't want her to not go to Uni because she has to look after me, and what's going to happen to her if anything happens to me? I can't do it, Izzy, I just can't do it.'

The tears cascaded down Megan's cheeks as the words tumbled out her mouth at a hundred miles an hour.

'Whoa whoa whoa, hold on Meg, we don't know what we're dealing with yet. How long before the results?'

'They have said it can be up to two weeks', explained Megan.

'OK, and it's already been a week? Then it can't be serious, can it, or they would have been straight in touch?' Luisa said hopefully.

Luisa's comforting words brought a glimmer of hope to Megan's eyes as she wiped away her tears. Luisa's reassurance that it couldn't be too serious if they hadn't heard from the doctors in a week made her feel slightly better.

"Do you think so?" Megan asked, between sniffs, seeking confirmation from her friend.

'Absolutely,' Luisa replied confidently. 'And you know what? Whatever they say, we will deal with it. Together. OK? You are not on your own.'

Megan's tears intensified at this, and Luisa went around to give her a hug.

'Come here', Luisa said as she wrapped her arms around Megan.

'Thanks, Lu; I'm sorry, I've been driving around for hours trying to figure out what I will do. I haven't even asked about Lucy yet. Have you told her about Zach yet?'

'Told her what about Zach?'

Luisa wasn't sure how long Lucy had been standing in the doorway, but it was long enough to hear Megan's question.

'What about Zach? Has something happened to Zach?' Lucy stood wide-eyed in the doorway, the panic making her fists clenched by her side.

'Mum! For god's sake, will you please tell me what's happening?! Why is Meg crying? Why are *you* crying, Meg, what's going on?'

Luisa took a deep breath.

'OK Lucy, sit down please, there's something I need to tell

you.'

* * *

'Right, so let me get this straight.' Lucy began, trembling, 'What I'm hearing is Zach, the boy I've been seeing for the past few months, is actually my half-brother?'

Lucy glanced across at Megan, who sat with her head in her hands and nodded solemnly. 'Yes. That's exactly what I am saying, Lucy'.

'And how long have you known about this exactly?' Lucy pressed.

Luisa sighed deeply, realising that her daughter was rightfully angry and confused. 'Lucy, not long, I promise, only the day of the accident. Martyn didn't even know at that point. I was going to tell him, then tell you.'

That was the first mistake.

'Oh right, so you were going to tell Martyn before me? Before your own daughter. Fucking Hell, mum, I think I'm going to throw up. This is the most fucked up thing I think I have ever heard.'

Luisa couldn't help but agree with her; she also couldn't even begin to chastise Lucy's use of language because she was correct; this *was* the most fucked up thing ever.

'Martyn needed to know; he needed to know that Zach wasn't actually his son. Can you imagine how devastating that is for him, Lucy?' said Luisa softly.

'And Dad? What does he have to say about this? Did he know?' Lucy asked.

Luisa hesitated, struggling to explain the situation. 'Kind of,' she finally replied, her voice tinged with uncertainty.

'Kind of? what does that mean?' Lucy inquired.

Megan jumped in to help, and Luisa was extremely grateful to take a breather.

'Your dad knew that he had got someone pregnant, but he ended it when he found out, so he didn't actually know what became of the child'. Megan explained before taking a sip of her tea.

'Christ. and you didn't kick him out at that point?' Lucy asked her mum.

'I never knew Lucy. I only found that out recently, too.'

'What a scumbag. Well, that's it; he can go fuck himself, the cheating rat.' Lucy exclaimed, crossing her arms.

'And he is still your dad, remember, he's still the same dad he has always been'. Luisa hated defending him, but this was more about her and him than he and Lucy. Whatever went on in their relationship had nothing to do with the relationship with his daughter.

'So when did he find out about Zach?' Lucy asked.

'The day of the accident. I only found out that day that there was an affair. It wasn't until he saw Zach's mum at the hospital that he realised who he was,' explained Luisa.

'Fucking hell, mum, this is a nightmare. What does he think is going to happen? We'll all spend Christmas together pulling crackers and eating mince pies?'

'I have no idea, Lucy, no idea what is going to happen. My only concern was for you; you and Zach have been quite close...'

'Stop right there, mum, before you say that thing you are about to say, just don't, OK?' Lucy said, shaking her head.

Megan stepped in again, 'You understand why we were

concerned, though, Luce?'

Lucy shook her head. 'It's not like that with me and Zach. We're just good friends. We thought it could be more, but we had joked that we get on more like brother and sister than girlfriend and boyfriend. What are the chances of that, eh?'

Luisa let out a huge sigh. 'Well, I will be honest, I'm relieved to hear that. I do have one more confession, though, Lucy'. Luisa continued.

Megan looked up sharply and shook her head discreetly. Luisa mirrored the shake of the head and gave her a reassuring smile.

'I have your phone; I've had it since we came home. I wanted to speak to you about Zach before you contacted him. I'm sorry, Lucy, I'll go and get it.' She got up and left the kitchen before Lucy could respond.

'You OK hun?' Meg asked softly. 'It's been a hell of a few days for you, hasn't it?'

Lucy nodded slowly, and fat tears plopped down her cheeks.

'It's OK to be upset; it's a lot to take in', Megan said kindly.

'I don't know why I'm upset,' replied Lucy. 'Whether it's because my dad is a rat, that Zach's just found out his dad isn't his dad, that my half-brother nearly died, that poor Martyn hasn't got a son, or my own mother has been keeping my bloody phone from me'. Lucy let out a laugh. 'I don't even know why I'm laughing; none of this is remotely funny', she wheezed at the absurdity of it all.

Megan giggled, 'Honestly, Lucy, you couldn't make it up, could you?'

Chapter 40

The phone sprang into life on the kitchen table as Luisa boiled the kettle. The continuous buzzing made her stop and look around to Lucy who was now scrolling across her screen like she was trying to spin the wheel of fortune, not that Lucy would understand that reference.

'Everything OK Luce?' She asked, eyebrows raised, desperately wanting Lucy to share who was contacting her.

'Hmm' replied Lucy, frowning at her screen as she studied her messages.

'Anyone we know?' Luisa continued.

'Mum, chill out, it's just my friends from school' replied Lucy without raising her eyes from the screen.

'Which friends?' Luisa persisted, trying desperately to sound nonchalant.

'OK Luisa, let's leave Lucy to catch up with her messages' Megan could sense the tension building between them ' I need to get back to Izzy anyway, I've been gone for hours'.

She got up from the table, gave Lucy's shoulder a squeeze as she passed and made her way to the front door.

'Are you going to be OK Meg? I feel like such a shit friend. Do you want to stay here tonight? the spare room is all made up?' Luisa asked her friend.

'No honestly, thank you, I just needed a cry and a natter. Like you said before, we don't actually know what we are dealing with yet' she shrugged her shoulders.

'Are you going to tell Izzy?' Luisa whispered consciously as Lucy sat in the kitchen.

Megan shook her head. 'no, not until there's something to tell, I don't want her worrying unnecessarily too'.

'OK well let me know the minute you do OK? Will they call you or will you have to go in? I'll come with you, tell me when it is, I'll take the day off work, I can drive us'.

'Lu, stop, I don't know, I guess I'll get a call and they'll tell me what the next step is, if there is one. ' She smiled at Luisa. 'I'm fine. Honestly. Looks like Lucy's going to be OK with the situation?' she added, nodding her head in the direction of the kitchen. 'That could have been much worse eh?

'Yes' said Luisa raising her eyebrows. 'Although I wouldn't like to be Jon when she catches up with him, ' she laughed.

'Shame' laughed Megan.

'And Luisa, do me a favour will you?'

'Absolutely anything' stated Luisa, 'just say the word'.

'Will you please call Martyn. Men like him don't come along that often. He's a good one. Don't let it drift to nothing, not now.'

Luisa sighed. 'I don't know Meg, honestly, I'm just getting things back on track with Lucy, I don't want to rock the boat. I also don't want to make things awkward for the kids, it's probably best we just forget about it.'

'Lu, I will not let you just throw this away, you deserve some happiness and it has been a very long time since I've seen you as happy as you have been with Martyn. All I'm asking for is for you to contact him'.

'OK OK' Luisa replied.

'Promise?'

'Promise' Luisa laughed. 'Now go home and spend some time with that lovely daughter of yours'.

Luisa popped her head around the kitchen door. Lucy was still sitting at the table, letting out a giggle now and again as she went through her messages. Once again, Luisa found herself wondering when she got so grown up? It seems such a long time ago since she bounded around in just her nappy and here she was, sitting at the kitchen table like a young lady. How close had she come to losing her? She shook her head as if to remove the thought from her head. 'You OK Lucy? Shall we put the film back on?'

'Not just yet mum, just want to catch up on these, I am literally a superstar at the moment, I should nearly get run over more often' she joked not lifting her eyes from her screen.

Luisa went upstairs, her mind heavy with the weight of her responsibilities and relationships. She was determined to keep her promise to Megan, her lovely friend Megan. Tears built up in her eyes as she thought about what she must have been through the last couple of weeks. Her guilt of being a terrible friend made her feel quite sick. Poor Megan, she'd been all alone with this huge cloud over her and no-one to talk to. 'Fucking hell' Luisa let out with a sigh, as she thought about the events of the recent few weeks, the drama, the upset, the hurt. Poor Megan. And come to think of it, poor Janet too. *I am genuinely in line for Shit Friend of the Year. I'm a Shit Friend and a Shit Parent and I deserve to be unhappy.*

Luisa had a lot of making up to do, she didn't have time for anything else in her life, did she? She pulled the duvet up over her head, which wasn't the most mature response to the situation but seemed a preferable option to making the call to the man who she had fallen in love with but didn't have the time or the energy to commit to. Or did she? Luisa lay down on the bed, taking a few minutes to considered her options. Ending her relationship with Martyn seemed like a tempting choice, as it would free up more time for her to focus on her daughter and friends.

Luisa also pondered the changing dynamics with her daughter Lucy. With Lucy soon returning to school and the uncertainty regarding Jon, she wondered how her time would be divided. There was an assumption from Luisa that Lucy may not spend as much time with her dad from this point forward, that situation had yet to be resolved. That would mean that Luisa would have her daughter back full time, she couldn't spend her evenings with Martyn then could she? Not every evening? Martyn would be spending time with Zach too, she assumed. So actually, there would be a bit of time now and again. And Lucy was 15, she was quite mature enough to be left on her own for a few hours. And it wasn't like Martyn and her hadn't met before, there was no reason why Martyn couldn't come around when Lucy was there? It seemed like a reasonable compromise to balance her personal life with her responsibilities as a parent. Or did it?

She was jolted from her thoughts by the Top Gun Theme as her phone sprang to life. Luisa's heart raced as she saw Martyn's name on the screen. Her initial surprise quickly gave way to excitement and butterflies. How inconvenient. In a flurry of excitement, she adjusted her hair and her top; she needed every bit of confidence to engage in this conversation. She took a deep breath to steady herself, and answered the call with a hopeful smile in her voice.

'Hello?'

'Hey, it's me, is it convenient to talk?' Martyn's voice was soft and calm and travelled down the phone line warm hot chocolate making Luisa melt inside a little.

Damn you Martyn

'Hey, yes, I mean it is convenient, yes' she stammered.

'Is everything OK? you seem a little flustered.'

'No, no all OK, just wasn't expecting to hear from you that's all.'

Why have you said that? You sound stroppy, don't sound stroppy, the poor man has had a shock.

'I won't keep you long.'

Damn.

'I just wanted to let you know that Zach's OK and out of hospital'.

'Oh Martyn, I'm so relieved. Is he back with his mum?'

'No he's with me, it was easier to make him a room up downstairs at mine, and actually Zach asked to come home to mine anyway'

Luisa took a deep breath, conscious of the lump in her throat but not wanting to make this about her.

'Oh Martyn, that's wonderful news, it really is.'

'And I've had the conversation about Lucy with him, it's not a problem, they'd already sorted it out. Turns out they're just really good friends so nothing to worry about. '

'Yes yes, I've spoken to Lucy too, she said the same' said Luisa, relieved. At least that was one awkward situation they had avoided.

'So there are no problems then, are there? Other than I need to get my head around the fact that I'm not actually Zach's dad. Although to be fair to the lad, he said it doesn't make any difference to him.'

'He's a good lad Martyn. You are a dad to him and that's all that matters.' Luisa was surprised how quickly they slipped back into their comfortable conversations. She just wished he was in her house and not at the end of the phone.

'OK well I'll let you go then' he added after a pause.

'Oh, OK, right then, yes, I'd better get back to it' she said flustered as she desperately tried to find something to say to keep him talking for longer. And to think she was putting off making the phone call.

'Oh and Luisa?'

'yes?'

'I miss you'.

Luisa lay on the bed and the tears flowed freely for what felt like hours, it could have been hours, she didn't care. The last few weeks of emotions that had built up inside of her had caused a tsunami and tonight was the night that it unleashed itself. The relief of her daughter Lucy being okay, the worry for her friend Megan, the shocking revelation about Zach's paternity, and the messy situation with her lying cheating rat of an ex had all come crashing down on her.

Martyn's declaration of missing her had prized off the lid and released the emotional outpouring. He was missing her, her,

Luisa Mulligan – the woman who had turned his world on its head because she couldn't keep a secret. She should never have gone to Jon's house that afternoon, she should never have confronted him. It would have come out anyway that Martyn wasn't Zach's dad, but she couldn't keep the secret, she couldn't bear the thought of Lucy and Zach unknowingly having a physical relationship. And now she had the burden of keeping Megan's news a secret. The overwhelming weight of all of that added to the added pressure of returning to work was too much.

And then there was Janet, her friend who was clearly dealing with her own troubles. Poor Janet who everyone will think is an alcoholic. Janet was her friend and of course she had to check on her, she couldn't bear the thought of her friend struggling at home. That situation was still a bit of a mystery. What was that all about? The vodka and the hidden bottle in the sanitary bin, what on earth had been going on there?

Luisa's anger and frustration welled up again as she thought about the reckless drink driver who had put her daughter's life in jeopardy. The police had told them they had arrested and charged someone but weren't allowed to give out any more details. Luisa sighed, she should feel grateful that justice had been done but she felt so detached from the situation, did this person not know what they could have done? They could have killed someone, they could have killed her daughter. She couldn't help but be haunted by the what-ifs and the danger that had lurked so close to her family.

There were a million thoughts battling for attention inside Luisa's head and she couldn't bear it any longer. Each tear that fell released a minuscule amount of pressure in her head, but the tears couldn't fall fast enough for her to feel the benefit. What the fuck was wrong with her, she should be grateful that she had her daughter safe downstairs in her house. She should be happy. She should be relieved that this situation had sorted itself out. She was torn between gratitude for having her daughter safe at home and the overwhelming sense of loss at the idea of never seeing Martyn again. She lay on her bed, and not for the first time in the last few weeks, she cried herself to sleep.

Chapter 41

'And you're sure you don't want a lift? I can literally drop you at the gates,' Luisa stated.

'Mum! Will you please just chill out? I can get the bus; I am perfectly capable.' Lucy laughed. 'I promise I won't get run over - too soon?' she added quickly when she saw the pained look on Luisa's face. 'Relax, I am winding you up, mum; I'll see you later.' She grabbed a slice of toast on the side and held it in her mouth as she checked her hair in the mirror.

'OK, but it's Wednesday. Are you sure you don't want to stop over at your dad's?' Luisa asked tentatively.

Lucy cut her a look and raised her eyebrows. 'Don't push it, Mother, I'm not ready to speak to him yet'.

'OK, OK, just asking. You will have to speak to him at some point, you know? He is still your dad.'

Me and probably half of Crosslands' Lucy retorted. She glanced over at Luisa, who was attempting to stifle a giggle unsuccessfully. Lucy paused momentarily, realising how long it had been since she saw her mum laugh.

'Right, better go - see you later mum'. The front door closed with a familiar bang, which made the glass panels rattle.

Luisa laughed to herself. *She may have a point there*, she thought as she picked up her handbag.

The first day back at work after the summer was always an INSET day at the primary school, and Luisa looked forward to catching up with all the staff gossip, particularly Pauline's dating stories. Luisa would have her own tale to tell from this summer. Despite being good friends with Janet, their summers were usually packed with everything they didn't have time to do during term time, which meant they rarely met up over the break. They would keep in contact via the odd WhatsApp message or photo, but they spent so much time together during the working week that meeting for coffee over the holidays seemed unnecessary.

Luisa was slightly disappointed that she wouldn't spend as much time as usual with Janet. The allure of working over at the high school had lost its appeal now that Lucy was back at home, and although the extra money would be helpful, she still had no idea how much that would be. There had been no contract, no terms of employment, absolutely nothing from the Trust over the summer. Luisa wasn't even sure where she was meant to be this morning, so she arrived at the Primary school early in case she needed to change location.

Luisa was happy that Janet's car was already in the car park when she arrived. , as was a rather shiny Range Rover in Head Jackie's space. Luisa and Janet often took the piss out of Head Jackie's car, not to her face, obviously, but the lime green Skoda she drove looked like it was about to die at any moment. Janet had once said it looked like Kermit the Frog on crack as it chugged onto the car park. Jackie must have upgraded over the summer, and what an upgrade it was.

There was a mug of Yorkshire tea waiting for Luisa on her desk. 'Good morning!' a voice exclaimed that sounded like Janet, but when Luisa turned around, she had to look twice.

'Janet?'

'Fucking hell Luisa what's up with you, don't you like it?' Janet asked, making the most of the fact that no children were in earshot.

'I love it, Janet – you look incredible!' Luisa shrieked.

'I asked Gareth to make me look young and sexy,' she added. Gareth had been her hairdresser for years. She often booked herself in just to spend time with him; she didn't even need her hair cut most of the time.

'He told me it was a pair of scissors, not a fucking magic wand,' she laughed.

'Well, I completely approve. What made you go for pink? I thought you hated pink!' Luisa said, touching Janet's new hair like it was a priceless artefact.

'I can change my mind, Lu; I'm fifty-five and menopausal; I can do what the fuck I like!' Janet declared.

Luisa laughed. 'Oh, I've bloody missed you, Janet', she said as she sipped her tea. 'Now sit down and tell me all the news.'

'No time, Lu, we've got a full staff meeting at nine. Bring your brew; you know what these things are like.'

The staff all shuffled into the hall, the hum of holiday talk and how quickly time off goes filtered through. Luisa scoured around. Pauline was just in front of them; it looked like she was showing her left hand around. 'Jesus Janet, I think Pauline's got engaged?' Luisa whispered. 'What again?' Janet gasped. Before Luisa had time to respond, the hall chatter had reduced to a hum. She stretched her neck, looking around for Head

Jackie. 'Where's Jackie?' she mouthed at Janet, who then also cast her eyes across the room and shrugged her shoulders.

'Thank you, colleagues, thank you, yes, can we get started, please? We've lots to get through', a voice boomed around the hall. The hum fell to silence, and all eyes turned to the lectern on the stage.

'Welcome back, colleagues; I hope you have all had a restful summer. Here we are again, a new term full of new opportunities.' Luisa and Janet locked eyes. Luisa looked away quickly before she laughed. Simon Randall was the executive head of the trust; they only saw him a few times a year, usually when something was kicking off or an inspection was due. He had called Janet, Jeanette on more than one occasion, which caused Janet to rage. 'For fucks sake, he can't even get my name right; it's not exactly hard, is it?' and referred to him as Simone from that point on (not to his face, obviously).

'Now, many of you may wonder why I am standing here. As you know, my role as executive head means I oversee all of our academies. Jackie won't be returning to her post here at High Trees.' There was an instant hum of muttering as staff turned to one another in disbelief.

'OK, OK, settle down, please. I know this must come as a shock to you, but we need to think about moving forward, not looking back.

'brutal,' exhaled Janet.

They sat for the next hour listening to updates to the framework and welcoming new staff members, who were made to stand up and wave. You could tell the newly qualified teachers, all smart with their new clothes, shiny shoes and new bags, just like the young children in Reception. They gave an awkward wave and a nervous laugh before they sat down again, red-faced. The more seasoned teachers took it in their stride, a confident hand up and nod of the head before sitting back down and recrossing their arms.

'Do you think it's Cardiac Colin with the false leg?' Janet whispered.

Luisa looked at her and frowned. 'what are you talking about?'

'Pauline's fiancee!'

Luisa shrugged her shoulders. She was more preoccupied with where Jackie had disappeared. Surely, she would have said something at the end of the term if she had a new role. And where did this leave Luisa and her new job? Would she now need to give Simon a nudge with her contract? She was starting to get a bit nervous. She recalled the conversation she had with Martyn just after her interview. He had found it odd that a Trust position did not go out to advert and that only one interviewer was on the panel. And Lucy had found it strange that no one was expecting her that day at the high school. And come to think of it, no one had mentioned it at the primary school either. But then Jackie had asked her to be discreet about the whole process. She made a mental note to speak to Simon as soon as possible.

'What the fuck has happened to this?' asked Janet, trying to open her drawer.

'Ah, that would be me,' laughed Luisa. 'Remember me telling you I was looking for the emergency tea bags, and it got stuck? That's when I found the vodka.'

Janet stopped wrestling with the drawer and sat back in her chair. 'Christ, yes, I'd forgotten about that; mind you, I forgot what I went into the bathroom for the other day, so that's nothing new.'

'Coooeeeeeee ladies, I have neeewss. ' Pauline had not actually entered the office; she had thrust her left hand through the door and wiggled her fingers vigorously.

'Christ, be careful, Pauline, you'll have someone's eye out with that', explained Janet. 'come in then and tell us all about it'.

'Well, ladies, Colin and I are getting married. Eeeeeeeek,' she squealed.

'Well, well, well', Janet responded. 'is Colin the one with the dicky ticker?'

'The one you went to the Cotswolds with?' Luisa chipped in before Janet had a chance to mention the leg.

'The one and only. And its cardiomyopathy. And he's OK as long as he watches what he's doing. Not exertion, so to speak. Although not sure how that will work when we're honeymooning if you know what I mean. Nudge nudge wink wink'.

She said the words' nudge nudge wink wink' while simultaneously tapping the side of her nose and winking. She actually looked like she'd developed a tick.

'Oh please, Pauline, it's too early for this sort of talk', Janet said as she pretended to wretch in the bin.

'Well, I am really pleased for you, Pauline. Honestly. It's so lovely to see you so happy,' said Luisa as she took another sip of her tea. 'So how did he ask you? Was it completely romantic?'

'Obviously' jumped in Pauline, extremely happy to be able to tell the tale again. 'So we'd been for a lovely meal; I had a feeling he was up to something; he kept dabbing his head with his hanky. 'Colin, what on earth is up with you?' I said to him after we'd eaten dessert. I thought it was the lamb shank; he shouldn't really eat a lot of red meat, anyway; he said he needed some fresh air, so we got the bill and walked along the high street. Have you ever been to Bourton on the Water? It's bloody lovely, like a picture book., you should go if you haven't been, really.'

'Christ Pauline, it will be half term before long. Can we get to the main event?' Janet chirped up.

'OK, well, we were nearly back at the cottage when Colin asked me to stop for a moment. 'You need to think about losing some weight; I said to him; we've only walked from the bloody restaurant, and you're already knackered. Anyway, when I turned around, he was down on the floor. I thought he'd bloody fallen the daft sod. He hadn't, though, had he - guess what he was doing?'

'He wasn't, was he? Was he on one knee? Gasped Luisa, who loved a bit of romance.

'He was, with this little beauty in his hand. Told me I was a firecracker, and he didn't know how long he'd got on this earth, but however long it was, he wanted to spend it with me.'

'Oh, that is lovely,' Luisa gushed. 'Isn't it Janet?'

'Well, yes, but how did he manage that with his leg, Pauline?' Janet asked.

Pauline ignored the question. So, obviously, I said yes. I mean, he's a bit of a catch, right? Dodgy heart and leg aside.'

'Well, if you're happy, then we're happy, aren't we, Janet?' Luisa stated, giving Janet an encouraging stare.

'Oh yes, yes, you're happy, we're happy', she recited. 'congratulations. Are we having a knees-up to celebrate?'

'Ooooh yes, of course, we must!' Pauline clasped her hands

together. 'I can't believe I'm getting married at my age! God bless Tinder,' she lamented.

Janet looked over at Luisa, who rolled her eyes before they both repeated, 'god bless Tinder'.

Pauline leaned in closer and looked behind her before whispering, 'So what do you reckon about all this then?' as she nodded toward the head's office.

Janet re-engaged in the conversation instantly and wheeled her chair closer to Pauline.

'what do you mean ?' whispered back Luisa.

'Head Jackie. I am not one to gossip, you know me, but I heard she's been in a bit of bother over the summer', Pauline said, nodding her head knowingly.

'Really?' asked Janet wide-eyed, 'what sort of bother?'

'Well, again, not one to gossip, but I heard she'd been caught driving while under the influence', she said, overly exaggerating the last three words to ensure Luisa and Janet heard them correctly.

'What? Jackie?' said Luisa, wide-eyed. 'Are you kidding me? I sincerely hope you've got that wrong, Pauline,' she added sternly. She felt herself prickle inside, and colour rushed to her cheeks. 'Are you sure you have heard that correctly?' Luisa asked, conscious of the red rash rising up her chest as the anger started to build.

'Fucking hell, Pauling, you better be sure about that; that's a hell of an accusation', said Janet, her eyes wide.

'Been arrested and everything,' added Pauline, ' so she won't be back here in a hurry, if at all.'

'Well, if that's true, then I hope they throw the bloody book at her; she could have killed someone, she could have...' Luisa choked up, unable to get the rest of her sentence out.

'Oh Luisa, don't cry', said Pauline, desperately looking around for some tissues.

'Luisa's daughter had an accident over the summer, Pauline, involving a drunk driver; it's a bit raw still,' Janet explained. The colour drained from Pauline's face.

'And are you absolutely sure about the facts, Pauline? 'Janet pressed.

'As sure as I can be, Colin's mate Jack works at the custody desk down at the station. He was working that night.'

'Christ so much for confidentiality, eh? Remind me never to do anything illegal; it would be all over the bloody news before they'd had a chance to say, 'You're nicked'.'

'Well, it wasn't exactly as clear cut as that; we'd already read about it in the paper, and Colin had been caught up in the traffic that night; he asked Jack if he'd been on shift that night. Jack had been, and he told Colin she was a head teacher, and together with the description of the car, I just put two and two together, and also, there had been some rumours, you know, about her drinking on the job' she added this last bit so quietly they only just made out what she'd said.

'Drinking on the job?' Luisa whispered back. 'Here? Drinking at work?'

'Well, that would explain the vodka bottle', said Janet ', the fucking cheek of her, trying to pin it on me!'

The three of them all sat in silence for a minute, digesting the information.

'Right, OK, I don't know if this is the right time to mention it, and you didn't hear this from me; I heard that there were others involved, a couple of kids who were on the crossing over in town…' Pauline added quietly.

Janet looked over to Luisa, sitting with her hand over her mouth, her complexion ghostly white. Luisa took a moment to compose herself before looking at them both, 'I swear to god, if this is true, Pauline, then if I ever see her again, I'll fucking kill her,' Luisa hissed, red-faced desperately trying to contain the rage that was building inside.

There was no time for her to explain; Simon popped his head around the door. 'Errr Luisa, isn't it? Hi, just wondered if you had a minute. I could do with a chat in the office.'

Luisa stood up, swallowed hard, and wiped her hands on her thighs. 'Yes, of course,' she said and left the room.

'Oooh, wonder what that's about?' asked Pauline, eyebrows raised.

Janet shrugged her shoulders. 'No idea, Pauline, but I'll tell you now, whatever Jackie has done, I wouldn't want to be in her shoes when Luisa catches up with her. '

'Thank you for popping in, Luisa. Are you OK? You seem a little flustered? Simon asked as he shuffled some papers on his desk. 'Please, take a seat,' he instructed as he sat down on the leather chair before her, not waiting for Luisa to respond to his question.

Luisa sat down in the seat at the other side of the desk, still seething about the information that had just made itself known to her.

'OK, so, just wanted to check in with you about a conversation you may have had with Jackie before she, err, before she left her post.' Simon looked awkwardly at the papers on his desk. Again, there was no time for a response from Luisa. 'Anyway, about your role, can you tell me a little about what you and Jackie had discussed regarding what you would be doing this term?' He looked up at Luisa, relieved he had finished the sentence without stumbling.

'OK, well, Jackie had told us about the Trust administrator role and asked us to apply.'

'Us?' Simon asked.

'Yes, me and Janet, although Janet said it wasn't the right time for her, so she didn't apply', Luisa informed Simon. She was confused as to why Simon was asking her these questions; he should know exactly what had happened. Simon nodded, encouraging her to continue.

'So I had the interview and was successful'.

'OK, and who interviewed you, Luisa?' Simon asked solemnly.

'Jackie'

'Just Jackie?'

Luisa frowned. 'yes'.

'And did you receive written confirmation of the job offer?'

'Nothing, I was going to chase it, actually; I just guessed with it being the summer and all that it would be followed up once we were back?'

Simon hummed to himself and flicked through some more papers. Luisa started to feel uncomfortable.

'The thing is, Luisa, ' Simon started up again, 'I think there has been some confusion in terms of the role; I wasn't aware there was a role to be filled. We still aren't quite sure why Jackie thought there may have been,' he didn't look up, his eyes still intently looking at the papers in front of him.

'I'm sorry?' asked Luisa, struggling to understand what Simon was saying.

'There was no job Luisa. Jackie wasn't well, shall we say. There are a few anomalies that we are uncovering, and this was one of them.'

Luisa sat back in the chair. *What the hell was this? Bloody typical,* she finally got herself a better salary and more responsibility, and it turns out the job wasn't even real.

'We are genuinely sorry that you have been caught up in this, Luisa, and as you can imagine, this is a sensitive matter, so we can go into too much detail. We cannot honour a role that isn't required. Do you understand?'

'So basically, I didn't get the job because the job didn't exist?' Luisa replied.

'Exactly that,' Simon added, 'but Luisa, the trust is still extremely grateful for the work you do here at the Hilltop, and to recognise this, we would like to honour part of Jackie's offer as a gesture of goodwill.'

'OK,' Luisa replied, unsure of the protocol when someone told you you didn't get the job you were offered because it wasn't a real job.

'So basically, if you wanted to, we could release you to the high school for one morning a week to help them out - unfortunately, there wouldn't be any remuneration.'

Luisa looked at him. *Seriously, does this get any worse? They are asking me to do what they initially offered but for no extra pay. What an absolute joke.*

Luisa pursed her lips together, mindful that the response waiting to explode from her mouth was probably inappropriate.

'Do you need to have a little think about that?' Simon asked, raising his head to meet her gaze.

Luisa nodded her head slowly. *Don't open your mouth, Luisa, just nod.*

'That's all then; thank you for your time', Simon said, still shuffling papers.

Luisa felt the rage unleash inside her as she left the room. It was a boiling rage, fueled by a mix of frustration with Jackie's incompetence in her job, the terrifying near-death experience her daughter had endured, and Simon's aggravating paper shuffling on the desk. She needed to get away, to let out her emotions, so she quickly shut the door to a cubicle before having a bloody good cry.

In the solitude of the bathroom stall, Luisa felt a wave of embarrassment wash over her. No wonder the staff at the high school had been acting strangely that day—they likely had no idea what was going on with her. She cursed herself for getting too ahead of herself, for thinking that this new job would be the answer to all her problems. She realised how fortunate it was that she hadn't gone on a shopping spree for new work clothes; not only would they be unnecessary, but she wouldn't even be able to afford them now. And Jesus Christ, was it Jackie who had run Lucy over? She felt her breathing getting out of control and steadied herself in the cubicle.

With a heavy sigh, Luisa muttered to herself, 'Fuck my life. Fuck my whole fucking life.'

Chapter 42

The pale green paint on the front door still looked tired, Luisa considered as she stood on the doorstep. She had been shafted again with some guaranteed comfort bullshit - she really should start ignoring these sorts of claims on footwear; it was clearly just a ploy to get forty-something women to buy shoes. She had no idea why anyone would think that was amusing, but, nevertheless, despite the pain she was feeling from her shoes, she smiled to herself as she pushed open the door and kicked them off down the hallway.

'Good day?' a familiar voice called from the kitchen. Something was cooking that smelt delicious, and her stomach rumbled in appreciation.

'Oh, you wouldn't believe the day I have had', she responded, hanging her coat on the peg in the hallway. She had come to terms with the whole 'here's a job, there is no job - sorry, not sorry' situation. At least she actually still had a job and a job that she enjoyed, working with people that she loved. In the grand scheme of things, she was doing alright.

She entered the kitchen, her nose instinctively following the scents of something roasting in garlic. Her smile soon turned to a frown as she immediately clocked Meg sitting at the table, cradling a mug of tea in her hand.

'Meg! What are you doing here? I didn't see your car? Is everything OK?'

'They called me today, Lu, the hospital.'

Luisa sat hard on the opposite chair and reached for Meg's hand. 'Right, OK, what's the plan? What's happening? Do you need me to come with you? I'll drive us,' she said at a hundred miles an hour.

'No, no, Lu, there's no need for that,' Megan interjected.

'NO, Megan, I am your best friend, and I would never let you go through this alone. I will not hear of it. I'm taking you, and that's that.' Luisa frowned and pursed her lips, hoping she was disguising the fear and dread she felt inside.

'Lu, please no', Meg squeaked, tears forming in her eyes.

Luisa sat back. She already knew - she already had the news.

'Oh Meg, OK, OK, what's the situation? What have they said? Whatever it is, we'll face it together,' she told Meg, her voice soft with a slight wobble.

'For God's sake, mum. Will you just give her a chance to bloody well speak?' Lucy laughed, wooden spoon in hand.

Luisa cut her a look. Now was definitely not the time to be joking around. Honestly, that girl could be so insensitive sometimes.

'Sorry, Meg, ' Luisa whispered. 'Why are you smiling? It's OK to be upset; you don't have to put a brave face on for me,' she insisted.

'Lu, will you please just stop talking for one minute?'

'but...'

'No, Lu. Please let me just speak. My car isn't here because I got a lift.'

Luisa lowered her head. 'Shit, Meg, can't you drive? Have

they told you not to?'

Megan laughed again, much to Luisa's confusion.

'Why does everyone find this so amusing?' she asked. 'Am I the only one taking this seriously?' she asked, getting more exasperated by the minute.

Lucy and Megan locked eyes and burst into a fit of giggles.

'Right, what the hell is going on?'

'Oh Lu, I do love you. Look, I haven't driven because if I had, then we couldn't drink this!' She pulled out a bottle of prosecco from underneath the table.

'What the fuck is going on?' she asked, glancing between Lucy to Meg.

'I'm not dying, Lu! I own a rather stubborn cyst, but it won't kill me.' Megan stated triumphantly.

Luisa looked around the kitchen at the beaming faces of the two people she loved most in the world and did what any respectable person would do in this situation: let out a colossal whooop.

A bottle of prosecco later and nearly a whole box of Kleenex and Megan had explained how she'd received a call from the hospital saying that there was no need for her to go in as Mr Kepe, the consultant, had received her results and told there was nothing sinister going on there. So that was that. All clear.

'I tell you what, though, Lu', slurred Megan, 'this whole situation has made me restock things.'

'What, like prosecco?' giggled Luisa.

'Huh? What are you on about?'

'You said it made you restock things.'

'No, not restock, you know what I mean, take stock, that's it, it's made me take stock of things - I have decided that I'm going to embrace things wholeheartedly from now on. My baby is going off to Uni soon, and I am going to start having some fun.'

'Oooh yes, fun' clapped Luisa. 'Remind me what that looks like?'

'Well', Megan put her wine glass on the side table and placed her hands on her thighs. 'Firstly, I'm redecorating.' she declared.

'Okay', Luisa responded slowly, 'not exactly the height of fast-paced living though, is it?' she questioned, disappointed that Megan wasn't getting a tattoo.

'OK then, secondly, I'm going to get my hair cut short.'

'OK, this is better', said Luisa excitedly

'And then, I think I'm going to go on holiday,' she declared.

'Oooh yes, now you're talking?' Luisa said, sitting back in her chair. 'Oh, how I'd love some sunshine'.

'Oh, me too, it feels like forever since I've lay by a swimming pool in the sunshine. I can read my book, drink wine, and do whatever I want.'

'Oooh sounds like heaven' swooned Luisa. 'And you bloody well deserve it, too.'

'Actually, mum, you should go with her!' Lucy piped up

'Oh no, I couldn't do that.'

'Why not?' Lucy and Megan said in unison.

'I don't know, it just seems so extravagant, and what about you, Lucy, what would you do?'

'Mum, I'll be sixteen in a few months; I'm sure I could manage by myself for a week.'

'No, I couldn't do that,' Luisa said dismissively.

'Yes, you could', Megan corrected.

'Or, there is another option', Lucy said looking a little

sheepish

'Which is?' Luisa asked.

'I could stay with my dad?' she looked up and winced as she said it.

'Oh?' Luisa replied, 'and you're OK with that?'

Lucy nodded. 'I can't avoid him forever, I know he's been a knob, but he's my dad at the end of the day, and if I'm honest, I miss him a bit'.

Luisa put down her glass and went over to Lucy, hugging her so tight Lucy gasped for breath. 'OK, Mother, that's enough; I'm going round for tea next week. I called him. I didn't tell you because I didn't want you to be upset', Lucy said sincerely.

'Why would I be upset? Of course, you should see your dad, Lucy,' said Luisa. 'I'm just so pleased that you've not let this whole situation ruin things between you', Luisa blubbed. 'I'd hate for you to not have a relationship with him.'

'Thanks, mum,' Lucy added, 'now let me go and see to tea.'

'Yeah, that would be awful, wouldn't it?' Meg added, looking at Luisa accusingly.

Luisa frowned, 'meaning?'

'Well, I'm just saying, yes, it would be awful if you let the whole situation ruin things, wouldn't it?' she smiled.

'I don't know what you're talking about', dismissed Luisa

'Yes, you bloody well do', said Megan.

Luisa picked her glass back up and downed the contents.

'And it's no good ignoring me,' Meg declared.

'Hold on, hold on, I'm only just getting my head around a holiday; I can't deal with anything else just at the moment.'

'So what I'm hearing is that it's yes for the holiday though?' Meg asked excitedly.

'Well, yes, I guess so, as long as you don't mind paying school holiday prices?' Luisa reminded her.

'Oh shit, yes, I'd forgotten that you work in a bloody school', Meg frowned, 'But hold on, if we have to go in the school holidays, then why don't we all go? Take Lucy and Izzy, too! Izzy will be home from Uni, you will have finished your exams, Lucy, what do you reckon, girls' trip?'

Lucy beamed. 'Really? Can I come? Mum? Can I?'

Luisa shrugged her shoulders. 'Well, that's sorted then, girls' trip it is!'

'Yes,' both Lucy and Megan fist-bumped the air together.

'Oh shit', Lucy suddenly remembered, 'the bloody chicken!'

'Really, Lu, please tell me we can really do this; we would have such a giggle,' Megan said, her eyes wide with excitement.

'Well, I guess there's no reason not to, is there?' Luisa replied, raising her glass. 'But also, what the hell is Lucy cooking?' she whispered.

'She wanted to celebrate, I told her earlier because I wanted to come and surprise you - she's a good girl, Lu, she really is.'

'I know, I'm fortunate,' reflected Luisa.

'Dinner's ready,' Lucy shouted from the kitchen. Meg and Luisa exchanged a look. 'Can she actually cook?' Meg asked. 'I guess we'll soon find out.'

'Right, mum, you sit there, Meg, you're here next to me, no mum, not there, the other side, that's it, sit down', Lucy bossed.

'OK, Lucy; Crikey, I feel like I'm in North Korea', Megan laughed.

'Also, you may be able to knock up a roast chicken, Lucy, but you can't count,' Luisa said, 'are we expecting someone?' she asked as she refilled her glass, noting the extra place settings at the table.

Meg looked at Lucy, who quickly turned around and busied herself at the kitchen counter.

'Lucy?' Luisa asked hesitantly, 'what's going on?'

'I'll have another glass of that,' Megan interrupted. 'Ooh smells lovely Lucy, aren't you clever, now where's my bag? I'm sure I put it down here somewhere.'

'STOP!' shouted Luisa. 'WILL THE PAIR OF YOU JUST STOP MESSING AROUND AND TELL ME WHAT THE HELL IS GOING ON?'.

Silence fell across the kitchen. The whirring of the oven took sole responsibility for trying to break the awkwardness. The three of them darted their eyes backwards and forward to each other, trying to throw the responsibility of answering the question between them.

The shrill of the doorbell shattered the vibe, and Megan visibly sunk into her chair as she exhaled.

'Megan? Who is at the door?' Luisa asked suspiciously.

Megan shrugged, took a sip from her glass, and averted her eyes downward.

'I'll get it then, shall I?' Luisa exclaimed, putting down her glass.

Chapter 43

Luisa padded down the hallway. She knew who it was before answering, and she laughed as she opened the door.

'You could have given me the heads up!' she whispered affectionately as she held the door open, 'I've just nearly lost my shit in there! You know how much I hate surprises, Martyn!'

'I'm sorry', he said, leaning down and kissing her. 'I should have warned you about their plan, but I needed your surprise to be genuine; they were so excited.'

'And how is the leg, Zach?' Luisa asked.

'Not too bad, a bit achy, but getting better all the time', he responded.

'So let me get this right: Lucy and Megan have arranged for you to come for dinner tonight to celebrate Meg's news?' Luisa asked.

'I actually think they are plotting to try and get us back together,' Martyn replied, rolling his eyes.

'Lucy's been planning this for ages', added Zach. 'She's so nervous', he laughed.

'OK, how are we going to play this?' Luisa whispered. 'Can we just string this out for a bit longer first?' He smiled cheekily and nodded slowly, mirroring her mischievous eyes.

'ARE YOU KIDDING ME?' she shouted as she slammed the front door.

Zach giggled, and she put her finger up to her mouth. 'Shhh', she whispered.

As they walked into the kitchen, Meg and Lucy sat stony-faced and pale, and neither spoke.

'So whose idea was this?' Luisa demanded.

Lucy and Megan both said 'hers' at the same time. It took all of Luisa's strength not to laugh out loud. Bless them both; they thought they were helping.

'Oh right, you've both ganged up on me then?' she continued. 'And as for you ?' she directed her head to Martyn,' why on earth did you agree to this?'

'I was hungry', Martyn replied, shrugging his shoulders.

Luisa put her hand to her mouth to stop the giggle from escaping.

'Well, you know I hate to see good food go to waste; you'd better sit down', she pointed at the empty chairs next to her. 'Go on, sit!'

The five of them sat in silence for what seemed like an hour, although in reality, they'd barely even started the main course.

'I must say, Lucy', Megan was first to speak, 'this chicken is amazing; I didn't know you could cook!'

The other guests nodded in agreement before another minute of silence, other than the clink of cutlery and the occasional 'hmmm' in appreciation of the food.

'So, we're thinking of going on holiday next year,' Lucy stated, desperately trying to ease the tension.

'Really?' offered Martyn as he looked at Luisa. 'when?'

'Not until the summer', Luisa replied, avoiding eye contact

and quickly following it up with, 'Not that it's any of your business!'

Another minute of silence.

'Right, enough is enough', stated Megan, slamming down her cutlery and startling the rest of the table. 'I'm supposed to be celebrating my being disease-free. Lucy here has spent all afternoon cooking this meal, bless her, and we thought this would be a nice surprise because sometimes Luisa Mulligan, you are a right royal stubborn pain in the arse,' she declared.' Megan took a deep breath before starting again. 'Martyn, tell Luisa what you've told me. Tell her how much you've missed her. Tell her!' she pointed at Luisa to make sure Martyn knew who to direct his speech to.

Before Martyn could respond, Megan continued, the three glasses of prosecco clearly kicking in.

'And Lucy, tell your mum, I mean it, tell her that you and Zach are OK, tell her! Go on!' Lucy looked at her mum with an apologetic face.

'Honestly mum, me we're fine, aren't we, Zach? There's no awkwardness at all, I promise,' she confirmed.

Luisa looked at Zach, who nodded in agreement.

Luisa burst out laughing. 'I can't do it anymore,' she managed to say through the laughter.

'What?' Megan asked, 'can't do what? I'm so confused'.

'Well, that Martyn and I, well, you know', she suddenly came over shy and blushed. Martyn reached for her hand and gave it a squeeze.

'OK.' Martyn cleared his throat and tapped his knife on the

side of his glass. 'Right, Christ, I'm nervous, OK, so as you know, it's been a hell of a few months.'

'You can say that again,' murmured Megan.

'And Lucy, Zach, you know that both Luisa and I think the absolute world of you, and we wanted to make sure you were happy with everything.'

'HAPPY WITH WHAT???' Megan was getting exasperated.

'OK, we won't keep you in suspense any longer; yes, Luisa and I are back together', he said proudly.

'I knew it!' exclaimed Lucy. 'I knew you were; I told you, Zach, didn't I? I told you something was going on!'

'Oh, so now look what you've done', Meg bawled as the tears shot down her cheeks. 'you absolute bunch of fuckers - and how on earth have you managed to keep this secret, Luisa?' Megan looked over at Martyn, 'Something you should know, Martyn. Luisa Mulligan can't keep a secret to save her life!' Megan laughed.

'You have a point', Luisa laughed, 'but I honestly can't believe you hadn't already guessed!'

'Well, now it's all out in the open, finally, I declare we should make a toast' said Martyn proudly, raising his glass. 'To the future.'

'abso-fucking-lutely', gushed Megan. 'This is just the best news ever.' The chink of glasses and general hubbub of celebratory hugging was interrupted by the doorbell.

Lucy left the table and reappeared in the kitchen doorway shortly after.

'Mum? You've got another visitor,' Lucy announced. 'And I promise this one had nothing to do with me!'

'Whatever that is cooking I bloody hope there's some left

for me,' a familiar voice called down the hallway.

'Janet!' Luisa gasped. 'What are you doing here?'

'Missing out on a bloody party by the looks of it', she gushed. 'Be a doll, Lucy, and pour me a glass'.

When Janet was up to speed with the talk of moving in and the plates had been cleared away, the conversation turned to the holiday.

'So where are you thinking of going?' Janet asked.

'Well', replied Megan, 'I don't really care where it is as long as there's a sunbed with my name on it', she stated. 'Actually, you should all come!' she gushed. 'Oh my god, please say you'll all come; we would have the best bloody time!' The prosecco had definitely fully kicked in.

'I'd be up for that', Martyn said,' how about you, Zach?'

'Errr, yea, obvs', he replied, a huge smile on his face. 'as long as we don't go to some old codger resort', he added quickly.

'Cheeky sod' chipped in, Janet laughing.

'That's it then, group holiday, Janet, are you going to ask Simon?' Megan enquired.

Janet shot her a look.

'I'll take that as a no, then, shall I?' she winced.

'Janet, come on, a break away will do you both the world of good. Come on, bring him; it will be a blast!' Luisa added.

Janet smirked to herself. 'Well, I guess I will need someone to carry my bags and keep my glass topped up', she added. 'Aah, sod it, why not? It's about time we let loose a bit', she declared.

'Eeeeeeek, this is going to be the best,' Megan gushed.

'Good job, I bought another bottle.' Janet reached down to her back and produced a celebratory bottle of fizz. 'Seems that we're celebrating'.

'And you're sure you're OK with this, Lucy' Luisa had inter-cepted a toilet break to speak to her daughter. 'Mum, I have never been happier. You and Martyn are made for each other. Honestly, he's so kind and caring; you deserve it.'

Luisa smiled at her. Her lovely Lucy, her kind, caring, meat-eating daughter. Standing here looking like a young lady, intelligent, funny, beautiful. How lucky she was. She reached out and pulled her close.

'Christ mum, chill, you're going to burst something', she laughed, pretending to pull away. 'And Mum? You really need to work on your deception skills. I've known Martyn's been sneaking around and leaving early in the morning for ages. It is quite sweet that he parks his car further down the street, though,' she mocked.

'oh god, Lucy', Luisa laughed, slightly embarrassed. 'we just really wanted to make sure it was right before we ran it past you; you are my absolute number one priority, you know that, don't you?'

Lucy nodded reassuringly.

'Martyn wanted to ensure Zach was OK with it all, too; you've both been through a lot.'

'Mum, stop, honestly; Zach and I have been laughing about this for ages; Martyn is as useless as you!'

'oh, come here', Luisa gushed and pulled Lucy in for another hug.

'Lucy, do you want to know a secret? 'Luisa whispered in Lucy's ear.

Lucy pulled back quickly, 'Mum, you really are useless at this, aren't you?'

'Well, do you want to know or not?' Luisa laughed.
'Well yes, obviously'.

Chapter 44

'Megan, here, grab this', Janet shouted as she maneuvered around the sunbeds, her hand laden with something that looked suspiciously like a round of tequila sunrises.

'Janet, it's 3 p.m. Are you sure we should be doing this? Shouldn't we wait an hour or two?' Megan said, checking her watch as she shot up to help before the contents landed on the hot stone floor around them.

'We're on holiday! We can do what the fuck we want!' Janet laughed. 'I might have another in a minute; this all-inclusive is bloody brilliant'. Janet had thrown herself into holiday mode; she'd joined in the aqua aerobics (although that may have had something to do with the young animation guy whose shorts were so tight they looked like they might split at the seams whenever he bent over, which he did, often).

Janet and Simon had taken part in the 'Mr & Mrs' show at the evening entertainment, much to everyone's amusement, and she'd been a constant source of entertainment around the pool - including the afternoon that she lost her HRT patch somewhere in the Jacuzzi pool and spent a good half hour wearing a pair of Zach's goggles searching for it.

'If you see an old man with boobs who didn't have boobs

when he got here, then he's got my patch stuck to his arse', she said. 'I don't want to be responsible for that!'

The temperature was starting to shoot up, and Megan and Janet were sitting in the shade of the blazing Spanish sunshine in a vain attempt to keep cool and prevent their faces from being beetroot red and getting sweat patches on their outfits. 'Where's Simon?' Meg asked as she sipped the extremely strong Long Island tea.

'He's having a last-minute shower', said Janet between sips. 'Christ, this is strong, isn't it?' she stated, examining the contents of her glass.

Megan nodded. 'Better just have the one, eh? Not sure Luisa will be too impressed if we're shitfaced,' she grimaced.

'No, good point', agreed Janet. 'We'll hold off until later, shall we?' Megan nodded, and she sucked on her straw. 'Maybe just *one* more', she said, 'because we *are* celebrating after all'. They chinked their glasses in agreement. Today would be a day to remember for all the right reasons.

* * *

The sun had burned out its full force and was starting to think about switching down the heat a little as it settled a little lower in the sky. A cool breeze had picked up, enough to bring some relief but not enough to be a nuisance. Simon sat fanning Janet, who was suffering from the internal and external heat. 'This fucking menopause', she said, 'I feel like I'm going to internally combust', she whispered to Simon, who looked at her and smiled.

'You're bloody gorgeous', he said, looking into her green

eyes, 'even with bright pink hair' he grinned. Janet went to swat him with the fan.

'Don't you dare bloody come any closer, Simon, I swear, I'm melting here'. She reached for his hand and gave it a reassuring squeeze. Luisa had been right; this holiday had been the break they needed. Janet had come back to life since starting her medication, and Simon saw his old Janet reappear. She still had that spark, that zest for life that he fell in love with all those years ago. They'd talked on the balcony for hours; she'd told him how she'd been feeling, how worried she'd been about her health, her memory, her dryness down there, and her weight gain.

'I wish you'd have said something earlier', Simon had told her,' I could have helped; I had no idea how much you've been suffering'.

Janet shrugged her shoulders. 'It's not something people tend to talk about', Janet said. 'My mum had just said she was going through the change, and that was that -there were no details, no advice, you just got on with it'. They still had their fiery rows, which also happened before menopause; the difference now was that they made up again afterwards like they used to.

Megan looked across at them both and smiled. She nudged Izzy beside her, 'goals', she said as she nodded towards them both. Izzy laughed and leant into the handsome young man sitting next to her. Izzy had fully embraced her first year at Uni, both socially and academically. She passed her first-year Psychology exams with a 2.1 and had met Ben when he'd taken her under his wing at a social where things had gotten a little out of hand. They'd been inseparable ever since. Megan approved entirely, particularly as he was extraordinarily studious and owned his own car, meaning trips home were now more frequent.

The tinkle of Ellie Goulding's 'How Long Will I Love You' emerged from the tiny speakers in front of them, and the five of them, plus a couple of random people who just so happened to be on the beach at the time, stood up and turned around.

'Oh fucking hell', bawled Janet dabbing her eyes. Simon put his hand on her shoulder and gave her a squeeze. She cast a look across at Megan, who had already gone and wasn't being discreet about it. 'Mum Christ, stop snorting, you're ruining the moment', Izzy said, laughing and reaching for her mum's hand.

Luisa and Lucy approached them arm in arm, Luisa's loose-fitting cream chiffon dress blowing in the gentle breeze and the golden throw of sunlight illuminating her face, perfectly framed by her dark hair. Lucy walked proudly beside her in an equally stunning pale coral dress, her dark curled hair falling perfectly around her tanned shoulders. They both looked at each other as they began to walk between the beautiful coral-coloured orchids that lined their path along the beach towards their closest friends standing waiting for them. Megan looked backwards at Martyn, who was mesmerised by the sight before him. Lucy, this beautiful, intelligent, sassy young lady whom anyone would be proud to have as a daughter, and Luisa, his rock, his best friend, and, any moment soon, his wife.

* * *

'And so please raise a glass to my beautiful wife, Luisa, my wonderful son Zach, and my enchanting stepdaughter, Lucy' Martyn raised his glass in the air.

'To Luisa, Zach and Lucy,' their guests responded by raising their glasses as instructed. They had also attracted a few other guests along the way who had wanted to celebrate with them, and so they had now quite a merry band of followers.

Luisa meandered through the revellers towards Megan and Janet. 'Everyone OK?' she asked.

'Oh bloody hell, Luisa, the whole day has been perfect. And look at you, you look like a goddess in that dress,' Janet said as she picked up the chiffon layers and let them fall from her hand. 'You said you wouldn't wear an actual wedding dress'.

'Well, Lucy quite rightly said that if I'm going to do it, then I should do it properly and feel like a princess for the day,' Luisa stated

'And do you?' asked Meg.

'Nope', replied Luisa with a straight face. 'I feel like a bloody queen who is on fire; it's so bloody warm', she laughed, fanning her face with a beer mat.

Megan and Janet laughed out loud. 'Of course, you're a bloody queen', Janet eventually said, smiling at her friend. 'You bloody deserve this'. She grabbed a bottle and an empty glass off the table. 'Here, get your chops around this before I drink it all,' she said.

'No, not just yet, Janet, got to keep a clear head for this bloody first dance', she said, cringing. 'Honestly, I thought the beauty of getting married abroad was that you could ditch all the cringy traditions', she said, rolling her eyes. 'but Martyn is insisting'.

Megan laughed. 'Aww, it will be sweet', she said encouragingly, 'what's the song? Or is it a secret?'

'Well, if it is a secret, you can bet your bottom dollar that she'll tell us,' Janet butted in. 'because we all know…'

'Luisa Mulligan can't keep a secret,' the three of them said in unison before falling apart laughing.

'Oh shit', Megan let out in a panic. 'We can't say that anymore, can we? Luisa Woodhouse can't keep a secret. It doesn't really have the same ring, does it?'

'Well, maybe Luisa *Woodhouse* can keep a secret', Luisa said with a wink, tapping her finger to the side of her nose before swishing her dress and heading across the bar to find her husband.

Lucy and Zach were watching the celebrations from the side of the pool. 'I don't think I've ever seen my dad smile so much,' said Zach, sipping his coke. Lucy nodded, 'She keeps insisting things won't change, and I keep telling her, so what if they do?'

'Yeah, same with dad, he keeps banging on about how things will be different. But I'm quite excited, Lucy, are you? I mean, with everything.'

Lucy nodded and smiled. 'Oh yes, absolutely. I cannot wait.'

Chapter 45

'A ladeeeez and a gentlemans, please can you come and stand here, the bride and groom are a going to start their first dancing' the Spanish DJ Disco's voice boomed through the microphone. An eruption of clapping and cheering rose from both the invited and uninvited guests. Martyn led Luisa by the hand to the centre of the dance floor as the iconic first few bars of Ben E King's Stand By Me started playing. Martyn pulled Luisa close to him, and their bodies moved in perfect harmony as they gazed into each other's eyes, lost in each other for a moment, the whole world carrying on around them as they marked their first dance together as man and wife.

'Here we are,' Martyn whispered lovingly to Luisa, his voice filled with emotion.

'Here we are,' she repeated, a smile fixed across her face.

'Mrs Woodhouse'

'Mr Woodhouse'

They swayed together for a moment longer before Martyn whispered into her ear, 'Are you ready?'

She pulled back slightly and nodded, 'I am if you are,' she replied.

'OK then, deep breath, let's do this,' she said confidently, her cheeks slightly flushed with anticipation. She turned and nodded to the DJ, who stopped the music sharply. Luisa reached across the DJ's desk and took the microphone from him.

'Errr, hello, everyone. Can I have your attention for a moment, please?' Luisa pulled away from the microphone slightly, startled by the volume of her voice. Her words hung in the air, a hushed anticipation settling over the crowd, and faces started to turn to theirs, the newly wedded couple standing on the dance floor.

'I'm sorry, *we* have something we would like to say', Luisa said, giggling, and a rose tint appeared on both cheeks. 'Can I just ask Lucy, Zach, Janet, Simon, Megan, Izzy and Ben to step forward, please?' she continued. Luisa continued with a mischievous smile. 'Right, OK, so firstly, can I just say a huge thank you to you all for making this day so special for us both?' she started, 'and as you know, now that Martyn and I are married, Lucy and Zach complete our family.'

'Cheers to that', Janet piped up as she raised her glass. The rest of the bar joined in with a 'here here', happy to be part of the celebration, even if they weren't 100% sure what the celebration was.

Luisa laughed. 'OK, well, as I was saying, Lucy and Zach complete our family, or rather, we thought they did'.

Megan looked over at Izzy and shook her head, confused. 'what does that mean?' she mouthed. Izzy shrugged her shoulders.

'Well, it turns out that maybe our family wasn't quite as complete as we thought it was because, in around six months, we are due a new addition.' Luisa smiled, turning to look at Martyn.

Janet looked around to Megan and back again; 'a new addition to what?' she asked.

Martyn laughed, 'To us, Janet, a new addition to our family'.

'You're never getting a bloody dog! Not after what you said about them licking their balls, Lu? Surely not,' Janet piped up.

Luisa bent over laughing, 'Not a dog, Janet, better than that! We're going to have a baby,' she declared, her hand resting on the bump disguised by the flowing chiffon of her wedding dress.

The room erupted into cheering and chinking of glasses. "Congratulations to the happy couple and their little bambino' DJ disco declared as Big Mountain's Baby I Love Your Way emerged from the speakers. Martyn took Luisa in his arms and kissed her tenderly. 'I love you, Luisa Woodhouse', he said.

'Never mind all this soppiness,' Janet barged between them. 'Come here, you absolute fucker and give me a hug'. Megan wasn't far behind, visibly caught in the excitement. 'Oh my god, oh my god, we're going to have a baby,' she squealed. 'I'm so bloody excited, Lu, I can't cope with all this emotion; I'm going to need another drink', she declared, 'so that's why you've been avoiding getting a round in!' Megan said wide-eyed.' You've been keeping a bloody secret!'

Luisa chuckled, 'See! Told you I could!' she said smugly. Lucy and Zach appeared beside them, 'and here they are, big sister and brother,' Janet said proudly. 'and did you know about this too?'

Lucy and Zach exchanged a knowing glance and then grinned. 'We might have had a little inside scoop', Lucy admitted with a mischievous glint in her eye.

'I've already bagged chief babysitter', Lucy said, 'when I'm home from Uni anyway,' she added quickly.

'Well, then, I'm deffo next in line', chirped Megan.

'Errr and me!' Janet declared defiantly, a twinkle in her eye. 'I'll have you know I'm a bloody brilliant babysitter.' She declared. Simon, always quick with a witty remark, said, 'If you don't mind late nights and secret snacks.'

Janet nodded enthusiastically. 'Exactly! I shall be the really cool aunty figure,' she proclaimed, 'always has the snacks, always up for a good laugh, and always on hand to smooth out any drama.'

Megan had her own role in mind. 'And I'll be the one they call at two in the morning when they need a lift home because they know I won't let on how drunk they were,' she joked, earning a round of laughter.

Luisa chuckled at the enthusiasm. 'Well, let's just get past the baby stage first, eh?' she teased.

DJ Disco was clearly getting impatient and wanted to get the party started as the familiar tones of La Bamba caused a massive swell of extremely merry holidaymakers to the dance floor. 'Congratulations to the new Mr and the Mrs, come to the dance floor and let's shakey shakey', he instructed over the microphone.

* * *

A welcome cool breeze fanned across the beachfront where three friends sat on abandoned sunbeds looking out across the ocean.

'Well, if you'd told me this time last year that in a year I'd be on holiday with my husband, I'd have told you to stop being a twat', Janet said.

Luisa laughed. 'well, if you'd told me this time last year that in a year, I'd be on holiday with *my* husband, then I'd have said the same.'

'And if you said the same to me,' Megan joined in, 'I'd have told you to fuck off'.The three of them giggled.

'But I have my beauty Izzy here with me, and that's worth more than anything', she added quickly. 'We're all fortunate, aren't we, in the grand scheme of things'

The three of them nodded silently.

'Actually', said Megan, tentatively looking at her friends on either side of her, 'I may have a secret of my own', she said and bit her bottom lip.

'Oh my god', said Luisa, her mouth wide open.

'Tell us this minute,' demanded Janet, sitting herself upright in preparation to hear whatever Megan would tell them.

'Well, firstly, I stand by my first response, that if you'd have said to me this time last year that in a year I'd be on holiday with my husband, I'd have told you to fuck off', she reiterated.

'OK', said Janet and Luisa simultaneously, both frowning as they tried to second guess what was coming.

'And actually, if you'd have said that I would be on holiday with any man, I'd have said the same thing', she added.

'Well, you don't need a bloody man to be happy, Megan', Janet declared. 'I mean, some of them are OK, but a lot of them are just hairy-arsed narcissists.'

'Bit harsh, Janet', interjected Luisa laughing.

'Maybe', replied Janet, shrugging her shoulders.

'However', Megan continued slowly.

She had a captive audience in front of her, two pairs of eyes willing her to spill the secret, two friends who would do anything for her, who just wanted her to be happy.

'Come on, for fucks sake, Meg, I need a piss', Janet was laughing, 'at my age; you daren't leave it too long.'

'And I'm bloody pregnant', nodded along Luisa, 'hurry this along, please.'

'Right, OK, I've had the best week ever; honestly, watching you and Martyn tie the knot just filled me with so much happiness, and seeing the four of you together...'

'Soon to be five,' added Janet interrupted, knowingly.

'Yes, well and the baby and everything else, it's just been brilliant, and having here too, and all of you, it's just been the best.'

'That better not be the secret', said Janet sternly.

'No, no, the thing is, as much as I've loved being here, I also cannot wait to get home because, well, there is someone special who I've been seeing for a while now'.

'Oh my god, she's blushing!' Luisa stated, 'Megan, you're bloody blushing! Who is it? Do we know him? Where did you meet? Was it Tinder? Oh my god, this is so exciting.'

Megan looked at the ground and let the sand run between her toes before taking a deep breath.

'You don't know them, no, we met at the gym' she informed them

'Ah ha!' Luisa chirped. 'I knew you'd been going to the gym more often lately. Oooh, is he a big beefcake?'

Megan shook her head.

'Come on then, tell us his name at least!' Janet said, shuffling herself on the sunbed, desperate to hear the news, before she ran off to the toilet.

'OK,' she took a deep breath and let it out slowly. 'We met at the gym; we've been dating for a while. We've both said we love each other.' Her cheeks were flushed, and the smile across her face was so wide it made her cheeks ache.

'Oh my god', Luisa gushed, 'this is the best news ever.' She clapped her hands together in excitement.

'So if you'd said to me that this time next year, I'd be on holiday with a man, I'd still have told you to fuck off; however, if you'd said this time next year, I'd be on holiday with a woman,, then I'd probably have agreed with you.'

The mouths of the two faces in front of her dropped wide open.

'Her name is Susie,' Megan jumped in to fill the silence.

'Oh my god! Susie in the back seat with the sweaty top lip!' Luisa recalled. 'Oh my god!'

Janet frowned with confusion at Luisa's slightly odd description. 'Well, I can't believe this', she stated, folding her arms.

Megan looked over at Luisa for some words of encouragement.

'Neither can I,' Luisa agreed. 'My best friend has fallen in love, and this is the first I've heard about it!' she gushed.

'Not that; I can't believe that you didn't bloody invite her here; then we could have all met her!' Janet huffed.

'Oh, come here right now', Luisa managed to get out before the tears started. She stood, arms wide open, and Megan fell for the tightest hug. 'Make room for me', Janet said,' but it will have to be quick; I really am going to piss myself'

The three stood there on the beach, the cool breeze a welcome relief around them. The stars blinked at them in the velvety, deep blue sky above them. In the background, they heard the party-goers belting out Oasis' *Don't Look Back in Anger* as the evening took a rest from the traditional holiday floor fillers. Side by side, they made their way back to the bar, Megan walking a little taller, Luisa one hand proudly placed on her protruding three-month bump, and Janet jiggling about in an attempt to not wet herself.

They stopped just before they rejoined the party. 'Well, here's to this time next year' Luisa smiled at her friends. Megan and Janet nodded as they smiled back. Three friends, all with their own stories and secrets, but facing it all as the best of friends.

Chapter 46

Two Years Later

'Oh, come on, Meggie, please, we'll be late!' Luisa pleaded, exasperated and hot. Dressing a toddler on a time limit was like trying to run in a dream; the harder you try, the slower you get.

'Don't want to', a defiant blue-eyed Meggie retorted before giggling and thumping off down the hallway, waving her tights in one hand and a half-eaten biscuit in the other.

'Of course, you don't,' Luisa exhaled under her breath, giving in easily.

'Everything OK here?' Martyn poked his head through the doorway. He could see Luisa was doing her best to keep it together; there was a lot going on today, and she was so brave. 'Let me grab her, and I'll get her dressed; you go and finish getting ready', he said softly. Luisa looked up at him and managed a half-hearted smile. She didn't want to be stressed today; she tried to be calm and at least appear to be happy. It was a massive day for Izzy.

'Thanks. I just need to finish my makeup, and then I'm done.

Little madam, there needs dressing if you can get her to keep still for more than a minute.'

'OK, no stress, deep breaths, the car is packed, Meggie's bag is packed, I've checked the traffic, we're good for time', Martyn assured her. 'And Lucy has already texted three times to ask if we've left yet; I think someone has missed their mum since going to Uni, ' Martyn added reassuringly. Luisa looked back at him. Lovely, lovely Martyn, he'd taken all of the drama in his stride. He'd continued to be a fabulous dad to all the kids, to Zach, Lucy and now little Meg. He'd sat in the car with Zach and Lucy as they each learned to drive, which Luisa attempted to do once, but Lucy declared that if she did it again, she would be in danger of ruining their relationship forever. Luisa gratefully bowed out and handed the reins over to Martyn, who never once grabbed the door, covered his eyes or yelled, 'Jesus Christ will you slow the fuck down'. All in all, it was a much calmer experience for everyone involved.

It was Martyn, whom Zach went to when he needed help with his apprenticeship application, and Martyn, who stepped up and looked after Meg while Luisa was at the hospital with Megan. Today, they were travelling up to Liverpool to see Izzy graduate. Lucy had been up at Liverpool John Moores since September, fully immersing herself in all Uni life. Her exam results had been a welcome reason to celebrate amidst the dark days. The moment was bittersweet. Luisa was filled with pride, knowing her daughter was leaving home to chase her dreams. This was what the years of parenting had been building up to - the moment Lucy could fly off with the confidence to go it alone. 'It's a sign you've done an excellent job, Lu, ' Martyn assured her. Luisa knew this, but part of her heart weighed heavily, knowing there was one less heartbeat in the house.

She made her way upstairs. She should be skipping them two at a time; today was the day they had all been focusing on if we could just get to Izzy's graduation. 'I just want to see her in her cap and gown, and then I'll be happy', Megan told Luisa.

'You'll be there, Meg, ' Luisa told her, squeezing her hand tightly, 'I promise'.

Luisa sat on the edge of the bed and let out a sigh. She could feel the emotions collecting, just waiting for the go-ahead to make their way out. They were going to escape at some point. Luisa didn't want to be the one who fell apart today; she wanted to stand clapping and cheering as Izzy collected her certificate. Luisa needed to be there for Izzy. Luisa gave herself a few minutes to cry before blowing her nose, wiping her eyes and continuing with her makeup.

A small photo booth photo of her and Meg caught her eye, tucked into the corner of her dressing table mirror. Luisa smiled. 'Well, we made it, Meg, ' Luisa spoke softly as she brushed bronzer onto her cheeks. 'She's done it; she's going to be there in her cap and gown, just like she told you she would'. She traced around Megan's face with her finger. It was taken just after they got home from the wedding, their faces still glowing from the hot Mediterranean sun. Megan still had her hair here, taken just before she started her treatment. She had not worried too much about the other lump she found; she had assumed it was just another cyst. It wasn't; she should have checked it sooner; when she did, it was too late.

'Right then', Martyn said as he slammed the car boot shut. 'I do believe we're ready to go, finally!' Meggie was strapped in her car seat, still in her pyjamas. 'Before you say anything, Lu, I've got her clothes in the bag. We can change her when we get there; it will save any little accidents'.

Luisa nodded in agreement; good thinking, batman,' she replied. She went to open the passenger side door but stopped. 'Martyn, just hold on one minute; I need to get something, ' she turned and raced back into the house.

'Be quick, Lu, ' Martyn shouted behind her. 'You know what the motorway can be like!'

A few minutes later, Luisa reappeared with a black canvas bag. She placed it on the front passenger seat, attached the seat belt around it and clicked it into place.

'Are you serious, Lu?' Martyn asked. 'On the front seat?'

Luisa climbed into the back seat beside Meggie. 'Totally serious, Martyn', she told him. 'Come on, let's go'.

Delete Created with Sketch.

'You go in, I'll be right behind you', Luisa insisted. Since their arrival, they fully immersed themselves in weepy re-unions with Lucy and Izzy, having numerous photos taken, each trying on the mortar board. The place was fizzing with excitement, with proud parents watching on with teary eyes and a mass of graduates adjusting their gowns and beaming for photos. They filed into the venue, glad to escape the cool December breeze.

'You sure?' Martyn asked her, 'Are you OK?'

'I just need a minute,' Luisa assured him. 'You go in, I'll catch up with you'.

Luisa placed the black canvas bag on the bench beside her. 'Well, Meg, we made it. I promised you that you'd get to go to Izzy's graduation,' she stated, patting her hand on the bag. 'And here we are'. She took a deep breath. 'You'd be so proud of her', she added, swallowing back the tears. 'No, no', she said, shaking her head. 'I promised I wouldn't do this', she said defiantly, 'I promised you that we would be here today, and the least I can do is get through the ceremony without being a blubbering wreck'. She stood up and wiped her hands down her coat before picking up the bag containing the urn of Meg's ashes.

'I miss you.' She looked up to the wintry sky. 'Sleep tight, Meg.'

THE END

Also by Jane Betteley

If you enjoyed reading Luisa Mulligan Can't Keep A Secret, please consider leaving a review on Goodreads or Amazon - these are really valuable to authors and very much appreciated.

To keep up to date with all the news, sign up for the newsletter at www.janebetteley.co.uk

These Thoughts Are Yours

These Thoughts Are Yours is a collection of 20 short stories which are connected by the female experience, the magical complexity of the female mind and the raw, honest emotions that accompany it. It exposes the beautiful defiance that hides away in those who have been hurt. It reveals the shocking truths that we often feel but never speak. It responds to the child who lingers within all of us, that part of us which maintains hope in an often cruel and unforgiving world. These are snapshots of life seen through the eyes of the female – the woman, the child, the girl.

www.ingramcontent.com/pod-product-compliance
Lightning Source LLC
Chambersburg PA
CBHW060655190726
48289CB00002B/425